10/12

Over the Edge

a&b

Over the Edge

STUART PAWSON

This edition first published in Great Britain in 2004 by
Allison & Busby Limited
Bon Marche Centre
241-251 Ferndale Road
London SW9 8BJ
http://www.allisonandbusby.com

Copyright © 2004 by STUART PAWSON

The moral right of the author has been asserted.

A catalogue record for this book is available from
the British Library.

10 9 8 7 6 5 4 3 2 1

ISBN 0 7490 8302 6

Printed and bound by
Creative Print and Design, Wales

To Doreen

Also by Stuart Pawson

The Picasso Scam
The Mushroom Man
The Judas Sheep
Last Reminder
Deadly Friends
Some by Fire
Chill Factor
Laughing Boy
Limestone Cowboy

STUART PAWSON had a career as a mining engineer, followed by a spell working for the probation service, before he became a full-time writer. He lives in Fairburn, Yorkshire, and when not hunched over the word processor, Stuart likes nothing more than tramping across the moors, which often feature in his stories. *Over the Edge* is the tenth novel to feature Detective Inspector Charlie Priest.

Acknowledgements

Many thanks to the following for their assistance and encouragement: Dave Balfour, Bill Buckley, Paul Bishop, John Crawford, Geoffrey Gibson, Clive Kingswood, Dennis Marshall and Dave Mason.

1

"A million pounds is a lot of money when you were brought up on bread and scrape."

"Aw, come off it, Peter. It wasn't that bad. Who told you that – your dad?"

The Range Rover peeled off the motorway on to the slip-road without signalling and braked for the red light at the bottom of the ramp. The two men in the front seats were in shadow until the light changed to green, and as the car moved forward again the illumination from the streetlights slid upwards to reveal their faces. The driver's was expression-less. His effigy wouldn't have looked out of place on Easter Island, gazing out to sea, but his passenger was the opposite. A generation older, this face was creased and mobile. It was the type of face that usually has a cigar poking out of it as the owner barks percentages into a telephone.

"It's still a lot of money to turn down," the driver said. He glanced into his rear-view mirror to confirm that the Lexus and the Audi had followed him, and looked for the signs to the city centre.

"I'm turning it down because it's unrealistic, that's why. OK, so we were poor, but we got by."

"It's a fair price and you know it," the younger man argued. "A million for the club, split between you and Pixie and Dixie, and a little sweetener on top of your cut to bring it up to another million. That makes it £1.6 million we're paying for the Painted Pony."

"Which is worth five times that amount. You've done the sums, Pete. I've seen that clown of yours there, counting the punters every night, seeing how much they drank, writing down the prices. For Chrissake, they laughed at me when I told them a million. Even if I split the money a straight three ways they'd still laugh at me."

"That's because they're accountants; think on the long

term. They're happy if a deal goes into the black after what, eight years? Five years? You and me don't think like that, though, do we, Joe? Twelve months max, and we want our money back. That right?"

"Yeah, well, that's how it used to be. But things have changed. Sorry, Pete, but it's still no deal. You're doing OK. Your dad would be proud of you. He'd have loved the new restaurant. That beef Wellington was the best I've ever had, and that's no kidding."

"Thanks. And the wine? What did you think of the wine?" The streets were bathed in orange light and deserted. Traffic lights went blindly through their cycles and crossing beacons blinked irrelevantly on the empty pavements. Two taxis were parked nose-to-nose, one of them on the wrong side of the road, as the drivers shared a cigarette and stories, and a gust of wind sent litter swirling across the street. Standing sentinel over all this were tower after tower of blacked-out office blocks, with only an occasional illuminated window high in the sky to indicate the existence of a netherworld, peopled by invisible men and women who emptied waste paper bins, polished floors and cleaned toilets. The Range Rover carved across three empty lanes and made a right turn.

"Ah! You know what I think of the wine. I've had nearly two bottles of it. What was it again?"

"You had nearly three bottles of it, but who's counting. Chateau Margaux. I was hoping it might make you more amenable to a deal."

"Ah! Nice try, Pete. Nice try. I'll have a head like an anvil in the morning but I'll still own a third share in the Painted Pony. 1980, did you say?"

"That's right."

"Can you get me a case?"

"No problem."

"You'd no need to bring me home. That's what I pay a driver for."

"Duggie, your faithful manservant? He's following us. I wanted to talk. And I wanted to ask you about a site near

14

your place, on the waterfront. Thought maybe we could have a look at it."

"It's the place to be, Pete. Leeds is jumping, at the moment. Those apartments are going for a million a time, and they're sold before they're built, unseen. That's the way to do business."

"A 24-hour city."

"That's right. Blair's Britain. Politicians wear their shirts out of their trousers and drink out of the bottleneck. I don't know what your dad would have thought about it."

"He'd have thought the same as you and me: how do we get a share of the action?"

"Yeah, I guess so," the older man agreed. "We had things cut up fairly well, me and your dad. And you've done well, too, Pete. But don't get greedy. The yardies are moving in, but there's room for them. We're in a different market. Remember what your dad used to say about when there was a gold rush? Don't buy a shovel and go chasing off into the hills. Open a shovel shop. It's the same with drugs. Let the dumb black bastards go round selling them and shooting each other. Meanwhile, we give them what they need: BMWs; a nightlife; and women. The cops leave us alone and we rake off the cream. No problem. Turn left here, Pete; we're nearly there."

"Here?" He braked hard and made the turn. The road was now narrow and bounded on each side by walls of MDF sheets, hiding the development going off behind them. A huge sign claimed the site for one of the major construction companies and an artist's impression portrayed an elegant lifestyle that owed more to the artist's holiday in Greece than to the realities of northern weather.

"That's right. Listen, Pete. I was sorry to hear about your mother. Grace was a lovely lady. We all thought the world of her. The big C's a real downer, no mistake. I hear you've opened a fund or something, in her memory."

"That's right. The Grace Wallenberg trust."

"Well, we'll be more than happy to make a contribution, Pete. A substantial contribution."

"But not the Painted Pony?"

"Ah ah! No, Pete, not the Pony. And you've bought Heckley football club, too. That could be a not-very-smart move. I hear they're a bunch of cripples."

There was a silence for a few seconds until the younger man said: "That's unkind to cripples."

"Sorry, Pete. No offence. So what's it all about?"

"Respectability, Joe, and access."

"Access?"

"That's what I said. Access to local government, politicians, big business. And tradition. The club is over a hundred years old, and I'm saving it for the community. Peter Wallenberg, pillar of society, saviour of Heckley Town FC, that's me, and they're falling over each other to shake my hand. Haven't you noticed how every Member of Parliament you hear about claims to spend all his Saturday afternoons on the terraces, cheering the local side on? It's the common touch, except that I give them a warm seat and a bottle of claret."

"You're smart, Pete, I'll say that for you. Your dad would be proud, real proud."

"But you won't sell me the Pony?"

"Ah! No way. Left here. Be careful, it's blacker than a Rasta's arse and there's no wall. It just drops straight into the river. What is it you wanted to show me?"

"Where is the river?"

"'Bout twenty yards away. Stop here." There was a hint of alarm in his voice. "Don't go any closer, it gives me the willies, this time o' night. That's near enough."

"And you live on the top floor of that block?"

"Sure do. A New York loft, the estate agent called it. That means there's no ceiling between you and the roof. Saves on construction costs but it's a bugger to heat. Wanna look-see? A coffee, maybe?"

"No, I don't think so. And the Pony's in the basement. That's handy."

"Damn right it is. Helps me keep an eye on things. We close

Monday nights, otherwise it would be buzzing around here, this time o' night."

"It's quiet now. And spooky." He pressed a button to adjust the door mirror and saw the other two cars edge round the corner, their lights out. They stopped in the shadows fifty yards back and waited.

"Sure is. One time this wharf was where all the wool was unloaded. See the bridge up there? That's Leeds Bridge. We used to stand on it when we were kids, your dad and me, and count all the barges, tied up side by side, wondering where they came from. The first ever moving pictures were taken on that bridge, by a man called Louis Le Prince, back in the nineteenth century. Now it's all yuppie apartments and three-quid-a-cup coffee houses. Well, thanks for bringing me home, Pete, and it's been a pleasure talking to you. We should do it more often, for old time's sake. Wanna change your mind about that coffee?"

"I want the Pony, Joe."

"OK, it's yours. The price is eight million. I'll take a cheque."

"1.6, no offers. We could come to some arrangement where you still had an interest. It'd be a nice pension for you."

"Sorry, Pete. I told you, the partners aren't interested."

"Fuck the partners, this is between you and me. OK, Joe, how's this for a sweetener? There's this girl coming over. Nineteen, blonde, figure enough to drive you blind. Thinks she's landed a job as a nanny to a brain surgeon's kids, at the HGI. All hush-hush and off the record, of course, to get round all the red tape nonsense. I was saving her for myself, but you're welcome to have first lick of the jam in the bagel, so to speak. How does that sound?"

"Ah! It sounds as if you're trying to appeal to my weakness, but you're too late, Pete. These days I need all the help I can get, not resistance."

"That's not what I hear."

"Well, you hear wrong. I'm not interested in your deal and neither are the partners."

"They will be if I make them an offer over your head."

"What are you getting at?"

"One last time. Do we have a deal?"

"No way."

The younger man pressed a button on the dashboard and the Range Rover's hazard lights flashed once. "OK," he snarled. "Get out of the car."

"Hey, what's that?"

"What does it look like?"

"A fuckin' gun, that's what it looks like."

Behind them the Lexus and the Audi began to creep forward until they were close up behind the Range Rover. The doors swung open and two men climbed out. The one from the Lexus was big, with a shaven head, wearing jogging bottoms and a t-shirt. His companion was more slightly built, but still muscular, wearing a hand-made suit and silk tie.

"So your eyesight's better than your hearing. I said get out of the car, Joe."

"*Uncle* Joe. That's who I used to be. *Uncle* Joe."

The two newcomers walked alongside the Range Rover and the well-dressed one pulled the passenger's door open.

"Get out!" the one called Peter Wallenberg ordered from the driving seat, pointing the gun.

"You heard what he said," the smart suit added.

"Hey! Where'd he come from?" the old man demanded.

"Need some assistance, Mr Wallenberg?"

"I don't think so, Dale. Mr Crozier is just getting out."

"What's going off, Pete? Dale? What's this all about? And where's Duggie?"

"He's here, behind me."

"Duggie. Why'd you let this happen?" He glanced at the faces surrounding him. He wasn't scared. He'd been in dangerous situations before, been beaten up a couple of times, but that was a long time ago. Things were different now. OK, so he'd lost this one, been out-manoeuvred, whatever it was about, but he'd bounce back.

"I'm wiv Mr Wallenberg now, Mr Crozier."

"You've betrayed me, Duggie. Betrayed me."

18

"Just get out."

He swung his legs out and dropped to the ground.

"That's it. Now, lean on the bonnet" The dapper one, called Dale, spun him round and forced him over the car's bonnet while Duggie dropped on to his knees.

"Hey, what y'doing?"

"We're taping your ankles together."

"What the fuck for?"

"This tape's not much good, Mr Wallenberg," Duggie said.

"Just do it. Put plenty round. And now his hands. Put your hands behind your back."

"Aw, c'mon, Peter," he pleaded. "A joke's a joke. Look, I'll have another word with the partners. Maybe we can find some middle ground."

"I'm not interested in middle ground. Do as you're told."

"You'll be sorry for this, Pete. Real sorry."

"No I won't. Put plenty round."

"Insulation tape would be better, boss," Duggie said, anxious to please. "This'll come off in the water."

The words hit the old man like a ten-ton truck. "The water!" he yelled. "Whadya mean, the water! Not the river! No! No! Please don't put me in the river..."

"Put some round his mouth, stop him screaming."

"No! Don't! Help! Help me... Aaarg... aaarg." His body undulated and twisted like an eel writhing on a fishing line in a desperate attempt to thwart his captors as Dale gripped him in a headlock.

"More, use more," urged the stone-faced one as Duggie wound the tape round and round the old man's head. "That should do. Well done, boys, he's all yours. Here, Dale. You'd better have this back." He handed the gun to the younger man, who put it in his jacket pocket. "I'll see you in the morning."

Gurgling noises came from the trussed-up old man as he tried to scream down his nose. Blobs of mucus bubbled out of it and his bowels and bladder released their contents in a last primordial defence.

19

"G'night, Mr Wallenberg," the dapper one called, softly, to the retreating back of his boss. "You take his legs, Duggie." "I got them. You OK wiv 'is shoulders?"

"Yeah, piece o' cake."

Their parcel strained at his bindings, his eyes bulging from their sockets as they flicked from one assailant to the other. He wanted to promise them the world, share his fortune with them, but all means of communication were denied him.

"After you, that way," Duggie directed.

"Arr! Dropped him. He's wriggling like a fish."

"Shall I fump 'im? That'd quieten 'im?"

"No. Mr Wallenberg sez there's to be no marks on him."

"Old Hopalong? He didn't stay long."

"He's OK, a good boss, but don't ever let him hear you call 'im Hopalong, or you're one dead person. Careful, don't bang his head on the edge."

The old man was weeping now, sobs racking his exhausted body as he gasped for breath. Their pity was his last hope.

"Right. Fanks for the advice. God, look at that water."

The river shone back at them like a hole in space. Broken patches of light from the apartments on the opposite bank sat on the water and gently merged into each other and parted again.

"I can't see it, just blackness."

"It's down there somewhere. Don't come too near the edge. Looks like oil, not moving. Rather 'im than me."

The old man prayed for the first time in his life. Not for rescue or salvation. It was too late for either of those. He had a pain in his chest. He prayed that it was a heart attack, that it would take him before the paralysing shock of the water racked his body and choked his lungs.

"OK, just roll him off the side." They pushed him over the edge as casually as they would drop a bag of rubbish into a dumpster. The lights on the water bobbed and shimmered, and broke up into smaller patches of colour that almost immediately began to reform again. "There we go, just right, hardly a splash, like the boss said."

"Can you see him? Is he floating?" They stood side by side, peering into the blackness.

"Can't tell. There's a few ripples. It's out of our hands, now."

"Phew! I'm out of breff. That's our first job together, Dale."

"Yeah. Pleasure doing business with you, Duggie."

"Likewise, Dale. Fuckin' likewise."

"Right. You put his car back in its normal parking place and we'll fuck off back to Heckley."

2

If I hadn't decided to go for a jog that morning I wouldn't have had just one slice of toast for breakfast, and if I hadn't had just one slice of toast I wouldn't have made the discovery.

The toaster went *ping!* and the square of bread was hurled completely clear of the machine, falling onto the kitchen carpet. The springs, it would appear, had been chosen for their ability to lift my normal two slices to the optimum level, not one. I threw the sullied portion in the bin, placed a fresh piece in the machine and pushed it further on to the worktop. While waiting for it to cook I had an idea. I placed a book under one edge of the toaster, to give it a pronounced list, and carefully positioned my plate next to the other side. I stood back and stooped to get a better view, considering the force with which the doomed slice had been ejected, estimating trajectories, and made a slight adjustment.

Ping! it went again, and one perfectly cooked slice of toast shot from the machine and fell on to my plate, untouched by human hand. The joy that welled up inside me was beyond belief. It was one of those unique occasions, experienced only when momentous discoveries have been made and known only to geniuses like Archimedes, Alexander Fleming, and now me, Charlie Priest. I scraped the last of the margarine across the celebrated slice and poured hot water onto coffee granules.

I was so pleased I decided to reward myself by not going for a jog. I'd settled down with yesterday's newspaper when the phone rang. The clock on the wall said ten to six.

"What's the trouble?" I asked. "At this time in the morning it's got to be trouble."

"Bugger me, Charlie," the voice at the other end said, "you're up and about early. Can't you sleep?"

"Been for a jog, Arthur," I replied. "Four miles before breakfast is a great way to start the day." No need to explain that it was only in my mind. I'd read a magazine article claiming that thinking about exercise was almost as beneficial as practising it.

"Blimey. How long have you been doing this for?"

"Um, well, actually, today was the first time. What's the problem?" Arthur is the controller at Heckley nick, I'm in charge of the CID. He wasn't ringing me to make smalltalk.

"Rodger's radioed in, Charlie, from an RTA up on the high road. It happened about an hour and a half ago. Car gone into a wall at high speed, driver killed. Rodge thinks there's more to it than meets the eye."

"Is he still up there?"

"Affirmative."

"What about a photographer?"

"He's already sent for him."

"OK, give me the location and I'll be off."

Rodger is our night detective. CID work normal office hours, plus or minus a few, but we have a representative on round the clock in case something crops up that needs a CID presence. Rodger is our regular night man. No doubt he would have told Arthur all about it, but I preferred to be up there, learning firsthand. I pulled my clothes on and finished the toast in the car, heading out of town up on to the moors.

It was a cold morning, drizzle and mist combining in a way that's special to this part of the world. According to the clock the sun should have risen, but it was only half-light and all the signs said that winter wasn't far away. I switched on the headlamps and wipers and groped my way upwards, wondering about the life that had been snuffed out, wondering who was waiting for him to come home.

The blue lights were visible from a mile away, blurry smears of colour on a grey background. The first set was a roadblock. Anybody using that route to work on a Thursday morning was going to be late. I lowered my window and the PC recognised me and waved me through. I paused alongside him long enough to say: "What's it look like?"

"Grim, boss," he replied.

Further up the road a cacophony of lights, flickering and dancing across the roofs of the assorted vehicles like static electricity, marked the scene of the crash. Two fire appliances and three police cars were clustered around a mangled wreck that sat in the middle of the road like it had been brought down by enemy fire. A deep muddy scar was gouged across the verge, then dislodged stones and shattered coloured glass marked its progress until it came to a halt, broken and silent, pointing in the direction whence it came. Fifty yards of evidence – one or two seconds of time – that told of the transformation of a technological masterpiece into a pile of scrap, and a living, feeling human being into a piece of carrion. Further away, waiting patiently, were a breakdown truck and a milk-float.

Rodger came to meet me as I took a waterproof coat from the back of the car. He introduced me to the fire chief who said they were going to remove the body, if that was OK. I had no objections if the photographer had finished.

One of the panda cars was from Lancashire Constabulary. We exchanged greetings and they told me that it had happened about two hundred yards inside East Pennine's jurisdiction, so it was all mine. I thanked them for their assistance and they went home.

"What's the problem, Rodge?" I asked.

"The milkman," he replied, nodding in the direction of the float. "He reported the accident. Apparently he was overtaken by two cars going at what he called lunatic speed."

"Racing?"

"Not directly. They were a minute or two apart. This was down the road, back near Oldfield. Then he came upon this and telephoned us. That's not all. He says that something similar happened about a month ago. Two cars, a minute or two apart, overtook him at breakneck speed. They were sports cars, not hatches like the two this morning, and he says they were all doing well over the ton."

"So you think it's more than youthful exuberance?"

"There's driving fast, Charlie, and there's racing, and

there's running away from something. This was more than driving fast. I asked the firemen to feel in his pockets for some ID. They didn't find any but there's an envelope. It's stuffed with money. All twenties. A few hundred quid at a guess. I've put it in an evidence bag."

"That's interesting. Have you had chance to check if there's anything on this one?"

"That's not all."

"Go on."

"They found this, too." He held a Ziploc bag up in front of my face, containing an automatic pistol. "Glock .38, at a guess."

"Sheest!" I exclaimed. "That will have to go to the lab for a full inspection. Back to the car. Have you checked it out?"

"Yes. It's registered as a blue VW Golf 1.8 GTi, which is what we've got, and it's not reported stolen. The owner is a Jason Smith, age 28, living in Scarborough."

"He's a fair way from home. Any guesses at the age of laddo?" I asked, nodding towards the wreckage.

"No, sorry."

"Dare we ring him?" Jason Smith might be at home in bed, or he might not, in which case we'd have some explaining to do.

"Hmm, I'd rather not."

"No, I don't think I want to, either. Let's see if we can find the VI number and take it from there."

But we couldn't. The Vehicle Identity Number is usually on a plate welded on the floor at the side of the driver's seat, but by the time they'd cut the poor chap from the wreckage there wasn't much left to look at, and what there was had a liberal coating of blood on it. We arranged to take a full statement from the milkman and sent him on his way. Couldn't have the kiddiewinks missing their morning cereals. We dismissed the breakdown truck, too, preferring to have our own take the wreckage to the police compound. It was ten o'clock when the fire brigade hosed the road clean and we opened it for normal business.

We asked Scarborough to do the dirty work and they sent a bobby round to the house where the blue Golf GTi belonging to Jason Smith was registered. If it was still there ours was a stolen car, marked up to look like that one; if it wasn't there he'd have to break the news that somebody might not be coming home and invite them to make an identification.

There are thousands of people driving round in cars that don't belong to them. They are stolen to order and passed on at about a tenth of their true value. They steal, say, a black BMW series 3 – it's usually an upmarket car – and sit at the roadside watching, or wander round supermarket car parks until they find a similar vehicle. They note the number and have identical registration plates made for the stolen one. That's it. Any perfunctory enquiry from a passing policeman shows it to be what it says it is, and his suspicions are alleviated. The owner of the original vehicle knows nothing about this, except that he receives the occasional summons for speeding in an area where he never goes, or a fixed penalty ticket for driving in the London congestion charge zone, although he avoids driving in London like a giraffe avoids overhead power-lines.

Scarborough rang back to say that Mr Smith was alive and well, but we'd already discovered that the crashed car was a ringer. The VIN number didn't tally with the DVLA records. It had been stolen three weeks earlier, from a house in Leeds. Burglars had broken in, found the keys and driven it away. Nothing else was taken. Nowadays, with all the sophisticated alarms and immobilisers on new cars, using the keys is just about the only way of stealing one.

We don't mourn when a car thief kills himself. Truth is, we all feel a little glow of satisfaction, happy that they haven't taken anybody else with them. Priority now was his identity, so his next of kin could be informed and the newspapers could announce to the world that justice had been done and the streets were that little bit safer. He'd be buried with all the pomp of a Third World dictator and the *Personal* column would have messages from all his friends and relatives saying what a kind, loving person he'd been. They'd make pilgrimages to the spot where he discovered that VW Golfs can't fly, and leave extravagant floral tributes and soft toys, to help him in the afterlife. Rodger asked if he could stay with it because he smelled something big underneath it all. I was happy to close the case and concentrate on the burglaries that make up our daily bread, but I said OK.

Saturday morning the report came through identifying him. He hadn't been carrying a passport, driver's licence or utility bill, so DNA samples and fingerprints were taken and sent for comparison with the databases. Two hits confirmed him to be Dale Dobson, a 26-year-old thug with a record of football violence, racial attacks and ABH. I tried ringing Gareth Adey, my uniformed counterpart, to dump it on him, but he wasn't answering. The sun was shining, it was Saturday morning and no grieving family had reported him missing. Gareth was probably wearing silly trousers and thrashing a small white ball around a big field, so I slid the report into my *Pending* tray and went home.

Many years ago I graduated from art college, with honours, for what it's worth. As well as strenuous activities like rugby, karate and scuba diving, we have policemen who write poetry and short stories, several who do watercolours, and I've heard it said that there's a sergeant in Barnsley who is a dab hand with the crocheting hook. But as far as I know I'm the only cop in the firm who knocks up the occasional abstract-impressionist work of art. I'd had a couple on display at the Heckley gala and they'd attracted quite a bit of serious attention, as well as the expected hoots of derision from my colleagues. But a local gallery owner – a man of taste and sophistication – had admired them and offered to show a couple in an exhibition he was organising in the autumn.

So that's why I spent Saturday afternoon on the roof of the garage, dropping blobs of red paint on to a six-by-four sheet of hardboard.

"What the chuff are you playing at?" a voice said somewhere below me.

I peered over the edge. "Look out," I warned, "or you'll get splodged." It was Dave "Sparky" Sparkington, one of my detectives and my best pal, with his teenage son, Daniel. Dave and I first met as schoolboy footballers, and then later when we joined the force. I've kept my boyish good looks and figure, but Dave, who is almost as tall as me, has spread slightly and lost most of his hair. We've shared a few scrapes, over the years, and he's kept me out of trouble more times than I care to remember. I'm his daughter's godfather.

"What's this: blood splatter analysis?" Dave shouted up to me.

"No, it's for the gallery. Or it would be if I could get it right. I really need to be higher, so it spreads out more on impact. It's not as easy as it looks. Have you been to the match?"

"Yeah. And do people pay money for this rubbish?"

"Listen, Sunshine. If I get this right I'll make more out of it than I ever did from coppering. How many did we lose by?"

"Just the odd goal."

"Practically a victory. 'Spect you want a cup of coffee."

"Wouldn't say no."

"Go put the kettle on, Dan, while I clear this lot up."

"OK, Charlie," Dan replied, heading for the door.

"Uncle Charlie to you," his dad shouted after him.

"You went to the fatal on the top road, I hear," Dave said when we were seated in the kitchen, eating custard creams with our coffees.

"Mmm. Who told you that?"

"Shirley."

"Shirley!" Shirley is Dave's wife, who teaches home economics.

"She met Davina in the supermarket." Davina is married to Rodger, the night 'tec, and is a sister at the General Hospital.

"I see. It's good to know that all lines of communication are functioning well. So what sort of holiday have you had?"

"Fantastic. Put a lovely shade of duck-egg blue on the wife's mother's ceiling. Why did he call you out for an RTA? Is he losing it?"

"No, I don't think so. There was some money in the car – about £500 – and he had a gun in his pocket. I've sent everything to Wetherton; see if the boffins can find anything."

"What sort of gun?"

"A .38 Glock."

"Hmm. I suppose he did the right thing, then, but guns are a fashion accessory, these days, and five hundred's not much to some of them."

"He did what he thought was right, and that's OK by me."

"Has the driver been ID-ed yet?"

"Umm..." I hesitated.

"What do you mean, umm...?"

"The results came back this morning, but I haven't done anything about it."

"Christ, Charlie. You mean you're sitting on it? He's dead, you know who he is and you're sitting on it. If it gets out they'll... they'll..."

I turned to young Daniel, saying: *"Hang me by the balls from the town hall clock* is the expression your father is looking for," and he grinned back at me.

"Well," Dave went on, "it is a bit much, don't you think. Do you want me to come in tomorrow?"

"He's a racist yob," I replied, "and I'm as entitled to my weekend off as much as the next man. It'll wait until Monday."

"I suppose so. Did you know that Tony Krabbe is giving a lecture at the Town Hall a week next Saturday?"

"Tony Krabbe?" I replied. "You mean Anthony Turnbull Krabbe? Conqueror of Everest and numerous other peaks?"

"That's him. Want me to get some tickets?"

"How much are they?"

"Twelve pounds."

"Crikey. No thanks."

"Why not?"

"I went to school with him. He's a... he's a ..."

Now it was Dave's turn to explain to Daniel. "*Twat* is the expression your Uncle Charlie is looking for," he said.

"An amiable cove," I told them. "I got on reasonably well with him. Everybody did, including the teachers. And the girls. Especially the girls. He was a good-looking so-and-so, and he knew it."

"Sounds like a bad case of jealousy to me," Dave said.

"You could be right," I agreed. "I took over from him as captain of the school team. He was a year older than me, which means a lot at that age. We lost six matches on the trot, then he broke his arm falling off the parallel beams – he was showing off in the gym – and I took over as captain. We won our next six matches but he came back and we started losing again. I don't think he was very academically minded. He was one of those golden boys who attracts all the attention but has nothing to back it up. You know the type."

"Yes, we have one or two of those in the firm. Where did 'e go when 'e left?"

"Presumably he joined the army. It must have been about ten years later that he started making a name for himself with his climbing exploits, writing books and all that, and he's always described as ex-SAS."

"He must have something, if he was in the SAS," Dave said.

I scowled at him. "The SAS," I echoed. "You must be joking. They're a bunch of hooligans."

"They're the elite of our army."

"No they're not. They're a bunch of trigger-happy incompetents."

Dave turned to his son. "Your Uncle Charlie doesn't like the SAS."

"I suppose he's done well," I grudgingly admitted.

"He's got the OBE for it, must be Heckley Grammar's most famous old boy."

"I know. He's the public face of mountaineering, knows the right people, always says the right thing, but I doubt if he can lace the boots of some of the others."

"Sure you don't want to come? Jeff's making one in." Jeff Caton is one of my sergeants.

"Go on, then. Get me a ticket. What about you, Dan?"

"Five-a-side," he replied, which was teenage-speak meaning that he was playing in a five-a-side football tournament on the evening in question and therefore would not be able to attend the lecture.

"Right," I said.

After Dave's disquiet about the dead body my conscience started troubling me, so Sunday morning I did some investigating. Dale Dobson's last known address was a bail hostel in Huddersfield, but a phonecall confirmed that he'd moved on. He was now lost to the system and had been living in the black economy – no taxes, no national insurance, no nothing. There's a whole cash-in-hand world out there, living on its wits, dependent on nobody, no questions asked. They're outlaws, and when we get on to them they just fold their tents, or leave the bedsit without paying the arrears, and disappear.

Fortunately for us, Marjory Dobson, his mother, believed in the work ethic, paid her community charge, and was therefore easy to trace. I decided to visit her.

She lived in a terrace house on the outskirts of Huddersfield, where the back streets were cobbled and the grime of the Industrial Revolution still clung to the walls. The rows of houses climbed up the hillside in steps, their redundant chimneys dominating the skyline, providing roosts for pigeons. They'd gone from desirable residences for workers in the wool industry to starter homes for young couples, then been snapped up by the Asian population who moved in during the last days of the mills. Now they were a cosmopolitan mix of older white tenants, Asian families, and students living in flats, all rubbing along in an uneasy truce. One day, perhaps, they'd be converted into bijou residences for the chattering classes, but nobody was holding their breath.

"Which one is it this time?" Mrs Dobson asked when we were seated in her tiny front room.

31

She was younger than I expected, with a face that had once been handsome but now bore the lines of constant disappointment. Her streaked hair was tied back in a ponytail and when she'd turned to let me in I'd seen a butterfly tattooed on her shoulder.

"Which one?" I queried.

"Dale or his dad?"

"I'm afraid it's Dale."

"What's he done now?"

"There was a car crash up on the top road, early Thursday morning. I'm sorry to have to tell you, Mrs Dobson, that Dale is dead. We've only just identified him as the driver."

She flinched at the word *dead*, but didn't look too surprised or upset. This wasn't the first time a detective had knocked at the door and asked if he could have a word. It was just another episode in the tragic story that began when Dale was born. She sniffed and forced her mouth into a grim smile but the corners were twitching as she stared beyond me, to a distant time and place where the memories were happier.

"It was a high-speed crash," I went on. "He was killed instantly."

"Was anyone with him?" she asked.

"Not that we've been able to establish."

"Well that's a blessing. Unlike Dale, though. He liked to make as much misery as possible out of everything he did."

"We haven't been able to find an address for him. Do you know where he lived?"

"No. I asked him, but he said he moved around. And…" She stopped before completing the sentence.

"And…" I prompted.

She shrugged her shoulders and blew her nose on a tissue. "And he said it was best if I didn't know, whatever that means." She rose to her feet, saying: "Will you excuse me?"

"Of course."

She left the room and returned a couple of minutes later. "I'm sorry about that."

32

I said; "It's been a shock for you. When did you last see Dale?"

"Last time I saw him? That would be about a month ago. He never came to visit me, but sometimes he'd just turn up and demand a bed for a night or two. It was as if…"

"Go on."

"As if… he was lying low for a bit, if you know what I mean."

"Lying low from what?"

"I don't know. He never had a proper job but always had plenty of money. He was a bad 'un, Inspector. I know that. These days, you imagine it's drugs, don't you? He was mixed up in something, that's for sure."

The kettle in the kitchen switched off with a loud click and Mrs Dobson went to make some tea. I had a look around the room and was surprised by the stuff she had. A big copper samovar stood in one corner, glowing like a sunset, and a tall jardinière filled with dried flowers was in another. The coffee table was jade and the sideboard was obviously antique. The photos on the wall were sepia prints of old Huddersfield.

"I've been admiring your stuff," I told her when she returned. "Is that what they call a samovar?"

"That's right."

"It's a beauty."

She placed my tea on the jade table. "I like nice things," she said, "but most of them are fake, like this table."

When she was seated again I said: "It sounds as if Dale has always been a problem, Mrs Dobson."

She sipped her tea, then said: "I lost him when he was eleven. Up to then he'd been a delightful little boy, but, overnight, something happened. He became a racist. You know what it's like around here, but you have to give and take. I've got Asians on either side, for about three houses, but we get along well. The children are polite and they'll run errands for you. But with Dale it was *Paki* this and *nigger* that. He didn't care who heard him. Then he got mixed up with the football crowd."

33

"What about his dad?" I asked, remembering her question when she'd asked me in: "Which one is it?"

"Him! Uh," she snorted. "Another waste of oxygen. I'm afraid he was probably Dale's role model, even though we split up when Dale was six. He's done time, too."

"What for?" I asked.

"GBH. He beat... somebody... up. And receiving, I think."

"Do you keep in touch?"

"He sends me a Christmas card, would you believe? He called here, about five years ago, but I wouldn't let him in. I told him where to go."

"Was it you he beat up?"

She looked down at her knees again and whispered: "Yes."

"When did Dale leave home?"

"Dale? It wasn't a sudden thing. He started staying out when he was about fourteen or fifteen. At first I assumed he was with a girl – he was a good-looking boy, never had any trouble attracting them. Gradually it built up until he was out more than he was in. By the time he was seventeen I hardly ever saw him."

"But you've no idea if he was working for anybody, or what he was doing?"

"Driving, at a guess. He was mad keen on cars and driving."

"Right. Dale's fingerprints and DNA were already on our files, and we've matched them to the person in the car. However, it's normal for us to ask a family member to formally identify the body. Do you think you'll be up to it?"

Her face clouded with alarm. "I thought you said it was him."

"It is. There's no doubt about it. It's not essential but we'd still like you to confirm it. And sometimes... you know... it helps if you can see the body."

"But you're certain it's him?"

"Certain."

"OK. When? When do you want me to do it?"

"Tomorrow morning, or will you be working?"

"My son is dead. I think that's worth a day off work, don't you, Inspector? And maybe I'll have another for the funeral. Then I can say good riddance to him once and for all."

3

After Monday's morning prayers in the superintendent's office we held our normal meeting in the CID office. It's when we compare notes to bring each other up to speed, and I hand out any new cases.

"OK," I began. "Mr Wood wants a result on the burglaries, so where are we at?"

"Which burglaries?" somebody asked.

"Any of them."

"Well," Jeff Caton began, "as you know, Charlie, we appear to have two different MOs, therefore possibly two teams at work. One is concentrating on properties at the lower end of the scale, mainly in the Sylvan Fields estate, and the others are more mobile and breaking in to more expensive properties."

I let him rabbit on about the burglaries. Jeff never uses one word if seven will do. Some stolen items had been recovered from Honest John's secondhand shop, but the seller had given a false address and Honest John's description was vague.

"He's a lying toad," Dave Sparkington informed us all.

Fingerprints had been found at one house, and blood from the glass of a broken window at another, but they weren't on the database. It was all bread-and butter stuff, like we have all the time. We'd eventually catch someone and put them in court, but they'd be a first-time offender and walk away with probation or community service.

"As you will have noticed," I said when we'd finished with the burglaries, "our night 'tec has graciously stayed behind to speak to the meeting. That's him in the corner, blinking like an owl, for those of you who've forgotten what he looks like. Over to you, Rodger."

Rodger came to Britain from Jamaica as a small boy, but he's no token black man. He's my secret weapon. Heckley is a small town, and most of us are probably known to all the villains, but not Rodger. Nobody expects a detective to be black, even if he is six-and-a-half feet tall and dresses like the Duke of Westminster. He and his wife have volunteered to work regular nights, rather than be on differing shift rotas, so they can see more of each other. And, as he sometimes says in a mock West Indies accent: when he puts on his shades and closes his mouth, nobody can see him.

"There was an RTA on the top road in the early hours of last Thursday," he told us, and went on to describe the accident. He read from the milkman's statement about seeing two sports cars apparently racing a month earlier. "This is where it gets interesting," he said. "Five weeks ago, on September twentieth, thieves stole an MG TF from a house in Tintwistle. Four days later a similar car was hijacked from a young woman in a multi-storey car park in Manchester. Neither car has been seen again, unless they are what the milkman saw."

"Hairdressers' cars," someone informed us disdainfully.

"The 1.8 VV's a flyer," one of the younger members protested.

"If you call nought to 60 in 7.7 flying."

"Whoa!" I interrupted. "We're not discussing the merits of MGs. Carry on, Rodge."

"OK. Now we come up-to-date. Two weeks ago, October 7th, a blue Volkswagen GTi was stolen from a house in Leeds. Like the first MG, the house was broken into and the keys taken. Three evenings later a similar car, but coloured black, was hijacked from a 25-year-old man outside Marsden station. The blue car was the one involved in the RTA, Thursday morning. Saturday morning the black one was found burned-out on the edge of Heckley park."

"They're stealing them to order," someone suggested.

"In pairs – his and hers," another added.

"The MGs were probably re-plated and passed on, so why did they torch the Golf?"

"Because of the accident? Maybe they thought it was too hot."

"Was he running away from anything?"

"Nothing we know about," I replied. "It'd been a quiet night."

It was all conjecture. I told them about Dale, the money and the gun, and asked Maggie Maddison to do the honours at the mortuary with the grieving mother. "I don't think you'll need the box of tissues," I told her when she gave me that *why me?* look. "She actually used the words 'good riddance'."

"Rodge wants to stay on this," I said, "so we need a new night 'tec. Can I have a volunteer, please?"

The first person whose eyes I caught nodded and said: "I could do with a rest."

"Thanks. Maggie and John, could you work with Rodge? I'd concentrate on Dobson's background, associates, *etcetera*. You know the score. Then maybe try to trace his route while things are fresh in people's minds. People may have heard the car, or cars, go by."

The route was easier to trace than expected. There are early risers, there are insomniacs and there are people who drag themselves reluctantly out of their pit, morning after morning, year after year, to travel to some tedious job that they hate. For all of them, a car careering by at over a hundred miles per hour was a break with routine and therefore memorable. Rodger, Maggie and John worked backwards from the scene of the accident. At each junction they would take a road each and knock on doors. One of them would soon strike gold, and off they would go to the next junction. Slowly, they found themselves working their way over the tops into the outskirts of Greater Manchester. On Tuesday an appeal was made on local radio and more sightings and hearings came in. Dozens of them. By Wednesday we had the route of Dobson's last journey, with a few gaps, marked on a map on the office wall.

There'd been two cars, and they'd gone round in a big circle, starting and finishing at Heckley, except that Dobson didn't quite make it all the way. They'd driven south, skirting

Huddersfield and Holmfirth, then headed over Saddleworth Moor into Lancashire. We lost them in one or two places but the return journey brought them back over the tops on the Oldfield Road. Maggie took me round and it measured 45 miles.

On the way we stopped at the crash scene to look at the flowers: spray after spray in their cellophane wrappings, stretching along the verge for fifteen yards. I don't know if it was hay fever or the sandwich I'd had in the canteen, but I felt unwell. It must have been hay fever, psychosomatic perhaps, brought on by the sight of all those blooms for a man whose mother had said good riddance to. When it was my turn to shrug off *this mortal coil* the force would chip together to send a wreath, and that would be it. If I'd lived a while after retirement, and memories had faded, pensions branch would remind them about me.

"Someone loved him," Maggie said, reading one of the dedications.

"It looks like it," I replied, adding: "Soon as you get chance come back up and collect all the cards."

In the car I said: "So you've decided they were racing."

"It looks like it," Maggie replied. "Two identical cars, going nowhere, and the same thing a month ago. Early in the morning when the roads are at their quietest. The gypsies used to do it years ago, with ponies and traps. You remember."

"That's right," I said. "And huge sums were gambled on the outcome. I wonder if that's what this was about."

"It's what Rodger thinks."

"He could be right. I spoke to the pathologist this morning."

"And…?"

"Death by multiple injuries consistent with a high-speed motor traffic accident. Traces of alcohol and cocaine in his blood. Minute traces, well below the legal limit for alcohol."

"Just enough to give him an edge?" Maggie suggested.

"Could be."

"In which case he was taking it very seriously. Professional, even."

"It's possible. Oh, and he's a long-term marijuana user"

"Has anything come back about the gun?"

"Yeah. It's a reactivated Glock, but there's no history for it. Bear it in mind: we're dealing with dangerous people. The money came to £500 exactly, in used twenties. Sparky said that's peanuts these days. Kids go out with that much in their back pockets. A few fingerprints but I haven't had a report on any matches."

We were having tea and sausage rolls in the canteen when Maggie asked: "How's Rosie? Have you seen her lately?"

It was between break times and there was nobody else in there, except the serving lady. "No," I replied, squeezing too much brown sauce onto my plate. "I rang her last week and she said she's OK,"

"But she didn't want to continue the relationship?"

"No."

Rosie Barraclough teaches geography and geology at my old school – Heckley Grammar. We'd gone out for a while but Rosie had called it off. She had, she said, too much baggage. My attempts to help her turned to ashes and Rosie was caught in a cycle of depression and remission that was never-ending. Much of the time she was delightful company – amusing and mischievous, with a giggling laugh that had people sitting nearby turning their heads and joining in the fun. But then the memories, the ghosts, would return and soon she'd be back to blaming herself for the sins of the world.

"I'm worried about her," I said. "I think she needs help, if help exists for that sort of thing."

"Pills," Maggie stated. "They work for some people, turn others into zombies."

"We've talked about it, but she says she needs her wits about her when she's in front of 30-odd teenagers, talking about grain production in Estonia."

"God, I bet she does. Is she back at school?"

"Yes, went back for the new term. I rang her the first day to see how it had gone and she was happy enough with things."

"But she didn't want to see you?"

"No."

"Do you want to see her, Charlie?"

"I'm not sure, Maggie. Not sure at all. Well, yes I do, but..."

"You could do without the hassle."

"I suppose so. I like her, like her a lot, and I want to help her."

"But you don't know what you'd be taking on."

"It sounds underhand, selfish, when you put it like that, but you could be right. I'd risk it, Maggie, believe me, I'd risk it, but maybe it's all for the best."

Maggie smiled at me. "No it's not, Charlie, and you don't believe it is, either. Talk to her. That can't do any harm, can it? Talking about things is usually the best way. Invite her out on a foursome, or dinner at our place." She jumped to her feet. "Can't stay here all day chatting or I'll have the boss on to me. Got some doors to knock on."

I met Rosie when I took an evening class about local geology. I do a lot of walking, and like to know what's under my feet and all around me. When the course ended I took her out a few times. The truth was, I'd have done anything for her. She'd had a tough life, with lots of disappointments, and had her problems, but she'd the figure of a fifteen-year-old school-girl and a grin that could halt a charging traffic warden at fifty paces. Her hair was silver and cropped short, and she wore scarlet jeans. My favourite memory was of her waving her geologist's hammer at me, saying: "Ammonites! Ammonites! Bah!" just because I misidentified a fossil. Every sixth-former in Heckley Grammar was in love with her, and at least one old boy.

There was no evidence that any other vehicle was involved so the inquest into the death of Dale Dobson rubber-stamped a misadventure verdict on him. We'd had a word with the coroner about the possibility that he'd been involved in a race but as the other vehicle was apparently miles away at the time of

41

the crash this wasn't mentioned in open court. I told the coroner about the fingerprints and DNA, Mrs Dobson confirmed that the body she'd seen was her son, and the coroner released it for disposal. As we emerged into the weak sunlight I caught up with Mrs Dobson and offered her a lift home.

It wasn't far, and we drove most of the way in silence. I prompted her to speak about Dale but she was deep in her own thoughts. "You don't know who he was working for, or associating with?" I asked, but she just shook her head and mumbled an apology.

"Has anybody contacted you, with messages of condolence or anything?"

"No. Sorry."

"That's OK, but if anybody does will you let me know, please?"

"Yes."

I stopped at her door and wrote my name on a CID card for her. She took it from me and unfastened her seatbelt, hesitating, not sure what to say. I thought she was going to ask me in for a cup of tea, which I would have politely declined, but she said: "The funeral. Who'll pay for the funeral? I can't afford it."

On the way back to the nick I got caught in the school run at Heckley's only private education establishment, and what should have been a fifteen-minute journey took me nearly seventeen. I marched into the office complaining: "What time do they finish at the Valleyside School for Young Ladies and Gentlemen, these days? In my day it was strictly nine till four. They only do half a shift."

There were nods of agreement. "And they get taken both ways in a four-by-four," someone said.

"Well, you can't expect little Coriander and Battenburg to walk there, can you?" another added.

"No, you mean Mezzanine and Lintel."

"Or Hernia and Placenta."

42

"That's enough," I said. "Any messages?"

"On your desk. One of your women wants you to ring her. How'd it go?"

"As expected. Misadventure."

I took my jacket off, trying to look nonchalant, and hung it behind my door. Back in the big office I spooned coffee into a mug and pressed the button on the kettle. When I'd made myself a brew I returned to my office and just happened to read the message.

It was from Mrs Dobson, Dale's mother. Not what I'd been hoping for. Would I ring her? Ah well, I thought, we live in hope. It was timed fifteen minutes ago, not long after I'd dropped her off. I dialled her number.

"There was a note for me," she said, recognising my voice. "A letter, been put through my letterbox. No stamp on it. It says: *Arrange a funeral with Golden Sunsets Funeral Directors. The bill will be taken care of.* That's all."

"No signature?" I asked.

"No, nothing."

"Do you mind if I send someone round to look at it?" I asked.

"No, I don't think so."

It was a slightly ambiguous answer so I interpreted it in our favour. "I'll send someone straight away. Maggie, who came to see you." I looked through my window into the main office and gestured for her to join me. "Meanwhile, try not to handle the note too much."

"What do you think I should do about the funeral, then?"

"I'd do as the note says, no expense spared. Give your son a decent send-off."

Maggie collected the note and we sent it to the forensic laboratory at Wetherton. While she was talking to Mrs Dobson, John Rose knocked on doors. Someone saw a car pull up and a man walk up to Mrs D's front door. It was a large car, but they didn't recognise the make. The man wore a suit and had broad shoulders, "like a weight-lifter."

The report came back about the money, and two days later we had the one on the note. Lots of prints on the money but no matches found. The note, on the other hand, was remarkably clean. Cleaner than would normally be expected.

"That's it, Rodger," I said. "You've given it a good run. It's all very fishy, but so were the Twelve Apostles. We'll see who's at the funeral, just for the record, then we'll have to drop it."

"Fair enough, boss," he replied. "Do you want me back on nights?"

"That's up to you, Rodger. You've done your stint. Do you want a spell on days?"

"No, I don't think so. With Dav on nights I hardly see her. It's ruining our sex life."

"Uh!" I snorted. "What's a sex life?"

It was back to burglaries. We caught a couple, and the CCTV camera in a cornershop enabled us to bring a halt to a string of robberies, so we were earning our corn, if not exactly repelling the rising tide of crime. Much of it has to do with perception. Ask anyone what they think of the crime rate in, say, Canada, and they'll say it is relatively low, people don't lock their doors and the streets are safe to walk down. The facts are different, and their murder rate is approximately twice that of the UK.

The troops handle all that. I was bogged down with the National Intelligence Model and Income Generation and Sponsorship. We were being encouraged to tout local businesses to see if they wanted to sponsor a police car, but I wasn't enamoured at the prospect. If they expected me to drive round in a car with *Pogson's Pork Pies* emblazoned on the side they were mistaken. I don't like Pogson's pork pies. They give me heartburn. And then there's the little matter of the National Intelligence Model. This is a scheme produced by NCIS to make people like me more professional and to be guided by intelligence. Instead of bashing down doors I should sit back with the *Times* crossword, the collected works of Proust and a glass of single malt, and wait until the blinding light of inspiration strikes. Lancashire had been running a pilot scheme for two years, so anything could happen.

It's all about catching big fish. I've nothing against catching big fish. I like catching big fish. Quite a few had fallen for my lure and found themselves in the pan with a glazed look on their faces, but if that big fish had felt a hook through his snout the first time he ever poked it out of the water, he might have led a different life.

Monday morning I was wrestling with POP versus SARA when big Dave came into my office and plonked down in the spare chair. Long ago I discovered that if you could only remember what the acronyms stood for you could not only get by, but you could pass yourself off as an expert. What they *meant* was irrelevant. So there I was, elbows on desk and head in hands, silently mouthing "Problem Orientated Policing" and "Scanning, Analyse, Response, Assessment" when I heard the chair creak and saw his size elevens appear near the left leg of my desk.

"Don't knock, sit down," I said without raising my head.

"Brought you a coffee," he said.

"You're a sweetheart," I told him, sitting back in my chair.

"What's that you're on with?"

"Bullshit from HQ. Did you know that there's a special department in NCIS, employing seventeen graduates, just to think up silly initials for things? I've been trying to sum up the way we work, in the real world. The best I can come up with is *Finger, Arrest, Restrain, Trial*, commonly referred to as FART. Think it will catch on?"

"It's bound to. And it's nice to know that our immediate senior officer is using his time gainfully."

"I do my best. Was there anything special?"

"A couple of things. Sophie's coming up at the weekend, so you're invited over for Sunday lunch, and Dale Dobson's funeral is on Wednesday."

"Great. Put me down for both of them. In fact, we'll both go to the funeral. If the flowers are anything to go by it'll be a big affair."

"You can say that again. Oh, and you owe me twelve quid."

"That's three things. What's the twelve pounds for?"

"The Tony Krabbe lecture. It's next Saturday."

"Right." I waved a weary hand at the papers on my desk. "It'll make a nice change from this lot."

Sophie, my goddaughter, is tall, beautiful and intelligent, and in her final year at Cambridge University, studying history. Her dad is fiercely proud of her and any young man who wants to win Sophie's hand in marriage will need the courage of a lion and the diplomacy of a Daniel. Daniels and lions' dens are what spring to mind when one thinks of big Dave "Sparky" Sparkington and his daughter. Which could mean trouble for a certain rugby-playing youth called Digby Merriman-Flint because Sophie is pregnant by him. I knew it but her parents didn't, and when they found out a Richter force ten would rock Heckley. I was already having doubts about accepting the lunch invite.

John Rose came into my office. "I've just been to the old Bridewell," he said.

"Don't worry about it, John," I told him. "We've only been out of there eight years. You're bound to forget and go back now and again."

"I didn't forget. I went to see what they're doing with it. One of the cells is full of new tackle for this National Intelligence Model initiative. There's all sorts of good stuff."

"Ah!" I exclaimed. "I'm supposed to be an expert on it." I shuffled the papers on my desk and found the one I wanted. "It's all in here. Except, as I understand it, we are to concentrate on NIM, or intelligence led policing rather than on POP, or people orientated policing, which is what we do now."

"*Problem* orientated," John corrected.

"Is it? Well, it's the same thing," I replied. "The people are the problem. Except there's a paper here somewhere that says the two are compatible. It's like the Bible – read into it what you want to hear. I'm asking the Staff Development Centre to organise a course or a training day, but first someone has to tell them all about it. Fancy taking it on?"

"If you want."

"Good lad. And we need some suggestions for the website. Just a couple of sentences. Have a look at what the others have said and pick the best bits out. Devon and Cornwall, or Hampshire. They've nothing better to do." Maggie appeared outside my door looking windswept, and made a knocking motion in mid-air. I waved her in and turned back to John. "So what sort of stuff is there?"

"All sorts. Must be tens of thousands of pounds worth. Cameras, VCRs, projectors, computers, software. Covert operations hardware. There's even a Land Rover according to the Intelligence Unit."

"Covert operations?"

"Yeah. Mini cameras, listening devices, you name it, we've got it."

"What's all this?" Maggie asked.

"New equipment for the DIU," I replied. "High-tech stuff. They're going to replace you all by robots. How've you gone on?"

"Well I hope they don't feel the cold. I've gone on OK. I've collected all the tickets from the bouquets and the wind is cutting like a bread knife up there. I intended coming straight back and preparing a list, but I decided that one of them – a large arrangement of lilies – warranted immediate attention, so I did some detectiving. The card says *Drive on, Mr Speed. In loving memory of Dale. Taken too early, but never forgotten. From Peter and Selina*." She handed me the card, adding: "I reckoned there must have been at least 70- or 80-pounds worth. That's a lot of money just to chuck down at the side of the road."

I said: "Peter and Selina. There can't be too many couples with those names. It'd be interesting to learn who they are."

Maggie pinned me with tight-lipped glare. "I said I did

some detecting. He is Peter Wallenberg and Selina is his delightful trophy wife."

"The new chairman of Heckley Town FC?" John exclaimed.

"The one and only," Maggie confirmed.

"How did you learn all this," I asked.

"Well, let's say one of your robots couldn't have done it, unless it just happened to have a sister-in-law working in Heckley's largest florist shop."

I drummed my fingers on the desk, turned the card over, tried to dislodge a piece of Eccles cake from between my teeth with my tongue. "Sister-in-law?" I said when I decided it wouldn't budge.

"She's Tony's brother's wife. That makes her my sister-in-law."

"Right. Well done, Maggie. There's no substitute for knowing the right people but let's not compromise her any more." I turned to John. "Would you say that this qualified as intelligence-led policing?"

"Spot on, I'd say."

"Me too, so all this covert observation stuff: let's have it organised for the funeral. Rodger is right: there's more to all this than we know about. Ask the surveillance unit if they'd like to try out their new toys and bring us photographic evidence of everybody who attends. Young Dale had friends we wouldn't normally associate with a little scrote like him."

We'd had a dry summer so all the trees had turned colour earlier than usual. Now we were in a cycle of changeable weather, with the wind working its way all around the compass every couple of days. When it was from the north and east we buttoned our jackets for the short trip between house and car, car and office. Soon, when the cold spells joined up, we'd extricate sweaters and vests from the drawers and cupboards where they'd hibernated for the summer. I like the cold weather, but the secret is to dress properly for it.

On the day of the funeral I put on the suit, with a white

shirt and respectful black tie. Then I realised that I'd bought the tie for my father's funeral and worn it at my mother's, too. I took it off again and found a beer-stained blue striped one from the staff college. Respect was one commodity I wouldn't be displaying. It was a good day for a funeral – bright and nippy – so underneath the shirt I wore a Helly Henson base layer, as worn by all decent mountaineers, fishermen and market-traders. I considered the longjohns but decided they were slightly over the top.

Superintendent Gilbert Wood hadn't been too pleased when I told him what I wanted to do, but he soon came round. He usually does. These days we're not allowed to use trickery or any of the other ploys expected of a detective in the pursuit of criminals. To do so is to invoke cries about the invasion of the culprit's civil liberties. And when we mount covert observation of a suspect we are supposed to inform the suspect first. My job is to go out and collect evidence to incriminate villains. Gilbert's job is the make sure that the evidence will stand up in court. Well, that's the way I see it.

"Perhaps he's a relative," he replied with impeccable logic after I'd told him about the flowers from Peter Wallenberg.

"Hmm, yes, I suppose he could be," I agreed.

"But it's unlikely."

"I'd say so."

"Is this the Peter Wallenberg who's the new chairman of the football club?"

"That's the man."

He rummaged through a pile of papers in his *In* tray. "There's an invite from him, somewhere."

"An invite?"

"Yes, to a charity do in the new hospitality suite in the grandstand. Raising funds for something. I've probably thrown it away. They send you a free ticket and it costs you about fifty quid in raffle tickets."

"Ah, the spirit of Scrooge is alive and well. So we can go ahead with it?"

He wasn't happy about photographing all the mourners,

but I pointed out that we had asked the grieving mother for permission, to which she had agreed, and he was pacified.

"It's cold, innit?" Dave whispered, two days later, as I joined him on the back row of the crematorium. "I nearly put my longjohns on."

"Me too."

"Like my socks?" He proffered a leg and hitched his trousers a few inches. The socks had little cartoon characters all over them.

"Very appropriate," I said.

"I've never seen so many red noses outside a circus."

I smiled. He was right. Everybody was white-faced from the cold and red-nosed from sniffing. I think that was the cold, too, rather than sniffs of grief, but I could have been wrong. A young woman with two toddlers was weeping copiously and I saw a few dabs from tissues. Dave and I were at the crematorium but there was a church service first at St Hilda's. I was surprised how many people came. Usually, I thought, all the business was done at the church, with the crematorium only dealing with the disposal of the body, as the businesslike language of the undertakers puts it.

Mrs Dobson was in the careful hands of Maggie. I didn't want any of Dale's friends talking to her. She was vulnerable, they were plausible and wealthy, and I needed her on my side. When they arrived from the church Maggie led her to the front and sat down beside her. We didn't exchange glances.

"36 here," Dave whispered. "Plus me, you and Maggie and three from covert ops."

"That's about 34 more than I'll get," I replied. "Wonder how many went to the church service." A woman in a black coat with fur collar and hat walked to the front to offer her condolences to Mrs Dobson. They shook hands and the woman made her way towards the back of the chapel again, looking to her left and right as she decided where to sit. "Who's that?" I asked. "I've seen her before."

"She's a DC at HQ."

"Is she?" If she had a camera hidden in her hat – and, I discovered later, she did – she had probably just recorded the entire congregation.

A vicar gave a diplomatic speech about Dale's life, making him sound like a misunderstood genius who'd lived ahead of his time, and not the racist yob we knew him to be. He stopped short of listing him alongside Van Gogh, Lawrence of Arabia and Elvis, but it was a close thing. Dale was snatched from us by a jealous God's fickle hand, and the loss was ours. This was a condensed version of the eulogy he'd spouted at the church, and I was glad to be spared the real thing.

A skinhead in a tuxedo stumbled through *Do not stand at my grave and weep*, his voice wavering and fading at the difficult bits due more to his inability to read rather than any emotion, and Dale Dobson, deceased, was sent on his last ride to the sound of Tina Turner's *Simply the Best* coming from a cheap ghetto blaster. Most of the men in the congregation went forward to lay a hand on the coffin before it went squeaking and jerking into the furnace. I rummaged amongst the literature provided – Bible, hymn book, order of service – to see if there was a sick bag.

4

We all went our separate ways after the funeral, picking up the threads of the other jobs we were following. Dale Dobson's standing in the criminal community wasn't such that crime came to a respectful halt while he'd been lying in state. That night the sky was filled with exploding fireworks, and bonfires lit up the countryside, but they were to celebrate another death, 400 years earlier. We were promised the photographs for Friday morning, so I called a meeting in the afternoon.

"Best funeral I've ever been to," Jeff Caton said. "The vicar did a lovely job. Everybody cried their eyes out."

"How many were there?" I asked.

"About 150, including children. There were three young women with toddlers who all looked similar. He appeared to have a penchant for anaemic looking blondes aged about seventeen."

Dave was Blu-Tacking a selection of the best pictures on the wall all down one side of the office and we crowded round to inspect them as each new image was revealed.

"C'mon, Dave, we haven't got forever," someone remonstrated.

"Leave him alone," another added. "He can't help it. It'll come to all of us, one day."

I said: "At the funeral he wore socks with little Mickey Mouses all over them. Very disrespectful."

"Mickey Mouses?" Jeff Caton queried. "You mean Mickey Mice."

I thought about it for a second. "No," I stated. "Mickey Mouses. One Mickey Mouse, two Mickey Mouses."

"There's no such word as mouses."

"I've just invented it."

"The plural of mouse is mice."

"Not if it's a name. If you were ordering two pints of Black

Sheep at the bar would you ask for two Black Sheep or two Black Sheeps?"

"Ah, you've got him there, Chas," someone said. "He's never asked for two drinks before."

Dave pressed the final picture against the wall and dusted his hands together to indicate he'd done his bit.

"Right, so who stands out?" I asked.

"Him," John Rose stated, tapping a picture with a pencil. "Bono from U2."

"Do we know who he is?" The image in question was of an unsmiling man in his thirties with his hair tied back in an apology of a ponytail. It's hard to tell from photos but I guessed him to be of below average height and with a dark complexion. He was wearing a long overcoat, buttoned up to his neck, with black leather gloves and just a flash of white shirt cuff showing. A beautiful woman with dark hair was permanently next to him.

"Peter Wallenberg," John told us. "Wealthy saviour of Heckley Town Football Club."

"So presumably that's his wife, Selina."

"I guess so."

"She's a stunner. "

"He walks with a limp. I wasn't sure but I think he was wearing one of those boots with a thick sole."

"Like when you have a club foot?"

"Or in his case, a football club foot."

"Hmm. So how does a runt like him with a club foot pull a bird like her?"

"Well, being able to afford to buy a football club must help. The word on the streets is that he met her in a Dutch brothel, but that may not be true. Want me to have a look at her?"

"Yep, might as well."

Dave chipped in with: "We used to play for them, didn't we, Chas."

"We certainly did. When they were winning games."

Someone said: "God, no wonder they're in dire straits."

"Anybody else?" I asked.

Names were reeled off, some familiar and some who were strangers to me, but all, according to the troops, prominent figures in the flashier end of business life in Heckley and district.

"Label them all up," I said, "and look into the ones we don't recognise. John, will you have a closer look at Wallenberg while you're looking at his missus. See how he earns his daily bread, please?"

"Already done, boss. No visible means of support other than inheritance. His father was Frank Wallenberg who earned a fortune in property speculation back in the Sixties. He came into the business high and went from strength to strength. According to Leeds he made his stake money out of protection, gambling and prostitution, although he was never prosecuted. Off the record, they say that more than one of his girls had a key to the judges' lodgings. His business partner in those days was a man called Crozier, Joe Crozier, known as Crazy Joe back then, who still lives in Leeds. Frank died of cancer in 1993 and his wife, Grace, took over the running of the empire. She died of the big C two years ago."

My parents died of cancer. It knows no boundaries, respects nobody, listens to no argument. It's the great equaliser, and a bastard of a disease.

"So it all came to him," I heard someone say.

"Looks like it."

"Can I ask a simple question, boss?"

"Fire away."

"Well, apart from two stolen cars and possession of a firearm, what's the crime?"

"Ah! That's a very good point. I'm glad you asked. There isn't one. But there ought to be. From now on we crack them before they happen. It's called Intelligence Led Policing, ILP for short."

"Right. Thanks for clarifying that."

"Any time. It's what I'm here for." There was a long silence, broken only by a cough from Dave, but nobody came out with an apt comment. "Maggie!" I snapped.

"Yes, boss."

"Any luck with the flowers?"

"Nothing special. We collected all the tags at the crematorium – it's what happens, so the bereaved can send out little *thank you* notelets to all concerned – and made a list. The only thing noticeable was that there was another wreath of lilies at the church from Peter and Selina but one at the crematorium simply from someone called S. 'With all my love, S,' is what it said."

"So he was knocking off the boss's wife?"

"Looks like it. Why else would she send a personal wreath to the crematorium, over and above the one she and her husband sent to the church? Want me to check with my sister-in-law at the florists…"

"No," I said, interrupting her. "We've pushed this as far as we need. Keep it all handy because I've a feeling that we'll be hearing about Mr Wallenberg again, one day. That's it, boys and girls. If there's nothing else I suggest you all dash off home to the bosoms of your families."

I stayed behind, writing it up in my diary and tidying a few other things. It's amazing how much you can get through when there are no interruptions. At 6.30 I rang Rosie. She was in.

"Hello, Charlie," she said. "This is a pleasant surprise."

"Which?" I replied. "Pleasant or a surprise?"

"Both, of course. How are you?"

"Fine, just fine. Nothing too heavy at work so it's all going hunky dory. How about you? Last time we spoke you thought a couple of girls in the new class might give you some grief."

"Hmm, yes. Something happens to them at about thirteen. They've had their navels pierced and walk around with bare midriffs. It's not a pretty sight, but the head has taken them out of class and told their parents to send them to school more suitably dressed. Are you still at work?"

"Just about to leave and I'm starving. Do you fancy a tea-time special at the Bamboo Curtain?" I have to be circumspect when I invite Rosie out. Make it sound casual, like we're just buddies and I'm going to the restaurant anyway because I need to eat. That way, I'm in with a chance. Any hint of romance, however, or any suggestion that it might be a *date*, and the portcullis comes down.

"Oh, I'm sorry, Charlie, but I've eaten already." Damn. I must have sounded too eager. "And I've just started stripping wallpaper from the hallway. Keeping busy, as per doctor's orders."

"Did he mean it so literally? Reading a book could count as keeping busy, couldn't it?"

"Hmm… perhaps, but I think there should be an element of physical effort."

"OK, so read a book while popping chocolates into your mouth."

"And then I'll get a big bum. Tell you what: I'll have done in there in about an hour, and it's thirsty work. A quick drink would be most welcome, if that's OK with you."

Oh! I thought. Perhaps I hadn't pitched it too badly, after all. I went home for a shower and to change my clothes and refresh the aftershave. We drove up on to the tops to a road-house with fake beams, a children's room and fizzy beer. Not the first choice for a connoisseur of real ale, but one I knew would be reasonably quiet on a Friday night.

Rosie was wearing her customary red sweater, but with black trousers, leather jacket and boots. As she slid into the passenger seat I wanted to tell her how terrific she looked, wanted to throw my arms around her slim shoulders, wanted to give her a welcoming kiss, but I didn't. I said: "Hi. Did you finish the wallpapering?"

"Wallpapering's tomorrow," she replied. "Tonight it was stripping the old stuff. You look smart. Thanks for coming over."

"Thank you. We aim to please. Not going to see your mother tomorrow?"

"No, I'll go next week. If I didn't go at all she wouldn't

know. She can't remember my name and two minutes after I leave she's forgotten that I've been. It's a tragic way to end your days. Where are you taking me?"

We sat in a corner, near a gas fire with realistic logs ablaze on it, and shared our week's triumphs and disasters. Rosie told me all the school gossip, which mainly concerned the diversion of funds from the school's sports facilities into yet more computers, and I told her all about the funeral. It was really cheery stuff, so I decided to change the subject.

"Tomorrow," I said, "three of us from the office are going to the Town Hall for a lecture by Tony Krabbe."

"The mountaineer? That should be interesting. He's climbed Everest, hasn't he?"

"Mmm. I never thought to invite you along. In fact, I was invited myself. If you'd really like to come I could tell one of the others that I needed his ticket."

"Ha ha, you wouldn't, would you?"

No, but I could have wheedled and pleaded with Sparky, told him how much it meant to me, until he handed his ticket over. I said: "I'd've tried, but they'd probably have told me where to go."

"It's made of limestone, you know. It was at the bottom of the sea, once." Rosie knows stuff like that.

"What, Mount Everest?"

"Chomolungma to the locals. Mother Goddess of the Universe."

"That's interesting. So presumably it just popped up out of the sea when India crashed into Asia?"

"Um, well, yes. Not the language I'd use, but the essence is there."

I said: "I know him, Tony Krabbe, went to school with him. We were in the same football team."

"Were you? What's he like?"

"He was OK, a bit of a golden boy, even then. Literally. He had fair hair, which was always on the long side. All the girls thought the world of him, as did most of the teachers. He was in the year above me. I quite liked him."

"Don't tell me: you had a schoolboy crush on him."

"Ha! You can read me like a book."

I took Rosie home, left the engine running as we stopped outside her house, thanked her for coming out with me. She said it was nice to have a change of scenery but didn't invite me in for a coffee. There was an awkward silence as she opened her door to go, then she leaned over, pecked me on the cheek and was gone.

I drove home feeling pleased with myself. Rosie has had her bad times, but was coping well, had her life under control. She once told me about the lines she'd drawn in the sand, beyond which she wouldn't trespass. *No alcohol in the house and never drink alone.* That made good sense, and just the odd drink at other times. *Go to work, even during the bad spells.* Quit once, ring in to say you couldn't make it, and the bar would be that little bit lower the next time. *Shower and change knickers and bra every day.* I'd pulled a face, saying I thought that was excessive, and we'd had a laugh. By being a friend, but not making any demands, I hoped I was helping her. My motives were suspect, entirely selfish, but it's the practicalities that count.

I hadn't had a crush on Tony Krabbe. In fact, the idea of boy-boy relationships of a sexual nature never occurred to me back in those days. Homosexuality was thought to be a product of the public school system, and just wasn't on the curriculum at wholesome, coeducational Heckley Grammar. But I had admired him.

Once every year we had a plum football fixture against the local private school, which we looked forward to for a variety of reasons: their pitch was level; the grass was short; they had hot showers; they fed us lemonade and biscuits after the game. But most of all we liked going there because they were useless.

We were leading four-nil with a minute left to play when Krabbe was brought down in their penalty area. He'd scored two of the goals and was now looking at a hat-trick. I was keeping goal at the other end and had made a couple of brilliant saves, but otherwise it had been a quiet game for me. Krabbe, the captain, placed the ball on the penalty spot, stood as if to compose himself for the kick, then turned and waved for me to come up and take it. He didn't have to do that. It was almost unheard of. I jogged up the field, slammed the ball into the back of the net and we won five-nil, with C. Priest on the scoresheet.

I've been on all sorts of courses while doing the job, and I have a certain amount of responsibility. My staff work long hours and are often exposed to danger. I ask them to do things, get into situations, which are above and beyond what an employer can normally expect of his workers. Until now I'd completely forgotten the Krabbe incident, but suddenly I couldn't help thinking that his generous gesture had taught me more about man management than all the training sessions and away days that I'd ever attended.

There was a message on the ansaphone when I arrived home. It was Rosie, thanking me for the drink, but the unspoken message was to thank me for not putting any pressure on her. I went to bed feeling reasonably happy. Totally confused, but reasonably happy.

There's a tourist attraction on the southern edge of the city of Leeds called Thwaite Mills. It stands on an island in the River Aire as part of the city's industrial heritage, preserved for posterity as a reminder of the days when work meant bending one's back, producing something. The river turns a pair of water wheels, the water wheels rotate a series of shafts, and an ingenious arrangement of pulleys and belts transfer the power to various applications. Grinding, mixing and grading. In the nineteenth century barges would bring stone, corn, oilseed and logwood to the mill, and sail away laden with flour, china clay, chalk, dyestuff, putty and fuel oil. Nowadays the wheels only turn as a curiosity, when there is an audience, to demonstrate the inventiveness of our forbears.

The schoolchildren showed more interest in the mill than

the teacher had expected. It was Friday afternoon and the weekend beckoned, but they listened politely to the guide, made notes and ticked boxes on the multi-choice questionnaire they'd been provided with. The place reeks of age, and it's easy to imagine the bustle and hubbub when it was working at full speed: the pulleys spinning; the transmission belts flapping and beams of sunlight slanting through the airborne dust. Sacks would be filled, hoisted on to strong but aching shoulders and carried to the waiting boats in an endless procession.

The kids gathered round as the guide told them how the big, eighteen foot wheels were controlled, then peered over the handrail as he started to open the sluice and the black water churned as if by some unseen monster of the deep.

As the wheel creaked and groaned and the first paddle rose out of the water they thought it was a joke, played on them by the staff in a feeble attempt to keep them interested. It happened all the time. Or perhaps it was somebody's left-over Guy Fawkes, tossed into the river rather than into the flames. When the streaming body lifted clear one or two girls giggled nervously, unsure of their first conclusions. When the head lolled over and they saw the bloated face and empty eye-sockets, there could be no doubt what it was, and the screaming started.

I heard it on the local news as I drove home from the office, Saturday lunchtime: "The body of a man found in the River Aire at Thwaite Mills is believed to be that of a local businessman who hasn't been seen for over two weeks." I used to work in Leeds and knew the location well. If he'd been in the river a fortnight he probably fell in somewhere near the city centre. Leeds Bridge was a good place for it. In my day it was all run-down warehouses near there, but now it has been redeveloped and turned into a yuppie colony. It's easy to fall into the river when you've done a few lines of coke on top of all that nouveaux Beaujolais. I thought no more of it, defrosted a chicken rogan josh for lunch and spent the afternoon doing damage limitation in the garden. I cleared the borders of dead stuff, mowed the grass – I never refer to it as lawn – and raked up the first flush of dead leaves. I was complimenting myself on being ahead of the game when it occurred that they were probably left over from last year.

Dave came to pick me up to go to the Tony Krabbe lecture, and Jeff Caton was already with him. Dave was wearing his Gore-Tex anorak.

"Thought I'd look the part," he explained. "Professional, like."

"Wally, you mean," Jeff said.

"Take no notice," I said. "You look just fine, and if it snows in the town hall you'll be prepared for it."

"Did you hear about Joe Crozier?" Dave asked asked.

"No. Who's he?"

"One of the names that cropped up when we were talking about Peter Wallenberg, yesterday. Don't you listen?"

"Not always. Sometimes, when Jeff and John are speaking I have a tendency to drift off. Give me it again, please."

Jeff took over. "Peter Wallenberg inherited his fortune from his father, Frank, who was a crook. His partner was Joe Crozier and between them they had Leeds and most of the old West Riding just about sewn up. Prostitution, protection – you name it, they controlled it. Well, yesterday, they fished Joe's body out of the river. A bunch of schoolkids were being shown around this old museum when up came a floater."

"How do you know all this?"

"Connections. Old friend Nigel is investigating detective. I rang him to see if he fancied a drink, later."

"As you do."

"Yes. As you do."

"Young Mr Newley?" I grinned at the thought of it. Nigel was one of my protégés and destined for high things, if he could shake off the cosy dust of Heckley and a few of the bad habits I'd passed on to him, and make his own mark in the force.

"I heard about the body," I said. "At a guess it went in somewhere near the city centre. So what's it to do with us?"

61

"Nothing," Jeff said. "It's just one of those strange occurrences. You go all your life without hearing a name and suddenly you hear it twice in two days. It happens all the time."

"Well," I pointed out, "when a person dies in strange circumstances they do tend to get their name in the papers. I bet you hear it a few times more in the next few days."

"Ah, but the first time was unrelated to his death."

"That's true. We must have put the mockers on him. Is foul play suspected?"

"No, I don't think so. According to Nigel they're looking into it because of Crozier's background. He lived near the river... enjoyed a drink or eight... Splash."

"Nige will sort it. Have we time for a snifter before this lecture starts?"

5

The talk was brilliant. Or the pictures were. For nearly an hour he showed us breathtaking shots, gathered over his early years, of some of the most beautiful places on Earth. You could imagine a climber being content to sit down on some of the peaks and freeze to death rather than turn away from the view and drop back down into humdrum normality. We saw vast snowfields, hanging by a breath on the mountain sides; jagged arêtes leading to unnamed peaks; ranges that stretched away forever into China and Tibet; tiny coloured specks of humanity dwarfed into insignificance on immense rock faces.

And then the mood changed. We were on Everest, it was late in the day and the weather was turning. He was climbing with his best friend, called Jeremy Quigley, but Jeremy was having trouble and dropped back at the Hillary Step, a 40-foot rock wall within spitting distance of the summit. Krabbe summited, took the pictures, then got down as fast as he could to camp IV, expecting Jeremy to be already there.

But he wasn't, and Krabbe never saw him again.

He made it sound like some sort of an epiphany. He brooded on the death of his friend for weeks, mooching around Kathmandu, witnessing the trend towards teams of well-heeled armchair adventurers and their guides heading towards the mountain, recognising the way things were changing. He costed the flash gear they brought for the Sherpas to carry for them and contrasted it with the dire poverty of the local people. At base camp he surveyed the mess: the discarded food packets; oxygen bottles; climbing gear and gas cylinders. Human faeces were everywhere, waiting for the brief summer to reduce them to something less offensive.

He was disgusted, and ashamed of the part he'd played in the desecration of the area. He loved the mountains, but didn't want to climb any more. He decided to do what he could to help the people who lived there; to help clean up the mess that richer people had imposed on them; to raise money to improve the health and education of the children. That's why he was there, that night, talking to us.

Dave bought the book. It cost £28 and weighed about the same.

"Are you going to introduce yourself?" he asked as we hovered on the edge of the small crowd waiting for a signature. Krabbe hadn't changed much in the intervening 30-odd years. We grow older, but the essence of a person always remains. Or perhaps the brain of the viewer makes compensations, subconsciously adjusting to allow for greying and receding hair, wrinkles and the effects of gravity.

"Hmm, no, I don't think so," I replied.

But Dave had other ideas. Krabbe scrawled his name across the title page of *Kingdoms of the Gods*, underlined it with a flourish and pushed the tome back across the table, saying: "Thanks. I hope you enjoy it."

Dave said: "I'm sure I will. Do you remember this fellow?"

Krabbe looked up, puzzled. He was as handsome as ever, I noted, still with rakishly long hair. Our eyes met, blue to blue: his the colour of glacial pools; mine, I'm told, more of a cornflower hue; then his craggy, tanned face split into a grin and he said: "Well I'll be damned, Charlie Priest."

His handshake nearly maimed me. His fingers were thick with scar tissue and calluses, and as powerful as hydraulic grabs. They had to be. His life had depended on their strength throughout his career. "Hello, Tony. How're you keeping?" I gasped, flinching.

"Fine, Charlie. Fine. This is a surprise. Are you still playing footy?"

"Um, no. I gave that up long ago."

"That's a shame. I thought you had what it takes. I always envied you, playing in goal. You're a cop, aren't you. It's coming back to me. I read about you in the papers – you caught that bastard who murdered the girls. God, that must have given you some satisfaction."

I said: "Well, we can't all climb Mount Everest. Some of us have more modest ambitions." The woman behind us coughed impatiently and we stepped aside so she could have her book signed. I told Krabbe that the talk was brilliant and thought-provoking and wished him well with his campaign.

"Listen, Charlie," he said. "We ought to have a chat sometime." He patted his pockets, saying he didn't have a card on him. "I'll be around for the next few weeks. Why don't you pop into the shop? You should catch me there, most mornings."

"The shop?" I queried.

"Art of Asia, in Heckley Mall. We import ethnic artefacts. It's all part of the mission, trying to earn foreign currency for them at a fair rate."

"I know it, but I didn't realise it was yours. Yes, I'll call in."

We exchanged handshakes again and Dave thanked him for the talk and the book. Ten minutes later, when we were seated in a quiet corner of the Spinners Arms, fondling our drinks, Dave said: "He's a nice bloke, don't you think?"

"Hmm," I agreed. "Very nice."

Jeff said: "It must be a fantastic feeling, standing on top of Everest, the highest point on Earth. The views across into Tibet were incredible. I know he disapproves of these expeditions where you pay, but I'd go on one if I could afford it. What's £30,000 for something you'd remember for the rest of your life?"

"Especially if the rest of your life was about two hours," I commented.

"How much did he say they charged for a permit? £15,000 was it?"

"That's right, or was it dollars? The Nepalese regard the mountain as a natural resource, and exploit it to the full. Some countries got the oil, they got a mountain. God help 'em, they didn't get much else. Let's have a look at the book, please, Dave."

He passed it to me, two-handed, and my arms sank under its weight. I sat with it on my knees, not wanting to put it on the table with its beer-rings, and opened it near the middle.

A photography geek at the lecture had asked what sort of camera he'd used, but didn't get the answer he wanted. Krabbe said that conditions were either so bad you couldn't take photos or so good, up there above the clouds, that you could take decent pictures with a pinhole camera. The only thing you had to do was have the camera acclimatised, so it would keep working at those temperatures and altitudes. The geek went home disgruntled, deprived of a long dissertation on f-stops and focal lengths. The rest of the audience sighed in relief.

Whatever he'd used, the photos took your breath away. I like the outdoors, enjoy being in high places, and thumbed through Krabbe's book with undisguised envy. It's all about dedication, I told myself. Krabbe had wanted these things, had made sacrifices to attain them. He'd probably turned his back on a career, perhaps ruined his home life, because he wanted to climb more than anything else he knew about. I'd drifted into being a cop, but I enjoyed it, most of the time, and it paid the rent.

Dave and Jeff were wittering on about the dangers of avalanches on the Khumbu glacier and the merits of prusiks and Jumars. Krabbe had won at least two converts. I was looking at the brown faces of two children in woolly hats, grinning at the white man's camera like a pair of idiots, although the hunger never left their bellies. I turned to the book's jacket to read what it said about the man himself. It was modest enough, mentioning his OBE and the fact he'd climbed Everest. I looked at the list of reviews and saw that all the broadsheets had lavished praise on it. I half expected to see one from the Dalai Lama - "If you have two loaves, sell one and put it towards a copy of this book" - but was disappointed.

The very last page had a list of companies and individuals who had sponsored Krabbe throughout his career. All the big names that you see on anoraks and boots and skis were there, plus a list of local businessmen who had presumably chipped in for the next expedition, when asked, providing a much-needed box of Kendal mint cake or simply a new set of tyres for his car. It was Krabbe's way of saying thank you to them.

Jeff was telling Dave about the death zone when I interrupted him.

"What, Chas," he replied.

"Coincidences," I stated. "Remember what you were saying earlier, about a name cropping up twice, close together, for different reasons?"

"You mean Joe Crozier?"

"Yes. It's just happened again. There's a list of Tony Krabbe's sponsors here, on the very last page of the book. They're in alphabetical order, just to show that he values the smallest of them as much as the largest. The final one on the list is someone else we've heard of, associated with Crozier: Peter Wallenberg Esquire, spinster of this county."

"Let's have a look," Dave said, reaching for the book, and I passed it to him. He studied the list for a while, head down, brow furrowed, before saying: "This is starting to look fishy to me."

"Do you think so?"

"Mmm. I wonder what he wanted in return. If this becomes part of an enquiry, will I be able to claim the book on expenses?"

We didn't stay long in the pub. Dave was driving and it was my weekend to be senior detective on call. It comes round every six weeks, starting at 10 p.m. Friday, and I was expected to remain alert and lucid. We dropped Jeff off at his local, where he would probably imbibe freely until loss of the use of his limbs indicated to him that he'd had enough, or his audience deserted him, whichever came first. Dave took me home and came in for a coffee.

It was nearly ten thirty and we were well into a discussion on investments and pensions when the phone rang. I gave

67

him the here-we-go smile and picked it up. A uniformed constable had been called to a body lying in the garden of a house just outside Heckley and he'd radioed in to say it was a murder. Now they needed a senior detective to confirm things and set the wheels rolling.

"What makes him so sure it's a murder?" I asked.

"Well, the deceased has a pickaxe embedded in his head," I was told, rather tartly. "Not a usual MO for a suicide."

"I'm convinced," I said, flicking the top off a pen and turning to a blank page on the memo pad. "Give me the details."

It was a nineteenth century mansion on the south side of town, surrounded by trees and converted into four luxury apartments. Once upon a time it had housed a local surgeon and his family and their small army of retainers. Rooms that had once been home to the pastry cook, the nanny and the maid now echoed to the clink of glasses of Chardonnay, the Opera Babes on the CD player and shouted conversations about the merits of personal trainers. The PC who'd raised the call had the good sense to turn his blue light off and was sitting in darkness just outside the electrically operated gates. I parked behind him and Dave – try to keep him away – pulled in behind me.

There's a popular misconception that for every murder we straightaway call in the pathologist, the scenes of crime people and all the other experts. We don't. We haven't enough of them and they cost money. Fortunately, most murders are committed by someone close who we just happen to find sitting there with his head in his hands, saying: "I didn't mean to kill her." If we are reasonably certain who did the deed we just get on with it and don't waste time with fingertip searches and DNA swabs of half the town.

But this didn't look like one of those.

"Any ideas who he is?" I asked the PC when he climbed out of the panda to meet me. He looked about seventeen.

"No, Sir."

"Boss or Mr Priest will do," I said. "So tell me about it."

"Well, Sir, I took the call at 21.40 and came straight here. One of the residents had come home and parked his car in the car barn and as he walked to the rear door of the house he came across a body, lying across the path. It was obviously dead so he rang the police, um, us."

"And is it obviously dead?"

"Yes, Sir. There's a pickaxe embedded in his head. It's in solid; must be about six inches into his brain."

"OK, you're right: it looks as if we have a murder on our hands. I'll ring the pathologist and the duty superintendent and we'll call in the experts." I looked at the imposing façade of the building, discreetly illuminated by concealed lighting. One window on the top floor was lit, all the others were in darkness. "Is that where the resident you met lives?" I asked.

"Yes, Sir. I told him to stay indoors, and it looks as if everybody else is out."

"But he didn't recognise the body?"

"No, Sir. He said he didn't know any of the other residents. Everybody liked to…"

"I know," I interrupted. "They like to *keep themselves to themselves*. It's a national disease."

"Um, aren't you going to look for yourself, Sir?" the PC ventured.

"At the body? Nah," I replied airily. "Seen one, you've seen 'em all. And stop calling me sir. Let's make these phone calls."

The PC looked disappointed that I hadn't rushed in to the crime scene, so I explained to him. We'd sent for the pathologist, who could tell us time and cause of death, and the SOCOs who would look for microscopic evidence. Neither of them wanted me blundering over the landscape. Anything I could deduce from a cursory examination of the body and its immediate surroundings, which I grandly referred to as the overview, would usually wait until they had finished. Not always, but usually. The secret is to know when to act swiftly and when to be patient.

Slowly the scene changed as people arrived to contribute their own special fields of knowledge in a process that would build up a picture of the victim and his death, and ultimately lead to his killer. I told the PC to record everybody who visited, and Dave wandered off to do his own investigation, knocking on the doors of the nearest neighbours. It was a black night, and everybody was working by torchlight. There was a danger that we'd overlook something obvious, lying in the herbaceous border, and were destroying evidence by trampling over the scene, so I decided to move the body, seal off the area and do a thorough examination in daylight. A photographer did his best to record the site in stills and video and a SOCO made a preliminary walk-through search, holding his flashlight close to the ground so that anything down there would cast a long shadow.

It was nearly two o'clock when the undertaker's van arrived and the pathologist told them where he wanted the body taking.

"I want to see it before you put it on the gurney," I insisted.

"C'mon, then, Charlie," the pathologist said. "I have to say, you've been very patient. What we have is a male, about 45 or 50, killed by a single, determined blow sometime between 21:00 and 22:30 last evening. His body temp is down by about two degrees and hypostasis has hardly started." Dave had rejoined me and we followed the pathologist through the gates and round the side of the house, along a path delineated by blue tape and then on raised metal stepping plates laid by the SOCOs.

The light of our torches flickered over the gravel, and shadows of plants loomed and swayed around us. I could smell wet compost, cut grass and, I imagined, the heavy scent of late roses like the ones Rosie grew. I wondered what she was doing. A pale cat strolled across our pool of light, emerging from the gloom like a spectre before mewing at our trespass onto his territory and moving off into the enveloping blackness again. Into his forests of the night. Oh, to know what you know, I thought. Not far away a leftover firework exploded, startling us all.

"There he is," the professor said, pinning the body with the beam of his torch. It was lying face downwards, legs towards us, one arm flung above the head and the other out sideways, as if he'd been about to make a right turn on a bicycle. A wooden shaft stood almost vertically away from it, the lower end firmly rooted in the skull.

It's always a shock when you see a dead body. None of us shows it, but I'm sure we all give a shudder and think about our own mortality. Those who don't probably never admired a sunset or were moved by an Elgar concerto. I stepped off the plates and Dave followed me, neither of us speaking. The head lay in a pool of blood which was black when our torches weren't directly on it, but startlingly red when they were. The victim's long hair was matted with it, pasted to the ground. I sank down to sit on my heels and reached a tentative hand towards the head, feeling under it for the chin. Dave kept his torch beam steady on where I was working. I grasped the chin and turned the head slightly until I could confirm what I already thought.

Dave said: "Well, bugger me."

I turned to the pathologist as I rose up again, saying: "That's his ID sorted, Prof. He's called Tony Krabbe."

"Tony Krabbe? You mean... the mountaineer?"

"Ex-mountaineer," Dave corrected. "His mountaineering days are over."

I visited the scene briefly on Sunday morning then spent the rest of the day in the office. It's all about teams and lists, and it was my job to manage them. We cleared the incident room of the stuff left over from the previous case: wiped the computers clean; took the maps and diagrams off the walls; and started to fill them with new stuff. I opened a diary and murder log and my admin officer, drafted in from HQ, supervised the creation of a property book, message book, job sheets, daily duty lists and correspondence file. An action allocator, statement reader and exhibits officer were appointed.

One team looked into the victim's background for any likely suspects; another into his family connections. We looked at

71

the MO – which was fruitless as this was a first – listened to various theories from members of the public and did a house-to-house. All this was routine, laid down in the manual. The only bit of creative thinking was to have somebody look into the Wallenberg connection, if there was one.

Monday morning we had a briefing and update meeting. The detective super who lorded under the title of senior investigating officer gave a pep talk to the troops, saying that this was a high profile case involving a media celebrity, so we had to be on our best behaviour, thanked them for working the weekend and handed over to the investigating detective: *moi*.

The post mortem findings revealed nothing relevant. It looked as if Krabbe had come straight home from the lecture and met his death after parking his car in the car barn, as the estate agents like to call the sheltered parking place that passes for a garage.

"…and he drove a TVR Tasmin," I was told.

"Wow!" somebody exclaimed. "Nought to 60 in 6.2 seconds."

Sometimes I wonder if I'm employing a bunch of petrol heads. I said: "Let's keep it relevant, please. What's next?"

Suspects. Most of all, we need suspects. The team looking into Krabbe's background had unearthed the fact that he'd lost a companion on Everest. What was the full story, someone asked? Had Krabbe done enough to try save him?

"Good point," I said. "Climbing's a close-knit community and the dead man no doubt had friends and family. Krabbe talked about him… I've forgotten his name…"

"Jeremy Quigley."

"Thanks. Jeremy Quigley. Krabbe talked about him in the warmest of terms at the lecture on Saturday. He sounded genuinely moved about it."

"Guilty conscience?"

"Could be. Stay with it. Who was looking into his family?" One of my DCs stood up and opened his notebook. "What have you found, Robert?" I asked.

"Something fairly interesting. First of all, he's only lived back in Heckley for about six months, since he bought the apartment in the block where he was found. His parents are still alive, in their eighties and living up in the Isle of Arran."

"Presumably they were informed."

"Yes. All dealt with. Krabbe has never married but he's had a series of relationships, mainly with women climbers. Two were Austrian girls and one New Zealander. But the longest, and most interesting, was with Sonia Thornton."

"The runner?" Sonia Thornton had been Yorkshire's golden girl a few years ago. She'd come second in the London marathon and had a string of high-profile successes at various distances. Apart from that, she was attractive and articulate, and the media loved her. Sonia was hot favourite to win the Olympic 5 000 Metres in Atlanta until, two days before the team flew out, she injured a leg in a car crash and her athletics career came to an end.

"The one and only. Apparently they were a couple from about 1989 right up to the accident, in 1996, although they spent a great deal of the time apart because of their various commitments. He was off climbing and she trained in Arizona for much of the year. They kept the relationship fairly secret because it was thought that living with someone might not fit in with Sonia's clean-cut image and damage her mar-ketability."

"And that's what it's all about, these days. Was he with her when she had the accident?"

"Yes, it was his car, but unfortunately she was driving. Their story was that a car came round a bend on the wrong side of the road. A couple of yobs were in the front seats but they didn't get any sort of a description. Sonia braked hard and lost control. Went off the road and hit a tree."

"That's right, I remember all the fuss. I don't suppose the misguided, misunderstood young people in the other car stopped to render assistance, did they?"

"'Fraid not, boss. Would you believe it, they kept right on going."

"How unfortunate. Have you spoken to her?"

"No, not yet."

"I'd like to be there when you do."

Little of interest was been found at Krabbe's apartment. It was decorated with artefacts from Asia, as one might expect, but he'd bought it fully furnished so his mark had not yet been stamped on the place. There was a magnificent panorama of the Karakorams on the living room wall, and above the desk in his study was a picture of him dangling one-handed from an overhang on El Capitan, in Yosemite, with a Dylan quote added: *He not busy being born is busy dying.* I'd never thought of the line in that context, but I liked it. The flat was remarkably free of climbing paraphernalia, but he had another place in Austria and, like most peripatetic climbers, tended to store his stuff anywhere he could: usually with friends who were slightly more settled than he was. When an expedition was due he'd just wander round and collect what he needed. It was a hand-to mouth existence, and until relatively recently he'd not been very well off, earning just enough money to pay for the next trip. Now, it appeared, money from his writing was starting to build up, he'd started manufacturing specialist climbing equipment under his own name and he had the shop in the mall. Things had been looking good for him.

"OK," I said. "What about the ground search team? Anything found there?"

"Fuck all, boss, so far, but we're pretty sure the body wasn't moved."

"Thank you. Succinct and to the point. And that brings us round to the weapon." It had come back from forensics and lain on the desk in front of me throughout the meeting, enclosed in a transparent ziploc bag. I picked it up and held it aloft. "It's an ice axe," I told them, "but it's an old-fashioned one. Years ago, when climbing was in its infancy, they carried what were called alpenstocks, which were about five feet long. These evolved into ice axes like this one, which I guess would have been about three feet long. They were used by climbers and ramblers back in the early days, say up to the fifties or sixties, when more technical stuff became available. This one could date from the thirties, but that's just a guess. We're trying to find an expert who'll tell us more about it. You can use it one way round as a walking stick, or the other way as an ice axe. It has a blade for cutting steps and a pick point for digging into ice. Or someone's brain if you have murder in your heart. Here's the interesting bit: like I said, they are normally about three feet long, but this one has been cut down. I'm told that the wood is ash, by the way, and the manufacturer's name is cast into the head. *Scheidegger*. There should be a metal spike on the other end, and a leather wrist strap, but they're not there now. The cut, however, is new. Bear that in mind, please: the cut is new. Somewhere, in a garage or shed, there's a little heap of sawdust underneath a Workmate. Keep your eyes open for it. But the question is this: 'Why would anyone cut the axe down by about a foot before going out to murder someone?'"

There was silence, until I made a shrugging gesture to invoke comments.

"To make it more easy to carry?" someone suggested.

I nodded agreement.

"Or easier to hide?"

"Possibly."

"Maybe they were more used to swinging a modern, shorter axe."

"Yep. Could be. Anything else?"

A DC from HQ raised a finger.

"Yes, George."

"Perhaps it belonged to the killer and he'd carved his name in the wood?"

"That's a good one. A very good one. We need the missing end, or that pile of sawdust. Only the killer knows the answer, so let's catch him and ask."

I love it when I finish like that, on an uplifting note. It takes years of practice and they don't teach it at staff college. Many years ago, when I played in the same football team as Tony

Krabbe, a schoolteacher with more optimism than judgement tried to drum a rough draft of modern history into my head. But the causes of the Crimean conflict did not grab the interest of a youth who was on the verge of having trials as goalkeeper for Heckley Town, and Picasso's early works were of far more interest to him than the fall of the Russian aristocracy. But one name, one bit of the story, stayed in his memory long after most others had been relegated to the recycle bin: Leon Trotsky.

Trotsky, with Lenin and Marx, was one of the founding fathers of communist Russia, but he fell out with Stalin and after a series of adventures settled in Mexico City. I had a certain admiration for Trotsky, back in those days, and felt that the world would be a better place if Stalin hadn't sent one of his hit men after him and Trotsky's views had prevailed. It was the mode of Trotsky's killing that made me think of him now: he was stabbed in the head with an ice pick.

All my life, until one evening in the cinema, I'd imagined that Trotsky had been killed with an ice *axe*. The film was *Basic Instinct*, with Michael Douglas and Sharon Stone, and Ms Stone played the part of a sex-driven, ice *pick* wielding psychopath. An ice pick, I learned for the first time, was a pointed, chisel-like implement used for chipping usable pieces of ice off a big block. A popular occupation in America, but unheard of the UK. It was a revelation, and answered one burning question that had troubled me for all those intervening years. Maybe it was the latent policeman in me, but I used to wake up in the night wondering: what was a mountaineer's ice axe doing lying around in a house in Mexico City, one of the most torrid, oppressively hot places on Earth? Now I knew the answer.

There was no such doubt or ambiguity about Anthony Turnbull Krabbe, though: he was killed by one blow from an ice axe.

"Anything of interest about the angle, Prof?" I asked, Monday afternoon, as I talked to the pathologist who'd done the PM.

He pulled a face, knowing that it's possible to analyse these things until you lose sight of the facts. I wanted him to say: "The blade went in at this angle, so, allowing for the length of the handle, the perpetrator must have been six feet tall." That's what I wanted him to say. The professor, however, knew that there were too many variables to be so certain. Did the perp. rise on the balls of his feet as he struck the blow or was he crouched low, stalking his victim? Was he holding the axe handle at the end or in the middle? Was the victim stooped or walking tall? Any of these could affect the angle of entry.

"If you push me, Chas…"

"I do, Prof, I do, but I promise not to hold you to it."

"You'd better not. I'd say the blow was on the low side. Krabbe was 185 centimetres tall. Indications are that the killer was about 166."

I wrote the heights down, for conversion later into something more meaningful to me.

"Call it six feet one and five feet five or six," the prof said, helpfully.

"Cheers. And what about the force of the blow?"

"You mean was it delivered by a man or a woman?"

"That's right."

"How many women do you know, Charlie?"

"Hmm, not enough."

"OK. So of the few you do know, how many would you say are weaker than the average man?"

"C'mon, Prof, it's a standard question."

"The blow was delivered with considerable force."

"A man."

"If you say so."

"Of below average height."

"Could be."

"Or a tall, strong woman."

"It's possible."

"That's it, then. We're looking for a jockey or a ballerina. You've been a big help, Prof."

"Anytime, Charlie. Any time."

6

The girl adjusted the sports bag that was hanging over her shoulder and followed the stream of travellers along the corridor. She read the signs – Arrivals, Luggage Reclaim, Customs and, most scarily, Passport Control – but took little notice of the arrows, content to follow the group. Everybody walked so purposefully, as if she were the only person who'd never flown before.

She was frightened, knowing that what she was doing was illegal, but excited at the prospect of a new life and opportunities that would be denied her at home. And it was only slightly illegal. She wouldn't be robbing anybody, or killing anybody, and the worst that could happen to her was to be sent home again. Her friends and what was left of her family would scoff at her, accuse her having ideas above her station, and the priest would counsel her on the evils of materialism and envy, but at least she would have tried. She would have tried to make a life for herself that didn't revolve around the small-minded village, the church, and ambitions that did not extend beyond marrying a local boy and having his children. And she was escaping, forever, she hoped, from a world where the past and all its evils encroached upon and shaped every aspect of daily life.

The man at Passport Control barely looked at it and gave her a hint of a smile. Was that it, she thought? A conveyor belt went around in a big circle and her fellow travellers were milling around it, waiting for their luggage to be offloaded. She had carried her bag, not handed it in when she boarded the plane, kept it with her when they transferred at Zurich, but now she was unsure of where to go next. She waited. Suitcases began to come round on the carousel and she saw a man in a business suit edge forward as he recognised his luggage. He manhandled it off the conveyor and started towards the sign that read Green Channel. She followed him.

This was the final hurdle. She was coming, her story went, on a fortnight's vacation, to have a look at the university in Leeds or Bradford, with the possibility of one day coming to study there. She was about to become a medical student in Tirana, but the opportunities were not great, and a British qualification would be much more useful in her homeland.

She stared straight ahead as she followed the man, but tried to take in the customs officers as she strode past them. It was true. Everything she'd been told was true. They weren't interested in her. In England, the people were free to come and go as they pleased and the whole country was covered in purple carpet. She turned a corner, leaving the customs officers and the purple carpet behind, and had her first genuine glimpse of her new world.

Faces turned towards her. Ordinary faces. Not smiling, as she had expected, but not lined with pain and fear like the ones back home. For a moment she did not realise that this was the outside world, but then she saw the taxi drivers holding their name boards, and realised that taxi drivers the world over all look the same. Some of the names they held forth baffled her. St James? Royal Court? The Duke of Wellington? Had the Duke travelled on her plane?

"Ludmilla," it said, simply, on the board she was most interested in. She hesitated, taking in the man who was holding it, thinking that he did not look like a taxi driver. Their eyes met and she moved towards him.

"You're Ludmilla?" he asked.

"Yes. Me Ludmilla," she replied. "You are...?"

"From the agency. I'm to take you to the house."

He turned and started to walk and she followed him, slightly dismayed that he hadn't offered to take her bag. Englishmen were polite and romantic, she'd always believed, and her first encounter with one was a slight disappointment. But then she noticed that he walked with a limp, and decided that this excused him. He wasn't handsome, but was interesting. He was dressed entirely in black and had a small ponytail. He was – what was the word – *cool*. She smiled to herself and trotted in his wake.

Outside, she failed to notice the hotel minibus with Duke of Wellington Hotel painted on the door. The man's car was the best she'd ever been in, which wasn't saying much because it was only the third she'd ever been in. It was like the one the President used. Her driver opened the door for her, put her bag in the back and climbed into the driving seat.

It was so silent – all the cars were – and didn't leave a trail of smoke behind. In seconds they were out of the airport and on a smooth road that led, the signs said, to Bradford. It would take her some time to become used to the strange names. She pressed her nose to the window like a kid outside a sweetshop and let the images flood her brain.

The land was flat and green, and buildings were everywhere. She read the names and smiled at the familiar ones: McDonalds; Texaco and Pizza Hut. One day, soon, she'd go into a Pizza Hut and order the biggest one they did. Her mouth watered at the thought and she realised that she had eaten hardly anything all day. The car swung off to the left without losing speed. Then round in a big arc to the right until it joined a motorway filled with speeding traffic. That was the most impressive thing: the speed of all the cars and lorries.

In fifteen minutes they were back on a small road, with green fields on one side and open moorland on the other. They passed through a village and she noticed how well-dressed and fashionable the people were. She saw the pub and the post office and, prominently situated, the square tower of the church. There'd been a lot of churches; many more than she'd expected in a country she'd been warned was Godless.

She'd meant to find a ladies' toilet as soon as she'd left the plane, but had forgotten in her nervousness as she'd followed the crowd. Now her need was becoming more pressing.

"Is far?" she asked, turning to the driver.

"Ten minutes," he replied. He turned to look at her, noting her pale blue eyes and long blonde hair. Real blonde, not from a bottle. He liked blondes, and that hair was just right for grabbing a handful of and twisting round your fist. She had nice teeth, too. That's a change, he thought as he shuffled in his seat and reluctantly turned his eyes back to the road. "Do you speak much English?" he asked.

"Very small," she told him, illustrating the words by holding her forefinger and thumb a little way apart. The driver nodded, the conversation evidently over. As if to confirm the fact he reached forward and pressed a button on the dashboard, and within seconds the car was filled with music: The Hollies, *He Ain't Heavy (He's My Brother)*. She recognised the tune and shuddered with delight. This really was going to be a new beginning for her.

There were more houses now. At first they were two-storey, nicely spaced and painted in different colours. Each had a garden with a neat patch of grass and shrubs. A car, sometimes two, stood outside every one. Then the houses crowded together in long rows, with a few steps up to the doors and small yards in front. People waited patiently to cross the road, shops spilled their contents out on to the pavement, like at home, and she saw a number of women wearing traditional Muslim dress. The car turned this way and that through the maze of streets crammed with parked vehicles. She tried to remember the route they were taking, but it was impossible.

They stopped outside a shop called Spar and the driver beckoned her to follow him. Inside, the shelves were piled high with all sorts of goods. He went to a refrigerated cupboard and pointed to the ready-packed sandwiches. She chose prawn and mayonnaise. He gestured for her to take another pack so she picked up a cheese and pickle.

In two more minutes they were at the house. It was in one of the long rows, next but one to the end, and the door wasn't locked. He pushed it open and led her inside. At first it was gloomy, but he turned on a light and she saw a staircase with a red patterned carpet. Other doors led off to both sides, with numbers on them, and she assumed that these were other apartments.

Upstairs he unlocked number eight and reached inside for another switch and she blinked at the brightness of the lights as they came on. A double bed was centrepiece of the room, with just enough room to walk around it. There was a cabinet of three drawers with a tray and kettle on it, and another door. It was standing open and beyond it she could see a toilet and a bath.

"I stay here?" she asked, wide-eyed. At home five of them had existed in a room smaller than this, with no water or electricity and a communal toilet fifty metres away.

"Yes, for the time being."

"When I see the doctor and his children?"

"The doctor? Oh, er, tomorrow. Tomorrow I'll take you to the doctor. You'll see his children then. Meanwhile, you are to stay here. Understand?"

She nodded. He took a banknote from his wallet, with a 20 in the corner, and handed it to her. "Buy another sandwich, if you need one," he said, "but don't talk to anyone. Understand?"

She nodded again. He handed her the keys and left. His parting words were: "I'll see you tomorrow, and lock the door."

She did as she was told and locked the door. She used the toilet, washed her hands and face and felt the water turn warm as she let it run. She'd never lived in a house with running warm water. Later, she thought, she would have a bath, but first of all it was a sandwich and a sleep on that inviting bed.

She slept all night and woke early the next morning. The room didn't have a window, so she could not tell what the weather was like. Someone was playing music in one of the other rooms, and she heard the occasional burst of laughter. She made herself a coffee, had the other sandwich, and unlocked the door.

A woman with hair even blonder than her own was coming up the stair. Ludmilla waited for her to pass and gave her a nervous smile.

"Hello, luv," the woman said, happily, and went into the room on the other side of the landing.

"Good morning," Ludmilla replied, trying to avoid staring at the woman's enormous breasts that bulged out of a mass of silk frills like the backs of two albino whales swimming through the surf, and started down the stairs.

In the Spar shop she studied the price of the sandwiches and calculated that if she bought one she'd have £17.51 in change. Instead she bought a small piece of Wensleydale cheese and a bread cake, for only a few pence more. Then she saw the cream buns and could not resist buying one of those, too. If the man was angry that she'd spent too much she would just have to pay him back next week, when she'd earned her first wage.

The driver had not said what time he would come back, so she didn't like leaving her room for too long. She had a bath, ate the cheese and bread and made herself a coffee. Later, she went for a quick walk around the square of streets that contained the house where she lived. There was no number on the door, but the house two doors along was number 45, her father's age, and the street was called Juniper Avenue. It was a bright, cool day, and as she strolled along the pavement admiring the goods on display the shopkeepers all spoke to her and gestured towards their wares, inviting her to buy from them. There was a fruit stall, a bakery and several selling furniture and carpets. Two Asian women in silk saris were arguing loudly with a man selling vegetables, and the Beatles were being played at a stall filled with CDs. She did a little dance step to the music and the man smiled at her.

To her surprise, she didn't feel self-conscious. Her clothes were shabby, but so were most of the others. Theirs often had designer names splashed across them – she recognised Cuba and FCUK – but they were not that much different from her own. Two black boys on skateboards startled her as they swept by, their wheels clack-clacking on the gaps between the flagstones. Their clothing was several sizes too large and emblazoned with numbers and letters that she didn't understand. Most of the girls of her own age had small children with them, but she assumed they were younger sisters and brothers. The girls walked around in scanty tops with their midriffs exposed, and she was slightly shocked. Back home they would have been taken off the streets by the police, except that they wouldn't have dressed like that in the first place. She smiled at herself and decided that she must stop thinking that way. This was her home now, and she would do everything in her power for it to remain so. Back in her room she looked up Juniper and Avenue in her dog-eared pocket dictionary and puzzled over the entries. They both mentioned trees, but there wasn't a tree in sight.

The man knocked at the door and said: "It's me."

Ludmilla turned the key in the lock and opened it wide, invitingly. He limped past her and she closed it behind him.

"Your money is there," she said, pointing to the pile on the drawers. "I spend too much. I sorry. I pay back."

He was carrying a long package, wrapped in a plastic bag, and wearing the same black clothes as the day before: long coat, trousers and leather gloves. He put the package on the bed and started to remove his coat.

"We go see doctor, now?" Ludmilla asked.

He'd been standing slightly sideways on to her. "Not just yet," he replied. His gloved hand came round without her even seeing it and smashed into the side of her face. She stumbled and nearly lost her balance, her mind a turmoil of pain and surprise. The hand came again and hit her at the other side, jolting her head back and rattling her teeth together. She fell against the wall, wondering what she'd done, if this was all a mistake, but as the hand came again she started to fight back.

He grabbed her wrists, slammed her against the wall and hit her again with the back of his hand. She fell over backwards, bumping her head against the cabinet. He stood over her, his face red with exertion or excitement, and reached for the package he'd been carrying.

When he unrolled the covering she saw he was holding

what looked like an aluminium tube with a red pistol grip. He did something with the handle then pointed the tube at her. She shrank away, not knowing what to expect, holding her hands defensively in front of her face.

He made a stabbing motion towards her and as the end of the tube touched her bare skin 10,000 volts shot up her arm. It felt as if she'd been hit with an iron bar, dislocating her elbow. Ludmilla screamed in pain and tried to hide in the corner, pulling her sleeves over her fists. He came at her again and caught her on the neck and then the ankle. She'd heard of this torture. The Communists did it to her brothers and other members of the KLA. Her world exploded into a violent maelstrom of her own screams and the hammer-like blows of the cattle prod as he came at her again and again.

When she thought she could take no more, when the pains were melting into each other, the blackness was all-enveloping and she was willing herself to die, he stopped. She was cowering on the floor, curled up in the smallest ball she could make, with tears and mucus streaming down her face and the taste of blood in her mouth. She heard his footsteps as he stepped back from her and she dared to peep out from between her arms that were folded over her face. He came out of the bathroom carrying a towel.

"Here," he said, throwing it down at her. She wiped her face on it and tried to stem her sobbing. "Now stand up."

She looked up at him, not understanding. He picked up the prod, switched it on and jabbed it against her ankle. "No! No!" she screamed as the electricity convulsed her body. "Please stop! Please stop!"

He did stop, and ordered her to stand up again, this time with a gesture. She reached up for a handful of bedclothes and pulled herself on to he knees, never taking her eyes of the prod. He held it across his chest, like she had seen the soldiers of both sides posing with their guns.

"Faster!" he demanded, but she couldn't move any faster. Every joint in her body felt pulled apart, and a searing pain pulsed behind her eyes. She leaned on the bed and pushed upwards with her legs, but the effort was almost too much for her. As she rose to her feet she lost her balance and started to sway. He caught the front of her blouse in his fist and swung her back on to the bed.

"Roll over," he said, pushing her towards the middle. She lay on her back, looking at him.

"This is my friend," he told her, holding the prod aloft and switching it off. "I'm leaving him there, where I can reach him." He leaned the device against the wall.

Ludmilla lay on the soft bed where she had earlier spent one of the happiest nights of her life and watched him. He peeled his gloves off and then his jacket. She could hear his breathing, heavy and hoarse, as he clambered on to the bed and leaned over her. He unfastened her jeans, pulled the zip down and began to work them over her hips.

It was almost dark when he left her, locking the door behind him and taking the key. Ludmilla lay on the bed sobbing, wondering what would happen next. Her body ached and she was sore where he'd done things to her. Tomorrow, she told herself, she would be taken to the doctor's house and would meet his children. She had been unlucky. Her driver was a monster. They existed in every country and it had been her misfortune to meet one in England straight away. She ought to tell the police, when she was free to do so, but then she would be sent home. What would she say to her parents and brothers? Perhaps the doctor would help her. She decided to sleep on it, wait until tomorrow.

He came back in the afternoon, with a bag of food for her and some clothing. There were two dresses and underwear like she'd seen in magazines. He ran the bath and gestured for her to take one. When she was in it he came in and watched her. She dried herself and he told her to put some of the underwear on, after unwrapping the cattle prod and drawing the tip of it across her breasts, with the switch in the *off* position. Ludmilla trembled with fear and did as she was told. He raped her again and left. As soon as his uneven footsteps faded she took another bath and put her own clothes back on.

That night two of them came. She was dozing when she heard the key in the door, and cowering with fear as they came into the room. For a brief second she'd thought they might be the police, to rescue her, but when she saw them her hopes crumbled. They had shaven heads and tattoos on their shoulders, and were carrying cartons of beer.

"Who... who you are?" Ludmilla asked, under the feeble pretext that this was her room and they were intruders.

"Who we are?" the bigger of the two mimicked. "Who do you fink we are?" He tore a can of Carlsberg from the carton and tossed the other eleven on to the bed. "Let's just say we're friends, luv, and we've come for the party."

They came back the following night, with three of their male friends and a video camera. When it was over Ludmilla cried herself to sleep, wishing she were dead. She wished they'd been captured and shot when they hid in the woods from Milosovic's soldiers. She wished she'd fallen into a ravine when they fled over the mountains into Albania. She wished she'd fought at her brother's side with the KLA and caught the bullet he caught. She wished the plane had crashed and killed everybody on board. She wished... she wished... she wished in vain.

For the plane hadn't crashed. She escaped the soldiers and the bullets and survived the dangerous trek over the Prokletije Mountains. She was special. Millions hadn't survived, and she owed it to them to keep their stories alive. Next morning she set to work. She systematically left her finger and palm prints on every surface in the two rooms. She pressed her hands on every inch of every wall. She left prints on top of the door, down the jamb and under the drawers. When she'd finished there wasn't a square foot of surface that was without her secret signature. There was no doctor, of that she was now sure, and they would probably murder her, but no matter how well they cleaned that room, proof of her imprisonment would always remain. She was bleeding slightly, so she left traces of her blood on the wall, behind the bed head. A light bulb had failed in the bathroom, so she left her mark on that, too.

The man with the limp came back later that day, but he didn't lay a finger on her. "From now on," he said, "you work for me and do as you're told. Remember, we have friends over there, and what would your parents think if they knew how you were earning your living? Clean yourself up and look nice for tomorrow night. I have a client for you. Just one, to start with. He's not a proper doctor but he's interested in anatomy." He laughed but she did not understand.

"Duggie will come for you," he went on, and she flinched at the sound of the name. Duggie was the bigger of the two men who brought the beer.

"Ah, you don't like Duggie, eh?" he said.

"No."

"That's alright. He won't hurt you. If he ever touches you again, let me know and I'll deal with him. Understand?"

"Yes. I think."

"Good girl. From now on, I protect you. *Comprendez?*"

"Yes. I understand." She did, and it was almost a relief.

7

The press office collected all the obituary announcements and I found them on my desk when I returned from Gilbert's morning meeting. Also with them was a report from John Rose about Selina Wallenberg, saying she had a conviction for running a house of ill repute in Kensington, back in the eighties. I marked it for filing and turned back to the new case and the obituaries. *Anthony Turnbull Krabbe, OBE* they were headed. I read each one carefully, then spread them out and read them again. The one from the *Times* was the most fulsome, probably because he'd reported directly to them from some of his trips. His record of first climbs was impressive and his bag of peaks over 8 000 metres put him in the top echelons of the sport. He was the complete climber, we were told. Be it on rock, ice, Alpine dash or big expedition, he was always up there with the best. His latest book, *Kingdoms of the Gods*, (£28, Times Books) was a masterpiece, and for the last few years he'd concentrated his efforts on fundraising for various charities.

I pinned them together with a compliments slip and directed them towards the incident room. They could go on the wall for the others to read. I wasn't sure how much of what they said was typical hyperbole, dredged up when any celebrity died, or whether he was really up there with the greats.

"Wallenberg," John Rose announced as he came into my office.

"I got your note on his wife," I said, gesturing for him to sit down and handed the cuttings to him.

"Good. She's been round the block a couple of times. What are these?"

"Tony Krabbe's orbituaries. They make him sound like something between Neil Armstrong and Nelson Mandela. What have you got?"

"Quite a bit, some of it off the record."

"OK, start with the concrete stuff."

"Right. First of all, he sponsored Krabbe to the tune of £5,000 for his recent trip to Nepal. And that wasn't to climb a mountain. He went on a fact-finding mission with a view to opening a school and a clinic out there."

"Mmm. Add Mother Teresa to the list. Have you spoken to Wallenberg?"

"Briefly, on the phone. I just said we were talking to everyone who had connections with Krabbe, and we'd read about the sponsorship in the book. He reckons he's only met him a couple of times, at charity functions, and Krabbe tapped him for a contribution."

"Sounds reasonable."

"Except he's lying through his teeth. Krabbe's shop in the mall – Art of Asia – is rented from a property company, which just happens to be part of the Wallenberg empire."

"That doesn't mean he knows who his tenants are."

"I've spoken to the staff who worked there. The shop's closed now, but I tracked down the manageress and her assistant via the security company. They both recognised a mugshot of Wallenberg. Said he called in now and again when Krabbe was there, and they would go into a huddle in the stock room. They knew each other, all right."

"I'm convinced. Anything else?"

"Yes. Wallenberg is bigger in this town than we've realised. Next to the council he's just about the biggest landlord, but did you know he owns that new restaurant on the Town Square: *L'Autre Place*?"

"No, that's a new one on me. They do a magnificent beef Wellington, I'm told."

"So they say. Word has it that he entertained Joe Crozier there a couple of weeks ago, and there's lots of other talk about him, on the streets."

"We've looked into Crozier and he's legit, these days. Only just – he's a club owner and into various other entertainment activities. Betting shops, that sort of thing. Nothing we can touch him for. What are they saying about Wallenberg?"

"Well, apparently he inherited a small fortune from his parents, but he has a weakness – gambling. He'll bet on anything, I'm told, and conducts his business deals with the same recklessness. The result is that he's had some heavy losses over the last few years, so it's back to basics. He's reverted to the original family businesses, namely prostitution and protection, and he's spreading his wings."

"Who have you been talking to?"

"I have my sources. They're reliable."

"Your Rasta friends?"

"They don't like him. They use him and he uses them, but there's no respect."

"Be careful with them, John."

"Don't worry, I am."

"It looks like we'll have to have words with Mr Wallenberg." I turned a pencil over between my fingers and tapped the blunt end on the desk, thinking what to do next. Gilbert answered his phone straight away. "You mentioned some tickets," I said, "to a charity bash at the football club. Did you find them?"

"Yes. I'd thrown them in the bin but they were still there. Do you want them?"

"When is it?"

"Let me see… um, next Saturday."

"I'll have them, then. I'd like to see Wallenberg on his own turf first, before I have a really good talk to him."

"Is he on your list of suspects?"

I didn't have a list of suspects. "No," I replied, "not for Krabbe's murder, but we'll think of something."

When John had gone I rang Nigel Newley in Leeds and arranged to meet him for a drink, later that evening. The Halfway House was conveniently situated, approximately equidistant from Leeds and Heckley, so we met there. Big Dave came with me.

"How's Sophie?" I asked on the drive over. "I haven't had chance to ask you."

"Alright," he replied.

"Only alright?"

"I hardly saw her, did I? We were working, remember."

"Mmm, sorry about that. Some people are inconsiderate about the timing of their murders. Did she bring the boyfriend with her?"

"Digby? No, he was playing rugby in France. Usually Shirley's OK. She knows the score, but this weekend she's been a pain. And Sophie wasn't any better. The little I saw of them made me feel like a pariah in my own house. I was glad to get out."

"Women," I said, as if that explained everything. I knew something Dave didn't, and thought about ways of changing the subject.

"Yeah, women," he agreed.

Nigel is a great one for shaking hands. He was late, as expected, but bounced in like a Labrador puppy on amphetamines, his arm already extended. I'm not a great shaker, but it's easier to comply than to make a point. He would have shaken our hands even if we'd spent all day working together, which I consider excessive.

Long time ago I was the youngest inspector ever appointed by East Pennine. Now it's my proud boast that I'm the longest serving inspector in the history of the police force. I was already in that rank, and had been for a long time, when Nigel joined the department. He was on the fast track, with a degree in law and a naïve belief in the innate goodness of everybody he met. Not just the crooks: he believed it about the police, too. How green can you get? They would have made mincemeat out of him, but I took him under my wing, hammered some sense into his receptive brain, and in double quick time he was the same rank as me.

Truth is, I saw a bit of myself in him, and it wasn't just the boyish good looks. If I'd ever had a son I would have liked him to be like Nigel. He would have stayed in Heckley CID forever, content to work for me, but I kicked him out, made him go for promotion. It was one of the hardest things I ever did.

"So how's the courting going?" Dave asked, when we were seated behind our drinks. Nigel had asked for a pint of lager shandy and I'd joined him. Dave was on the bitter.

"It isn't," he replied.

"What happened?"

"No, you're supposed to say: 'What did she do for a living?'"

"OK. What did she do for a living?"

"She was a chicken sexer."

"A chicken sexer? That's interesting."

"No! You say: 'Where did you meet her?'"

"Right. I see. So, um, where did you meet this, um, chicken sexer, Nigel?"

"At a hen party!"

He hooted with laughter while Dave looked at me, blank-faced, and I returned the look. "Good one, Nigel," I said, eventually.

"Yeah. A very good one," Dave agreed.

After Dave fetched the second round I said: "So tell us about your new case, Nigel. This could be your passport to fame."

"I knew it," he replied. "And I thought you'd invited me out for the pleasure of my company."

"Well it wasn't for your sparkling wit," Dave told him, unkindly, I thought.

I said: "Joe Crozier knew Peter Wallenberg. Wallenberg was some sort of business acquaintance of Tony Krabbe. I don't believe in coincidences. They were all mixed up in something."

"Perhaps we should have a joint meeting, see if it's worth combining the two enquiries."

"It's a bit early for that," I said. "For a start, we don't know if Crozier fell or was pushed, do we?"

"Ah! The leading question," Nigel replied. "No, but let me tell you this: Crozier owned a third share in a lap-dancing club called the Painted Pony. It's in the basement of the apartment block where he lived. The other two shares are held by a pair of accountants who sail close to the wind. We tried to talk to them, of course, but they clammed up. The DS who did the interview said they were scared stiff, but they did admit that they were selling their shares in the club."

"Who to, did they say?"

"Mmm. No point in them denying it. Your friend Peter Wallenberg. He'd made them a good offer."

"That they couldn't refuse," Dave added.

"Crozier," I stated, when I'd digested Nigel's announcement. "He was in the water about two weeks. Was death due to drowning?"

"Yes, and there wasn't a mark on his body and he still had his wallet in his pocket with £300 in it."

"Had he drowned in the Aire?"

"Yes. The diatom analysis showed he had."

"So he could have gone for a walk late one night, after having a bevvy or three too many, and fallen in," Dave suggested.

"It looks like it," I agreed, but Nigel remained tight-lipped. I took a sip of my new drink before asking: "Is there something you're not telling us, Nige?"

He took a longer draught of his pint before saying: "There was one small indication that his death may not have been accidental."

"Which was…" I prompted.

"Well, it just so happens that his ankles and wrists were tied with masking tape, and his mouth was covered with it, too."

I clunked my glass down on the table and a burst of bubbles exploded inside the golden liquid, causing a head of froth to rise and quickly subside again. "Well, you kept that quiet," I said after a while, feeling slightly annoyed.

"We decided to," he replied. "And we still haven't released it. You can imagine why."

"I suppose so," I agreed, and at least he'd had the courtesy not to tell us to keep it to ourselves.

"Did you say *masking* tape?" Dave asked.

"That's right."

"The stuff that decorators use?"

"Yes."

"It's only made of paper, isn't it? I'd have thought it would go soggy and float off."

"We thought the same, so we're doing some tests. As of this morning, it still hasn't gone soggy."

I'd have thought it would soften and float away, too. I'd have gambled money on it. Perhaps the murderer or murderers thought the same thing, but they were too impatient to do the tests. Wrap his hands and feet with the tape, put some round his mouth to stem the screams, and let nature do the rest. It sounded a great idea, but it hadn't worked. The inquest had been adjourned indefinitely, so this piece of information would be hidden from the public. And from the murderers. They could relax, safe in the knowledge that they'd pulled off the perfect deed, but we knew otherwise. I had to smile: Nigel was thinking like me.

Wednesday I rang Sonia Thornton and went to see her. She worked at a place called High Adventure, but this was her day off because she worked weekends. High Adventure was a new resort, as it liked to call itself, built on an old colliery site outside Oldfield, in Lancashire. Where once had existed slag heaps, a coke works and a hundred years' of industrial grime, there was now an indoor ski slope, with real snow, and lots of other associated activities. I'd been promising myself a visit since it opened.

Sonia lived in a Victorian terrace, one of the grander ones that had not yet been divided into bedsits, just outside Halifax. Robert, The DC who'd made the initial interview, was tied up with paperwork, so I made the journey there alone. I was happy to do so. Sonia Thornton was a dream to any man who liked his women fit and talented, and not looking as if they'd spent six hours applying their makeup. When she opened the door and I saw her for the first time in seven years, I wasn't disappointed. I extended a hand – it's only men I object to shaking with – and introduced myself. "Charlie Priest," I said. "DI. Um, Heckley CID."

She was taller than I expected, probably about five feet ten, and still had the runner's figure, although the baggy top she wore did its best to disguise it. When we were seated in her front room I smiled and said: "You haven't changed. You look just the same as when I watched you on TV, tearing down the back strait. I expected you to have put on about four stones."

"You said it was about Tony," she replied.

Ah well, I thought, perhaps some other time. "Yes," I confirmed. "I understand that you and he were partners for a while. Is that true?"

"Yes, but not for long."

"1989 to 1997. Eight years. That's a fair length of time."

"Not compared with most marriages, Inspector. Even by today's standards."

"But you never married?"

"No."

"Any reason why?"

"Yes, I suppose so. Tony was in a high-risk occupation, he said. He didn't want the commitment."

I noted the *he said*. It always implies disagreement. "What difference does that make?" I asked. "If someone you love gets killed, does it matter if you are married or not?"

"You should have asked him that," she replied. She was quiet for a while but I could see she was wondering whether to say more, choosing her words carefully. "At least, if you were married there'd be something to hang on to," she added.

"That's what I would have thought."

The room was furnished old-style, with cabinets and a sideboard and a big, soft, three-piece suite like my grandma had. I suspected it had belonged to her parents. One of the cabinets, with a bow front, gleamed with silverware from her athletics days, and there was a picture standing on it of her receiving a medal from some dignitary. I said: "Wow! Look at those trophies."

"There's more, upstairs," she told me, matter-of-fact, but didn't invite me to a private show.

"I have three football medals," I confessed, "in a drawer somewhere, wrapped in cotton wool, inside a tin box."

The corners of her mouth lifted into a smile, ever so briefly, and she said: "You probably worked just as hard for them as I did for these."

"I suppose so," I agreed. "The only difference is talent. You work at High Adventure, I believe."

"That's right."

"What do you do there?"

"I'm climbing wall manager-cum-instructor. There's a 20 metre climbing wall. Tony designed it, as a matter of fact."

"I didn't know you'd been a climber."

"Yes. I was a climber before I was a runner. I took up running to be fit for rock climbing, and found out I was good at it."

"And the rest is history."

"I suppose so."

"Until you had the crash."

"Yes."

"Tony was with you, wasn't he?"

"Yes. We'd been to a fund-raising function."

"Who was driving?"

"I was."

"Your relationship ended soon after."

"Not so soon after. We rumbled along for a couple of years, until he came back from Everest in '97, but we didn't see much of each other. It all ended just after Everest."

"Why was that?"

"I don't know. It – the accident – just put a strain on us. I missed going to the Olympics and... we'd been drifting apart. He'd achieved his goal, I'd failed at mine. He didn't seem to understand how I felt."

"Where were you on Saturday evening?"

"Am I a suspect, Inspector?"

"Ex-partners are always suspects, Miss Thornton."

"I was working. I was at High Adventure until after ten o'clock. I came straight home and it's a 25-minute drive. Will that do?"

"Sounds watertight to me." I looked around the room, patted my hands on the chair arms as if about to rise, then said: "Do you know of anyone who might have wanted Tony dead?"

"No."

"How about if I asked you for a list of the names of his friends?"

"Wouldn't his enemies be more appropriate?"

"Did he have enemies?"

"Not that I know of, but climbing's a competitive world. It's not just you against the mountain, you know. It's you against everybody else. There's a lot of jealousy."

"I need help, Sonia. Can you give me a list?"

"I have photograph albums, but it's nearly five years since I saw him."

"Can I look at them?"

"I don't see why not. They're upstairs." She rose to her feet and moved towards the door. When I didn't follow her she said: "They weigh a ton. You'd better come with me."

They were in the attic, along with loads of other gear that had belonged to Krabbe. Sonia told me that he left the stuff with her because one day he wanted it putting in a museum. There were climbing jackets made of canvas and oilskin, boots like Captain Scott might have worn, and a mass of complicated devices for climbing up and down ropes, belaying and abseiling. Several ice axes were leaning on the wall. They started with old-fashioned ones, a generation on from the wooden-handled device that killed him, and evolved right through to wicked looking shapes like the beaks of prehistoric birds of prey, designed for hooking into vertical walls of ice.

Everything had a parcel label on it, tied with a piece of string. I read them off: *Eiger N Face 1984* one said; *Napes Needle 1965*; *K2 1991* and *Weisshorn 1987*. On a shelf I saw a bundle bristling with steel teeth and picked it up. It was a pair of crampons, tied together with blue neoprene straps. They were designed for fixing to the climber's boots, to give him grip on glaciers and ice-encrusted rock faces. Each had a plastic sole, surrounded by twelve wicked teeth, like a crown of thorns. The front two teeth pointed straight forward, so he could tip-toe up vertical walls. Moulded into the sole, put there during the manufacturing process, it said *Krabbe Klaw*. The ticket read: *Everest 1997*.

I proffered them to Sonia, indicating the name, and she took them from me. "Yes," she said. "He'd started his own manu-facturing company, designing highly technical gear. These were one of his first attempts."

"Everest in 1997," I said. "Is that when he lost his partner?"

"Jeremy Quigley. Yes, it was. That was a bad time for him."

"Did you know Jeremy?"

"We'd met, but only a couple of times. Jeremy wasn't a close friend, and not expected to be in the first summit team."

I said: "I suppose reaching the summit was some sort of consolation," but she didn't reply. "Was there any criticism of Tony after the incident?" I asked.

"Not that I heard. These things happen in climbing."

"What did Jeremy's family and friends think about it?"

"You'll have to ask them that."

"Was he married?"

"He had a partner. Gabi – Gabrielle Naylor. I only met her once, at the memorial service. We exchanged phone numbers but never rang each other."

There were two photo albums, each about six inches thick. Far too many pictures for me to look at there and then and make any sense of. "How do you feel about me borrowing these?" I asked. "I'll really look after them."

"Take what you want, Inspector," she replied. "I long ago learned the pointlessness of possessions."

"Sophie's pregnant." My visitor's chair creaked as Dave dumped his weight on it, and I groaned inwardly at his announcement. This was the conversation I'd been dreading. "Apparently she was sick over the weekend, and eventually confessed to her mother. Shirley told me about it this morning."

"Yes, I know," I said, even though I'd resolved not to admit it.

"You *know*! *You* know!" he exploded.

"Don't get uppity about it," I told him. "And calm down. These things happen. Young people have different standards, these days. Her boyfriend's a good bloke and they're staying together, which is the way they do things. Two years from now you'll be buying him football boots and teaching him how to bend free kicks."

"So how come you know before I do? I'm only her father, after all."

"Sophie rang me."

"When was this?"

"As soon as she knew. She was crying, on the phone. She was upset and scared, didn't know what to do. She didn't know what Digby's reaction would be and she was frightened of telling you. I tried to reassure her. You might be her dad, but I'm her God dad, remember. It's my job to give spiritual guidance." That last sentence was an afterthought, but it sounded good.

"So you knew before Digby did?"

"That's right."

"And you say she was scared of telling me?"

"Yes."

"Why, for God's sake?"

"Because she knew you'd explode. She felt that she'd let you down."

Dave buried his face in his hands and let out a great sigh. "Oh Charlie," he groaned, "what a mess." I sat looking at him for a long minute, wondering if I'd done the right thing. He lifted his face, saying: "You say she was frightened of telling me?"

"Yes."

"My little girl was frightened of me?"

"It was bound to be a shock to you, Dave. She didn't know how you'd take it."

"It's him I'm mad with, not her. So what do I do next time I see him? Punch him on the nose?"

"No, Dave, not if you don't want to lose her. You shake his hand and give him a cigar." I retrieved the Post-it note Sonia Thornton had given me with Gabrielle Naylor's name and number on it. "Here," I said. "Track her down and make an appointment to see her in the morning. We'll go together."

Rosie was in when I rang her, after I'd dined and washed the dishes. "How are you?" I asked.

"Oh, so-so."

"Have you eaten?" If she hadn't I could always force something else down.

"Yes. Have you?"

"Meat and three veg, with an M&S bread-and-butter pudding to follow. Heaven. What did you have?"

"Poached egg on toast."

"That's not enough."

"I had a school dinner at lunchtime."

"You are what you eat, y'know."

"Then I must have eaten some rubbishy meals."

"School dinners. Aren't you feeling too good, love?"

"I'm… struggling, a bit."

"Listen, Rosie," I said. "No strings, no chatting you up, but I've managed to borrow Tony Krabbe's photo albums. There's some terrific stuff in there; I'm sure you'll find them interesting. I want to go through them and make a list of all the names. How about if I brought them round and we went through them together?"

"I don't… "

"C'mon, Rosie. It can't do any harm, and I promise to behave. Scouts' honour."

"You haven't caught his murderer yet?"

"No."

"Do you think there might be a picture of him in there?"

"I doubt it, but it's possible."

"All right then. I'll watch out for you."

She hadn't baked a cake, like she used to do, and something else was missing. Her face had lost its glow and the force field that normally surrounded and defined her was switched off. I missed its sparkle and crackle. She brightened briefly as she let me in and I noticed that she was still wearing her school-ma'am clothes: longish skirt and bulky sweater. Normally Rosie changed into jeans within seconds of coming through the door. She rinsed two mugs and made coffee.

We sat close together at her table and turned the pages of the albums. Apart from being a history of climbing they were also a catalogue of the changes in photography over the last 30 years. The first pictures were minute squares in fading black and white, the latest ones ten-by-eights in glorious Kodachrome.

"I've been there," Rosie said, as we peered at three figures sitting on a summit cairn in the Lake District. "Good place to explore the Borrowdale Volcanic Series, and there's supposed to be a Stone Age axe factory on the fellside, but I've never found anything."

"Me neither."

"And there," she declared. "Went with a chap I knew, briefly. And there."

"Me too."

But within two or three pages our amateur efforts in the Lake and Peak Districts were left well behind. The photos grew bigger, the slopes steeper, the names more romantic. Soon we were clinging to rock faces in the Dolomites, the Alps and the Karakorams. Napes Needle and Pike of Stickle were replaced by Lhotse, Annapurna and the dreaded K2.

As I turned the pages I could feel Rosie's arm warm against mine. I wanted to reach out across her shoulders and pull her close. Every instinct I had told me it was the most natural thing in the world to do, a thousand films and stories had imbued me with the belief that she would respond favourably, but I knew, deep down, that they were false. My only chance of staying friends with Rosie was to maintain the distance between us. *Softly, softly, catchee monkey*, but for how long I could play the game I had no idea.

We stared in wonder at vast landscapes of ice-clad peaks, me envious of the people who had the single-mindedness to sacrifice their careers and relationships, and sometimes their lives, to go off to these beautiful, inhospitable places. We didn't speak for the last few pages, because our superlatives sounded banal. I turned over the final page somewhat reluctantly, and there he was : Tony Krabbe with another man, each cocooned in full climbing gear, but with their hoods down to take advantage of the brief sunshine as they grinned at the camera. Their teeth shone like Aldis lamps in their scabby, sun-blackened faces, and the peaks behind the camera were reflected like a saw blade in their snow goggles.

The two of them were sitting on a snow step with their feet, bristling with the evil-toothed crampons, towards the camera. The caption read: *With Jeremy, Camp IV*.

I touched the photo with a forefinger. "That's on Everest," I said, my voice a whisper. "Last camp before they pushed to the summit. Jeremy is Jeremy Quigley. They became separated. Krabbe made it to the top and back down. Jeremy perished."

"Which one's Jeremy?"

"That one, I think."

"Poor chap."

"Yeah, poor chap."

The eastern leg of the M62 is probably the quietest stretch of road in the country. Its construction, and that of the Humber Bridge, was more to do with pandering to the electorate than with needs of the traffic lobby. Gabrielle Naylor ran an animal sanctuary, called High Chaparral, near Barton, on the south side of the bridge.

Dave touched 110 on the motorway, out of sheer

exuberance, and conned his way through the tollbooth by flashing his warrant card.

"I, er, had a word with Sophie last night," he'd said to me on one of the slower stretches.

"You rang her?"

"Mmm."

"How is she?"

"She's OK. I, sort of, told her it was all right."

"So you're friends again."

"I suppose so. She said you were good to her."

"We came to an agreement."

"An agreement?"

"Yeah. If it's a boy she's calling him Charlie."

"Over my dead body."

Once it was called Lincolnshire, then it became South Humberside, and now it's something else but nobody knows what. Businesses are waiting before they order new stationery in case the name changes again. Armies fought over the land and now county councils do the same. God knows why. It's flat, barren and bleak, fit only for growing potatoes, and the most prominent colour is mud. Everything about it feels as if it were designed by a committee. The people are good and nice, of course they are, and, when the sun comes out it's probably as pretty and welcoming as anywhere in the country. But on the few occasions I've ventured over there it's either been grizzling with rain or swept by winds from the Urals. The folks of South Humberside buy their clothes with the collars already turned up.

We were lost, thumbing through his book of maps, when Dave said: "I think we've found it."

I looked up and followed his gaze. A lugubrious head on the end of a long neck was peering over the hedge, studying us. "You could be right," I agreed.

"Can we call you Gabrielle?" Dave asked after she'd met us at the gate; our presence announced by three liquorice-all-sorts dogs that leapt and cavorted in a friendly way when they saw us. We'd seen her in the distance, heaving straw bales on to a stack, and were wondering how to attract her attention when the dogs did it for us. Gabrielle had ordered them away and opened the gate.

"Gabi," she replied. "Everybody calls me Gabi." She was small and dark, with a tip-tilted nose that no-doubt had a band of freckles across it when she was younger.

"Was that a llama we saw?" I asked as she led us towards her small bungalow.

"Yes. We rescued him – he's called Santiago – from a farmer who'd died and he didn't fit in with the new owner's plans. That's how we get most of our animals." Several donkeys were tethered in a field with a flock of geese grazing amongst them. Hutches outside the bungalow held rabbits and guinea pigs, and a purpose built run housed a selection of cats.

Another donkey was standing by the door. "This is Pedro," Gabi told us. "He's our longest-serving resident." Pedro stuffed his muzzle in Dave's jacket and he rubbed the donkey's ears.

"Behave, Pedro," Gabi said, pulling him away, adding, with a chuckle: "You'll have to excuse him, he's from Barcelona." We entered her tiny, cluttered kitchen and she spooned coffee into three mugs without asking if we'd like one. "Find a seat, if you can. Sorry about the mess, but this is tidy for me."

An Aga cooker took up almost one wall and a table occupied most of the remaining space. We pulled chairs from beneath it and sat down.

"Doesn't Pedro find it a bit cool in this part of the world?" I asked, grateful for the warmth of the Aga.

She stirred the mugs and put them before us, with a jug of milk, saying: "Sorry, but I don't have any sugar."

"That's OK," we said.

"Pedro?" she repeated. "No, he's happy here. He was rescued from a festival to one of the saints, by a tourist in one of the remote villages. They hold it every year, so Pedro was

105

lucky. The fattest man in the village rides around on the unfortunate animal until it's near collapsing, then all the other so-called men of the village climb on with him. The donkey is crushed to death."

Her hands were wrapped around her mug and I noticed that the little finger of her left hand was missing. Paperwork was neatly sorted into four piles on the table, each one held in place by a pebble. I said: "There are some evil people out there, Gabi. You probably see more evidence of it than we do."

"Animals don't let you down," she replied. "You always know where you are with them. I used to work here when I was a teenager. Then, when I was looking for a change, the owner became too frail to manage, so I took it on. You said you wanted to talk about Tony."

"How well did you know him?" Dave asked.

"Quite well. We'd met several times over the years, at various nights out and climbing functions. Book launches, fund raising, that sort of thing. First time I met him was on a rock-climbing course."

"You're a climber?"

"Was a climber, but never too seriously. I just went along for the beer." A smile lit up her face and the corners of her eyes crinkled into a patchwork of criss-crossing creases. In that moment I realised how beautiful she was. Outdoor girls, I thought. Give me an outdoor girl every time. "And then…" she went on, hesitantly now, "after Jeremy died, we started dating. Just a bit. He found me some work, but it didn't last."

"What sort of work?"

"With a TV company he was well-in with, as a researcher. We made outdoor documentaries. I loved it, but… it didn't last."

"How close were you to Jeremy?" I asked.

"We were engaged. We'd set a date, conveniently after the Everest expedition. But I never saw him again." Her head lowered and she lined her coffee mug up with the pattern on the table cover, equidistant from three corners of the design. "Tony came to see me, told me what had happened. He sounded grief-stricken, as I was. I suppose we comforted each other. At that level, Mr Priest, it's an incestuous world. Outsiders don't understand what drives them on. But... that didn't last long, either."

I reached across the table and touched the stump of her little finger with the tip of my forefinger. "What happened to that little piggy?" I asked.

She smiled again and withdrew her hand. "Climbing," she explained. "In Derbyshire. The leader dislodged a stone and it fell on my finger. Chopped it clean off." She illustrated her words with a chopping motion.

"I don't suppose it was Tony Krabbe leading?" I asked.

"No," she replied. "Actually, it was Jeremy. He was devastated. Leaders are not supposed to do that. He half carried me to the road and rushed me to hospital, but they couldn't save it. This may sound unbelievably corny to you, Mr Priest, but that's when we fell in love with each other."

"No, it sounds perfectly natural to me, Gabi," I replied, smiling at her, "and totally understandable."

Santiago and Pedro were standing by the door as we left. "It's their feeding time," Gabi explained, pushing them away.

"Do you need a hand with those straw bales?" Dave asked.

"No, I can manage. I'm as strong as an ox, but it's kind of you to offer."

"I think you took your eye off the ball," Dave declared on the journey back to Heckley.

"No I didn't. It's the way I work. I like to create the illusion that my mind has been diverted, but my razor-sharp investigative intellect is completely focused on the job in hand, all the time."

"You could have fooled me."

"Well... she is rather attractive, now you come to mention it."

"Chop her other pinkie off and she could be yours."

"So what did you think?"

"I'm not sure. She didn't sound too devastated, but Krabbe

certainly has an eye for the ladies. No wonder you were so jealous of him. Hey, you never told me how you got on with the other love of his life: Sonia Thornton."

"Didn't I?"

"No. And Robert's a bit dis-chuffed that you didn't take him with you."

"He'll get over it. Actually, she's an ice-maiden. I've had warmer conversations with the contents of my fridge. He can do a follow-up, if he wants."

"That bad, was it? And what about a follow-up with Gabrielle? Want me to do that one?"

"Um, no, Dave, I might just take that on myself. Inspector's prerogative."

We re-crossed the bridge and joined the motorway west-bound. As we drove inland the sun came out briefly and the traffic thickened. South of Leeds it slowed and finally ground to a standstill.

"Some people have to endure this every day," Dave said.

"Poor sods."

"So how's Rosie these days? You don't mention her much."

"I'm not sure. I saw her last night and she said she was OK."

"We could have a foursome, one night, if you wanted."

"Thanks. I'll mention it," I replied, untruthfully.

But I did ring her. I spent the afternoon filling in the diary, studying a summary of reports compiled by the reader and discussing the case with Gilbert and the SIO. Soon as I was home I rang Rosie.

"Listen, Rosie," I said, after asking about her well-being, "I don't want to crowd you but I've an invitation to a function on Saturday night. It's partly work – I want to have a look at some of the people there. It's at Heckley football club, in the new hospitality suite. Should be fun."

"If it's work wouldn't it be better to take one of your police-women?" she replied.

"Possibly, but their husbands object to me borrowing them on a Saturday evening. And… and…"

"And what?"

"…and they all have big calf muscles. We'd stand out like a pair of toby jugs."

"Charlie, have you ever kissed the Blarney stone?"

"Um, no, but I once had a romantic relationship with a bag of cement."

"Really?"

"I was all mixed up, those days. No strings, Rosie, and I promise not to ring you again for… oh, a month. No, a fortnight. How's that sound?"

"Saturday, did you say?"

"That's right."

"What time will you pick me up?"

"I'll let you know. There is just one other thing."

"Oh yes? What's that?"

"You'll have to watch a football match first."

8

"You're to put these on," Duggie said, handing her a small holdall. "And make yourself look nice. If you don't the boss will be very annoyed, and he'll come round wiv his little 'lectric friend." He made several stabbing motions towards her with a forefinger, laughing and hissing *pssst pssst* between his teeth just in case she was in doubt as to his meaning. "Understand?"

Ludmilla cowered and nodded. She knew too well what he meant. She took the holdall into the bathroom and slowly changed. There was lipstick and perfume in the bag, and a pair of high-heeled shoes; items she'd once dreamed of buying but now symbols of a world she hated. She applied far too much of the lipstick and perfume, achieving, at first attempt, the look and smell that were the trademarks of her new profession.

Duggie's car was not as luxurious as the boss's, as she thought of him, and it stank of cigarette smoke, but it was still far above anything else she'd known. They drove for nearly twenty minutes, over some hills where there were no lights from houses, until they were in another small town. She was in the back seat. Duggie had opened the door for her, and placed his hand on her head as she stooped to enter. She could see his face in the driver's mirror, his eyes constantly flicking her way, so she slid into a corner, out of his sight. At one point they stopped at a traffic signal and she could see a group of people waiting at a bus stop. She could run over to them and ask for their help. There were men amongst them. Duggie would be outnumbered.

Ludmilla slipped off the high-heeled shoes, slowly raised her hand and curled a finger behind the door handle. Very gently, she pulled it towards her but the door wouldn't spring open as she'd expected. She let go of the handle and sank lower in the seat as the light changed to green and they drove off.

The house was in a cul-de-sac illuminated only by the glow from windows and from carriage lamps on each side of every door. All the houses were big, with double garages, and one or two had a car standing outside. There were no fences or walls around the gardens, but most had small trees growing in them. A door opened and she saw a woman standing silhouetted as a cat sniffed the air before stepping decorously into the night. Ludmilla couldn't believe that ordinary people could live in such a fairytale world. The woman closed the door and was gone. The cat scratched the turf, arched its back and strolled around the corner, out of sight.

Duggie drove to the end of the street and stopped, peering at the numbers on the doors. "This is it," he said.

She tried the car door again but it still didn't open. Duggie walked round and opened it from the outside. "Childproof locks," he said, grinning, but she didn't know what he meant. "C'mon, it's pissing down."

He took her by the elbow and steered her up the short drive to the front door of the house. There was a name on the wall at the side of the door, but it meant nothing to her. She had no coat on, just a thin silk dress, and she shivered with cold.

Duggie pressed the bell and the door opened immediately. A grey-haired man was standing there, in a jacket and tie. "C'm in, my dear," he said in a soft, sibilant voice, taking her by the arm and nodding to Duggie. He closed the door, with Duggie on the outside, and turned the lock. "My, you're a bright young thing," the man told her. "And you're wet through. Let's get you out of those damp clothes. Would you like a glass of wine?" As the door closed Duggie had said: "Don't forget," and made the *pssst pssst* noise through his teeth.

Rosie rang me to ask what she should wear, and I'd been a big help. Well, that's what she'd said: "You're a big help, Charlie." She'd decided on a pinstripe suit – "My interview outfit" - with the inevitable red blouse, and looked terrific. I gave her a kiss on the cheek and told her so.

Heckley Town played their hearts out and only lost by one goal. Everybody agreed that the result flattered the other side, and that if Heckley played like that every week then success would surely follow. Rosie, knowing nothing about football, suggested that if the other side scored more goals every week, wouldn't all the results be defeats? I began to explain, then abandoned the task.

The hospitality suite ran the full length of the ground's new grandstand, behind where the crowd sat, and looked out over their heads. It had a glass wall facing the pitch with rows of tables and chairs. All the women wore dresses or suits, but the men were in everything from jeans to dinner jackets. Twenty minutes after the final whistle the players filtered into the function, freshly showered and powdered, identifiable by the huge knots in their ties and the silly hairstyles.

Young ladies in short skirts wandered amongst us with trays laden with wine, and a substantial buffet was laid out near the middle of the room. We stacked our plates – Rosie's modestly, mine to the gunnels – and shared a table with a couple from Tintwistle who manufactured rustic garden furniture.

"For *rustic* read *splinters in your bum,*" Rosie told me as we moved on. I'd seen Wallenberg circulating, exhorting everybody to give generously, but steered out of his way. Once we'd met, I'd have no excuse for staying longer, and would have to take Rosie home. Work and pleasure are not always mutually exclusive. At one end of the room was what could only be called a shrine to Grace Wallenberg, whom I assumed to be Peter's mother. A table covered in blue velvet bore a series of framed photographs taken throughout what looked like an active, prosperous life, with a portrait in oils hanging behind them. In her later years she was an elegant lady who wouldn't have looked out of place on the balcony of Buck house, flapping an indifferent hand at the adoring multitude. Earlier, she'd been an adventurer, but her adventures and hardships were of the type that usually had a flunky or two not far to the rear, bringing along the Harrods hamper. There were photos of her standing alongside cars bedecked with Monte Carlo rally plates, smiling from the cockpit of a Tiger Moth, and posing in shorts on the deck of a yacht. There was just one picture of her with the man I presumed to be her husband. She was wearing ski goggles and it said *Chamonix, 1958* in a bottom corner. We were there, a glossy plaque told us, to support the Grace Wallenberg Trust in its fight against cancer.

"A noble cause," Rosie said.

"Yep," I agreed.

"She certainly moved around in high circles."

I leaned closer to her. "All paid for by ill-gotten gains," I whispered. "Can't help wondering how much she knew about it."

"Sometimes, it's easier just to lie back and not ask questions."

"Mmm, but that doesn't make her any less culpable."

"The portrait's good," Rosie said.

"Do you think so?"

"Mmm. Don't you?"

"It's a bit amateurish," I said. "The eyes don't follow you round the room. That's how you tell a good portrait."

Rosie smiled at me. "Can you do portraits?" she asked.

"Yes. They're my speciality. Mainly for *Wanted* posters."

"Will you do one of me? I'd love to have my portrait painted."

Instantly I knew how I would do it. She'd be curled up in her favourite chair, barefooted with painted toenails. "If you like," I replied. I reached forward and took hold of a wisp of her hair between my thumb and forefinger. "I'll go to Halfords in the morning," I said, "and buy a tin of aluminium paint."

When she'd forgiven me I gave her ten pounds to buy raffle tickets and bought another ten pounds-worth for myself, which earned me a tut and a headshake from her. We wandered back into the throng and I positioned us where a collision with the ever-networking Peter Wallenberg and his wife was inevitable.

A girl in overloaded fishnet tights hove alongside and I lifted two orange juices from her tray. Wallenberg was talking to the couple standing next to us, holding the man's arm and occasionally laughing out loud. His wife was as tall as he was, dark and Mediterranean-looking, wearing a blue sleeveless dress that came high around her neck. A strategically placed keyhole displayed her cleavage to anybody who might be interested in that sort of thing, and around her shoulders was a shawl in muted colours that she held together with her left hand. The sparklers on her wedding finger would have bought my house.

"So how did Peter make his money?" Rosie asked, very softly, turning to me.

"You name it," I replied, stooping to place my lips close to her ear. "He was a gangster. Everything up to murder, at a guess."

Wallenberg shook the man's hand yet again and turned towards us, but his wife said something to him and moved off

"The ladies," Rosie stated. "I think I'll join her. See what I can find out."

"Rosie!" I hissed, but she slipped away and I watched her vanish behind the door into the secret world of the ladies' loo.

"Good evening," Wallenberg boomed, with all the confidence of a man who was paying for the booze and food but could afford it. This was his party. "I don't believe we've met."

"Charlie Priest," I said, taking the extended hand and shaking it. "As in Roman Catholic. I'm with Heckley CID. Thanks for the invitation."

"A policeman! Wonderful. If the evening descends into a fight I'll be depending on you, Charlie."

"I'd say it was unlikely. They look a docile lot. I understand you've bought the club."

"That's right. It's a wonderful institution and I'd like to keep it alive. We try to put something back into the community; that's what it's all about, don't you think? Are you a supporter?"

"Lapsed is probably the word," I said. "I come when I can." No point in hurting the man's feelings, but I'd rather watch the sink overflow. "I played for them, briefly," I boasted, "when I was a teenager."

"Really?"

"I was a goalkeeper. We had a weak defence. That's my excuse."

He looked around, conspiratorially, and placed a hand at one side of his mouth. "You wouldn't like to turn out next Saturday, would you?" he whispered.

"Ah! I think you'll be better off without me."

"Perhaps so. I envy you, though, Charlie. I envy all sportsmen. I love sport, but I have a slight handicap." He glanced briefly down at his leg, then continued: "I was hopeless at games. Had a rough time at school. Ironic, really, that I now own a football club, don't you think?"

"That's life, Mr Wallenberg."

"Peter, please. Have you bought some raffle tickets?"

I placed a hand on my top pocket. "Right here," I said, then went on: "Actually, I need to talk to you sometime."

"Oh? What about?"

"Tony Krabbe's murder. I'm the investigating detective. I believe you knew him."

"An unfortunate business but I don't see how I can help. I hardly ever met the fellow, as I've already told a police officer."

"We do follow-up interviews, especially when we're totally baffled. How about Monday morning?"

He looked thoughtful. "I'm not sure. You'd better ring my office."

"I'll do that."

Before we could continue the conversation his mobile phone rang. He apologised for the interruption and retrieved it from a jacket pocket.

"Yes, this is Peter," I heard him say. He listened for a few moments, then added: "Hi! How are you? Yes thanks, it's going well. I appreciate that it's not quite your scene… Listen, though. I'm glad you rang. It just happens that I might have something that interests you. My latest import. Guaranteed top quality. You won't be disappointed… Money back? Ha Ha! You drive a hard bargain… Yes, we have immediate availability… Same price as before, let's call it an introductory offer… Shall I have a word with my man? Good. Good. Give me the address and I'll get on to it."

He remembered I was there and turned to me, saying: "Will you excuse me, please, Charlie? Give the office a ring. Business never ends I'm afraid," and moved out of earshot, so I never discovered what the mysterious import was.

Duggie came to collect Ludmilla two hours later. She sat in the back of the car without speaking and shrank into a corner. Duggie said: "Not too bad, don't yer fink?" but she ignored him. All she wanted was to go back to her room and have a bath. They were nearly there when Duggie's mobile phone rang.

"Hi, boss," she heard him say. "Yeah, she done fine. No problems. Hang on, I'll pull over." He parked the car, listened for a while, then turned on the interior light and wrote something on the back of his hand. When he'd finished the call he switched the light off and turned to her. "Your reputation is spreading, girl. You have another client," he said.

It was an apartment in a block near the city centre. Duggie parked right outside the entrance and spoke into a grille on the wall. Something buzzed, the door opened and they were inside. They rode up in a lift but Ludmilla couldn't read the floor number where they alighted. The instant Duggie touched the bell push a dog started barking, and they both flinched at its ferocity and took a step backwards. His fingers tightened around her arm, and she gave him a pleading glance, but he wasn't looking. A light came on, a security chain scraped and the door opened. Ludmilla's second client stood before her.

He was wearing leather jeans and a startling white t-shirt that struggled to contain his bulging physique. The head was

116

shaven, as she expected, but the leather collar and wristbands, with their silver spikes, were a chilling novelty. He glanced briefly at Duggie and turned his gaze upon the girl. She felt his eyes strip her naked then crawl all over her body like maggots over a carcass.

When he'd seen enough for the moment he turned his head and called over his shoulder. "Hey Todd. Come and look at this."

Todd appeared a second later, one fist grasping the chain around the neck of a Doberman that tugged and strained to be free. Todd was even bigger than his friend, clad in a leather singlet to best display his body art. Fabulous beasts – dragons and serpents – squirmed around his arms and shoulders and writhed up his neck, their forked tongues reaching towards his eyes. Because of the dog he was stooped forward, displaying the swastika tattooed on his head. Ludmilla's knees gave way and only Duggie's firm grip prevented her falling to the ground.

Todd took a long look at her until his wet lips parted and one corner of them curled into a smile. "Oh, yes," he said, his voice hoarse with anticipation. "We'll have some of that. We'll certainly have some of that."

Duggie propelled the terrified girl towards them with as much concern as if he were delivering wet fish. "An hour," he said.

"That should be plenty of time," one of them replied, closing the door in his face.

It didn't take an hour. When they'd finished they pushed her out and slammed the door. Ludmilla leaned against the wall and sobbed.

The lift took her down and when she peered through the glass door she could see the car, with Duggie dozing in the driver's seat. She turned and saw a corridor leading off, with a sign that said Emergency Exit.

There was a door at the end of the corridor, with a bar across it and a notice about a fire alarm. Ludmilla pushed at the bar, the door swung open and a bell somewhere rang out its warning. She flung the door wide and started running, out into the night, towards the lights.

Her shoes came off in three strides and the pavement felt cold and clean beneath her feet. She ran like the wind, the dress riding up over her thighs, down a dark street with a high stone wall on either side. There were dead leaves under her feet now, like there'd been before, when they ran for their lives through the pine forest. Across the end she could see the warm glow of lights, with cars and buses passing by. Her chest was bursting and now her feet hurt, but the hurt was a small price to pay. She slowed as she reached the end and jogged round the corner, into the brightness of the city.

Duggie's arms clamped around her and he laughed in her face, his breath smelling of beer. "Where do you fink you're going, eh?" He lifted her off her feet and carried her back round the corner. When they were in the darkness again he dropped her, slammed her against the wall and grabbed a fistful of her hair. "I fink you and me had better have a little talk," he hissed, pulling her head back, his face an inch from hers. "Old Hopalong has told me not to lay a finger on you. No fingering the goods, he sez, or else. But he's also told me that if you misbehave or don't give satisfaction, I've to tell 'im, and then he'll give you a taste of his little 'lectric friend. *Pssst pssst.* So I fink we can come to a deal, don't you? Now, let's go back to the flat and work out the details, eh?"

I watched Wallenberg write the address on a napkin and make the call, repeating what he'd written to the person at the other end. I was behind him now, about five yards away, but couldn't read it. When he'd finished the call he folded the napkin into small squares and put it in his pocket with the cell phone.

He glanced around, choosing his target, then headed for an elderly couple who looked as if they'd be more at home on a cruise ship than at a football match. They smiled at him and the mental backslapping started all over again.

I turned to find a table to put my glass on and a napkin to wipe my fingers, and bumped into Rosie.

"Oh, I've missed him," she complained.

"Where've you been?" I demanded.

"To the loo. You know where I've been."

"I mean… what did you say to her?"

"I asked her about her shawl."

"Her shawl?"

"Yes. It's rather nice, if you haven't noticed."

Women's talk. I sighed with relief. "As a matter of fact, I did notice."

"I said to her: 'Is that what they call a pashmina?' and she said: 'Well, actually, this is the real thing,' and I said: 'It's lovely.' She thanked me and that was that."

"A… pashmina?"

"Yes. They make them in Kashmir and they're the finest wool in the world. They say you can pull one through a wedding ring. There's another sort… even rarer. They cost a fortune. Thousands of pounds. I can't think of the name but I read about them somewhere. In *National Geographic* at a guess. That's what she probably meant by the real thing." Her brow creased with puzzlement, but the name wouldn't come.

"You had me worried," I confessed. "I thought you were going to ask her if she knew her husband was a crook."

Rosie looked up into my face and smiled, and my heart skipped a few beats. "I meant to," she said, "but somebody was using one of the cubicles, so I couldn't."

"Thank the Lord for that. C'mon, let's go."

"I walked down them all, pushing the doors open with the toe of my shoe, like cops do on TV." She stood on one leg and demonstrated. "It's fun, isn't it?"

"We don't do that. C'mon."

"Not just yet; they're drawing the raffle."

9

Guess who won a team shirt, signed by all the players? I wanted to give it back but Rosie wouldn't let me. Monday morning I dumped it on Dave's desk, saying: "Give that to Danny."

He held it up and tried to read the names. "Where'd you get this?"

"Saturday night's charity bash. If you wash it the writing might come out. They wouldn't have the brains to use indelible ink."

"Danny wouldn't be seen dead in it, but Sophie might like it."

"There you are then. A present from Uncle Charlie. What have we got?"

The investigation had concentrated on identifying the people associated with Krabbe and interviewing them. Trace, Interview, Eliminate. Slowly, we were working our way through all the people in the albums, all his sponsors, neighbours and acquaintances. His climbing friends were scattered around the world, but if somebody was halfway up the highest peak in Mongolia there was little point in asking: "Where were you last Saturday night?"

"One thing strikes me, though, Charlie," the statement reader told me after we'd discussed his notes. "Everybody says what a brilliant climber he was. You get the impression that he's one of the best ever. There's tremendous respect for him as a climber. He's done all the big mountains, and nobody can take that away from him, but… but nobody says they miss him. Nobody expresses any regrets for his passing."

"Jealousy?" I suggested.

"Could be."

"And it's a high-risk activity," I added. "They're used to dealing with death."

"This is more than that. With the possible exception of his

parents, I don't think a single tear has been shed for Tony Krabbe."

We had a meeting with Mr Wood and the SIO. "How did the charity bash go?" Gilbert asked.

"Great. I won the raffle," I told them. "Only thing of interest that I picked up was that Wallenberg's parents holidayed in Chamonix in 1958. They were the type of people who would toddle off to the outfitters and buy the complete wardrobe, so I've no doubt they owned a couple of ice axes. I'd love to find them."

"Do you think they'll have kept them?"

"Probably."

"There's not enough grounds for a search warrant."

"I know. It was just a thought."

"Anything else?"

"Yes," I replied and told them about Crozier's death being murder.

"What's the link between Wallenberg and Crozier?"

"Crozier was a business acquaintance of Wallenberg Senior. Wallenberg Junior has just bought a nightclub called the Painted Pony that Crozier had a share in. They were mixed up in all sorts of deals."

"He bought it since Crozier died?"

"Mmm."

"What's the link with the youth who crashed the car?"

"Wallenberg knew him. His wife may have been having sex with him. Other than that, we assume he was just an employee. Apparently Wallenberg will gamble on anything, so it's possible they were arranging car races and betting on the outcome."

"My driver is better than yours?"

"Something like that."

"Sounds fun. So why would Wallenberg want Krabbe dead?"

"I don't know." I told them about the shop in the mall – Art of Asia – and suggested that there might be more to the relationship than we knew.

121

The SIO nodded sagely. "I think that's where I'd focus the investigation, Charlie," he suggested.

Thanks, I thought. Thanks a lot. I wouldn't have dreamed of it, myself.

Word about the investigation spread through the climbing fraternity like chlamydia through a polytechnic, and we had some feedback about it from a couple of rock-climbing constables. There was no shortage of theories about Krabbe's death, right down to it being divine retribution for the desecration of holy places. We'd had a look at the shop in the first days of the enquiry, but nothing leapt out at us. There were no hollow sandalwood elephants stuffed with hashish, or solid gold frames on tapestries of tigers drinking from a stream, destined for the walls of local restaurants. We even wondered about animal parts for traditional medicine, but found none. We looked at woollen rugs, hessian bags, incense from Tibet, silver jewellery and a variety of wooden artefacts. Some of it was elegant and expensive, produced by artists and craftsmen as good as any in the world, but much of it was tacky and cheap.

So we went back and this time we took the shop apart. Everything we could find was pulled and poked, weighed and measured, checked against the stocklist. The sniffer dog worked overtime but never gave a reaction. I wondered if it had been overwhelmed by the variety of scents, but the dog-handler threw the piece of impregnated rope he uses as a test piece behind some boxes and the dog found it in seconds.

The pashminas were on a shelf, priced at £250 each. I carefully lifted them off and put them on a table. The colours were gorgeous, rich and muted at the same time, and the pile of garments was as light as a feather. One by one I picked up each shawl and, without unfolding it – I'm not very good at folding – felt for anything hidden between the layers. When the dog had sniffed them and given its all-clear I replaced them on the shelf.

We looked for hiding places and copied all the addresses

122

off the empty packing cases in the stock room. The postman delivers the mail via the back door and there was a big pile. Jeff Caton divided it into two heaps: junk and non-junk, and analysed every syllable of the good stuff.

I went back to the office, dispirited. I found a postcard with a picture of Ingleborough from Crina Bottom with a light covering of snow and wrote: "Enjoyed Saturday, hope you did," on the back and put it in an envelope. I addressed it to Rosie and dropped it in the *out* tray. Jeff came in two hours later, long-faced and morose.

"Sod all," he declared, flinging his notebook on the desk as he removed his jacket.

There's a database somewhere in deepest Hampshire that lists thousands of MOs of murders in close detail. Krabbe's killing was peculiar in that the murder weapon was related to the way in which he earned his living. The word *poetic* came to mind. I asked Jeff to prepare a submission to them, then I wondered about Joe Crozier and rang Nigel to suggest he do the same.

"Already done," he replied. "No other similar uses of masking tape on record."

"Have you made any progress?" I asked.

"Ye-es," he replied, warily. "We've had one small development." I kept silent, waiting for him to volunteer the information. "We searched his clothes, of course, but didn't find anything interesting. But the scientific boys have given them the once-over and discovered something we overlooked. His jacket had a little pocket inside one of the other pockets. I'm told it's for keeping your condoms in but I think they're having me on. Inside there was a little scrap of paper, screwed into a ball."

"Which the scientific boys have unfolded with their usual care and read the message thereon," I said, hoping to hurry him to the point of the story.

"Yes," he replied. "It was the wrapping off a toothpick. A purpose-made one, with the name of a restaurant on it."

"Go on."

"Sometime, while wearing that suit, Crazy Joe Crozier had eaten at *L'Autre Place* restaurant in Heckley."

"Wow!" I exclaimed. "Do you know who owns it?"

"Mmm. Peter Wallenberg."

"That's right. Were there any credit card receipts on Joe?"

"No."

"That's a pity. So somebody else paid."

"There's more."

"Go on."

"Joe was famous for his dapper appearance. We found receipts in his office for a new suit, dated about the time he went in the river. We've checked with the tailor and it more or less looks as if that was the first time he'd worn the thing."

"So it could be that his killer invited him out to *L'Autre Place* and treated him to his last meal. Poor Joe put on his best bib and tucker for the occasion."

"Could be. The meal was beefsteak, incidentally."

"Any pastry?"

"Yes, I believe so."

"Speciality of the restaurant is Beef Wellington."

"I know."

"It sounds as if you've been straying on to my patch."

"I was about to ring you. We ought to have that conference."

"Have you spoken to Wallenberg?"

"No. We don't know when exactly Crozier died, so there's little point, yet. It was about the twentieth of October, give or take a couple of days, but that's not much help."

"I don't suppose he kept a diary."

"If he did we haven't found it."

"Old habits die hard," I said. "Never write anything down."

"So how're things going with the Krabbe enquiry?" Nigel asked.

"They're not. Yet."

I'd left some lamb chops and vegetables in the slow cooker, so I ate reasonably well that evening. I wondered about ringing Rosie but decided not to. I'd said a fortnight, so three days was a little premature, and she wouldn't have received the card, yet. The board with the paint splashes on it was in the garage, taking up space. The gallery wanted my pictures in four weeks but I wasn't happy with my early efforts so I decided on a fresh start. I sanded off the blobs and gave the whole thing two coats of matt white emulsion, ready for the next attempt. Time was tight, so I'd have to settle for a couple *in the style of* Jackson Pollock. They always go down well, and they're dead easy.

I was flicking round the channels, wondering whether to have some cornflakes, when Nigel rang. "We've had a break-through," he said.

"Go on," I invited.

"A woman came into the station, about half-past five, asking to see me. Apparently she's just finished with her boyfriend and was indulging in a bit of revenge therapy. He lives in Waterside Heights, ninth floor, bang opposite where Joe Crozier lived. This woman and her boyfriend were, to use her words, 'messing around on the balcony…'"

"Having sex," I interjected.

"OK, having sex, when she saw some figures down below. They appeared to roll something into the water. She wanted to report it but the boyfriend convinced her that it was some-one dumping a roll of carpet."

"Really? And this was when?"

"Monday the twentieth of October."

"Bingo. You've got your time of death."

"That's what I thought.

"So why didn't this woman call you earlier and say that they'd seen someone drop something into the river but they thought it was only a roll of carpet?"

"Ah, this is where the revenge bit comes in. They'd done a couple of lines of coke. We've just paid him a visit and caught him in possession, but he verifies her story. He was most cooperative, managed to fill-in a few blanks. The carpet dumpers – he thinks there were three of them – were in a Range Rover, but there were two other cars on the wharf. He estimates the time to have been between half-past midnight and one o'clock."

"Wallenberg drives a Range Rover."

"I know."

"How the other half live, Nigel. See what you're missing."

"Yep. He's a director with an insurance company and she calls herself a financial consultant."

"So what happens next?"

"I was thinking of visiting *L'Autre Place*, with your permission, to see if the manager remembers them being there."

"Good idea. Tonight?"

"Oh, I had tomorrow lunchtime in mind, but we're probably more likely to catch him tonight. Shall I pick you up?"

"I'll be waiting for you."

I did a quick change out of my painting clothes and was just going round with the electric razor when Nigel rang the bell. At half-past ten we breezed into Heckley's poshest watering hole and a flunky asked if we'd like a table for two.

"No, we'd like to see the manager," Nigel told him, showing his ID, and the waiter went to fetch him from the kitchen.

He wanted to talk standing in the doorway, but we persuaded him that his office might be more appropriate. "This is Inspector Priest and I'm Inspector Newley," Nigel had said.

"That's *detective* inspector," I added, "not environmental health," and I swear he looked relieved.

Before Nigel could say his piece I went on: "We're investigating the murder of Tony Krabbe, the mountaineer. You may have read about it in the papers."

"Yes," he replied, "but I don't see how I can help."

"Well, we're going through all Mr Krabbe's acquaintances and checking their alibis. Mr Wallenberg had business dealings with him. He tells us that he had dinner here on the night of Monday, the twentieth of October. Can you verify that, please?"

"Yes, no problem. He did have dinner here one Monday evening, which was unusual for him. It's our quietest night of the week. I'll just fetch the diary."

When he'd gone Nigel glared at me. "You shouldn't have done that, Charlie," he hissed. "We haven't spoken to Wallenberg yet. It'll be inadmissible."

"He's been spoken to about Krabbe, Nigel, and we've got what we wanted."

The waiter came back and spread a large diary on the desk. "Here we are," he said. "The twentieth of October, Mr Wallenberg, table for two, nine p.m." He pointed to the entry and I read the name.

"So he'd be safely in here at ten p.m.?"

"Most assuredly, Inspector."

"Does he always dine so late?"

"No, not usually."

"Who was his guest?"

"His guest? I'm afraid I don't know."

"Male or female?"

"Er, male, I believe."

"Could you describe him?"

"He was a small man, fairly old, going bald."

"Well-dressed?"

"All our customers are well-dressed, Inspector. Well, most of them."

I gave him a big smile. "You've been most cooperative, thank you. I think we can safely cross Mr Wallenberg off the list of possible witnesses, don't you, Mr Newley?"

"Oh, er, y-yes," he stuttered. Nigel dropped me off at the door and refused my offer of a coffee. He was displeased at the way I'd conducted the interview but he'd got the information he required: Joe Crozier dined with Peter Wallenberg shortly before he was murdered. He agreed that a talk with Wallenberg might be appropriate but it was doubtful if it would achieve much. Motive and opportunity were there, but we needed some forensics, desperately, and none was forthcoming.

I breezed into the nick, Wednesday morning, and saw this… this monstrosity standing in the foyer. I stopped short and gaped at it.

"What's that?" I demanded of the desk sergeant.

"What does it look like, Charlie?"

It was big and square, with illuminated Coca-Cola logos all over it, and stacks of cans visible inside.

"It looks like a drinks machine."

"Well done. CID strikes again."

"Does Mr Wood know it's there?"

"'Spect so, but it's over his head."

"What's wrong with going to the canteen?"

"The canteen? It's not for us, Charlie. It's for them."

"Who?"

"Villains. The enemy."

"You're having me on."

"No way. Human rights says they've to have access to fizzy drinks at all times. Otherwise, we're in bother for depriving them of essential E-numbers."

"Strewth! What next?"

"Don't ask, Charlie. Don't ask."

Jeff Caton was keeping an eye on Krabbe'shop, checking the mail. I was in Mr Wood's office when he rang to say that there was a message from Parcel Force, saying that they'd tried to make a delivery. I told him to collect the parcel and give it the full treatment. I kept the afternoon clear because Nigel had invited Wallenberg in for a talk, but Wallenberg cancelled at the last minute.

He kindly agreed to call in Heckley nick on Thursday morning, when it was more convenient for him, and he came with not one, but two briefs in his entourage. Nigel brought one of his sergeants and agreed that I could sit in on the interview. We didn't bother with the tape recorder. Those tapes cost money, and we weren't expecting anything other than a series of evasions.

"How well did you know Joe Crozier?" Nigel began by asking.

One of the briefs put his hand on Wallenberg's arm and whispered something to him. Wallenberg shook his head and turned to Nigel. "Fairly well," he said.

"How did you come to know him?"

"He was a friend of the family. When I was small I called him Uncle Joe."

A good one, I thought. Who ever heard of anyone murdering his Uncle Joe?

"So he was a friend of your parents?"

"Yes."

"Did you continue the friendship after your parents died?"

Nigel is slow but methodical. It gradually emerged that Peter Wallenberg had inherited considerable property interests from his parents. Grace Wallenberg had run the empire after the old man died and now the baton had passed to Peter. No, he'd had very few contacts with Crozier since then. Yes, he had put a bid in for the Painted Pony, but directly to the other two partners, who were accountants. He hadn't known at the time that Joe was the third shareholder.

"So when did you last see Joe Crozier?" Nigel asked.

A leading question, the answer to which depended on whether his restaurant manager had told him about our little visit, 36 hours earlier. Wallenberg stretched a hand out on to the formica tabletop and drummed his fingers, as if deep in thought. He pursed his lips, looked at me and then back at Nigel. He was wearing a long black coat and had declined to take it off, even though it was stifling in the interview room. Removing his black leather gloves was his only concession to the warmth. After an eternity, drawn out for maximum effect, he gave a big sigh and said: "I saw Joe about four or five weeks ago. It was a Monday night. We had dinner together. Is that accurate enough, Inspector, or would you like me to consult a calendar?"

"Monday the twentieth of October?" Nigel suggested.

"Yes. The twentieth does ring a bell."

"And you ate at *L'Autre Place*, in Heckley, which you own, I believe."

"Correct on all counts, Inspector. Have you ever dined there?"

"No, it hasn't been my pleasure."

"You should. You won't be disappointed. Tell Raymond that I sent you and I'm sure he'll look after you."

"Thanks for the offer. So how did Crozier get there?"

"His driver brought him."

"There were just the two of you? No wives."

"No."

"And what time did he leave?"

"I'm not sure, but it must have been around midnight. Joe was particularly taken by our Chateaux Margaux, finished nearly three bottles of it. He was legless."

Nigel looked across at me. I shuffled in my seat, sat upright, and asked; "Who organised this cosy little party, Mr Wallenberg?"

He turned his gaze to me. His eyes were dark and the brows almost met in the middle. "Crozier did," he replied. "He rang me, out of the blue, said he'd heard about the restaurant and wondered how things were with me. That's all."

I looked at my notebook. "Crozier went in the river at nineteen minutes to one on the morning of the 21st," I said, "and a Range Rover with the same description as yours was seen in the vicinity. Was it yours?"

His expression changed. He'd been in control up to now. Not quite cocky but ahead of the game. Hit them with a precise time and they start wondering how much you know; had the whole thing been captured on CCTV?

"No, of course not."

"Where were you at that time?"

"I went home. I'd be getting ready for bed."

"You didn't stay behind to have a nightcap with your manager?"

"No, I went home."

"Can anybody verify that?"

"My wife, I suppose."

"And poor Joe fell in the river."

"Yes. As I said, he was well away with the drink. Perhaps he went for a little stroll, or just mistook his directions. The apartments at one side of the river look much like the ones at the other."

"That's what you assume happened, is it?"

"It must be, mustn't it?" but he didn't sound so sure.

I wanted to hit him with: "So how do you explain the tape binding his hands and feet?" but it was Nigel's show and it might be expedient to keep that little cookie under wraps for a while longer. Nigel does things patiently and methodically and teases out the answers; I like to jump in and cause confusion and panic and then put the pieces back together. I had the stage, and we'd learned as much as we'd get, so I decided to go out on a high note.

I said: "You mentioned your wife, Mr Wallenberg. The lovely Selina. Is it true that you met her in a whorehouse in Amsterdam?"

That did it. The brief jumped up, Wallenberg's mouth dropped open and the sergeant nearly exploded.

"That's a disgraceful thing to say," one of the briefs protested as soon as the power of speech returned. "I demand an apology right now, or this interview is terminated."

All eyes fell on me. I held up a placatory hand. "I apologise," I said, "unreservedly. My information is that Mrs Wallenberg, in a previous existence, made a lucrative living administering sexual services to the rich and famous. I am apparently misinformed about Amsterdam, for which I apologise."

"We're not standing for this," the brief proclaimed. "And I'll be having a word with the chief constable. Let's go, Mr Wallenberg."

They were all on their feet, now. I said: "Did you know your wife was having an affair, Mr Wallenberg?"

"Yes," he replied as they ushered him towards the door. "Yes, I did. We have an open relationship." He didn't say: "So there," but I could feel it in his tone.

"And don't you mind?"

131

"No. We go with whom we please. We trust each other. You should try it, sometime."

"C'mon, Peter," the brief urged. "That's enough."

"Did you know who it was with, though," I shouted at him. "Did you know that her bit of rough trade was one of your heavies?"

It hit him like a double-decker bus travelling downhill back to the depot at the end of the shift. With no brakes. He twisted round and shrugged out of the brief's grip. "What did you say?" he hissed at me.

"You heard," I told him. "I said did you know it was one of your semi-house-trained thugs she was having it off with?"

The briefs put themselves between us and pushed him towards the door. "Ignore him, Peter," one of them said. "He's winding you up. They've nothing to go on so he's having to resort to desperate measures. Selina's not like that."

"You're a liar, Priest," I heard him shout. "And a disgrace. I've raised half a million for cancer research. What have you ever done, eh? Answer me that. Answer me that."

The voices faded down the corridor and Nigel turned to me, a big grin on his face. "Well, you fucked that up good and proper, boss" he said.

"Sorry," was the best I could do.

10

Appendix 1
<u>Crash Analysis Report</u>

Speed at instant of impact: 60 miles per hour (96 kph)
This equals: 88 feet per second (27 mps)

Impact + 0.1 second
Plastic bodywork at front destroyed
Crumple zones deformed

Impact + 0.2 second
Air bags deployed
Active seatbelts deployed
Driver and front seat passenger thrown forward against seatbelts
Front of vehicle crushed
Engine forced forward through radiator
Coolant hoses, petrol pipes ruptured
Windscreen projected out of frame and other glass shatters
Rear of car projected upwards

Impact + 0.3 second
Engine torn from mountings
Roof buckles inwards
Vehicle floor buckles upwards
Driver's arms and legs strike interior surfaces. Legs broken; internal injuries caused by seatbelts; head injuries against roof. Similar for front seat passenger
Fuel tank torn from mountings
Doors thrown open

Impact + 0.4 second
Front wheels, suspension and steering gear forced into cabin space

Engine forced into cabin space
Car body stationary
Occupants at limit of forward travel; begin to rebound. Severe whiplash injuries to neck of driver and of front seat passenger

Impact + 0.5 second
Car body rebounds
Rear of vehicle falls back to ground

Impact + 1 second
Vehicle comes to rest
Occupants fatally injured
Coolant, petrol and brake fluid released.
Danger of fire

"Have you seen the accident examiner's report?" Dave asked as he seated himself in the visitor's chair.

"Mmm, I've just been looking at it. What's this other thing in with it?"

"It's a paper he did for Police that he flashes around at every opportunity. It's his great crusade for road safety. If we all knew what happened in a crash in gruesome detail we'd drive more responsibly. That's the theory."

"Looks a good way to go, if you ask me. One second and you're dead. *Finito*."

"I agree. He reckons Dale Dobson was doing about a ton. There was a dip in the road and then a brow just before where he crashed and he says the car would have taken off at that speed."

I pinned the sheets of the report back together and handed them to Dave, saying: "Stick them in the file, please,"

"I think Nigel should spin Wallenberg's place," Dave stated.

"I don't think he'd get a warrant," I replied.

"You could get one."

"I'm flattered, but I doubt it. What would he be looking for?"

"The remains of the rolls of masking tape."

"Hmm. And what would *we* be looking for? I presume we'd tag along for a look-see."

"That pile of sawdust and the other end of the ice axe."

"I think the tape and the end of the shaft will be miles away by now. Probably in a landfill site." I sat back in my chair and thought for a few seconds. "There was another car accident," I said, eventually.

"Another one?"

"Yeah. The one involving Krabbe and Sonia Thornton, back in '97. I've been thinking about it. Have a word with traffic; see if you can find who covered it. Two celebrities like that; they'll remember."

I stayed behind for an hour, filling in the diary and catching up with report reading. There was one from Jeff Caton saying that the package that Parcel Force had tried to deliver was from a company in India. According to Jeff it contained "lots of little animals carved out of that smelly wood," and it was clean. I took a Chinese takeaway home and ate it sitting at the kitchen table, listening to *The Archers*. After I'd washed my plate I rang Rosie and left a greeting on her ansaphone. It was the fortieth anniversary of JFK's assassination over the weekend, and there were several programmes on TV covering it. I intended watching as many as I could and Dave had promised to tape them. Friday's was a straightforward documentary outlining the build-up to the president's visit to Dallas, with a graphic reconstruction of events and much playing of the Zapruder film. There was no conspiracy, I was sure of that. No big conspiracy, that is. There may have been somebody behind it all, encouraging him, but Oswald alone did the deed. There was just one little doubt in my mind: how did he manage to land a job in the book depository just four weeks before the president was due to pass under the sixth floor window? There was something we all agreed on, though: a little bit of each one of us died on that day in Dealey Plaza.

I was ready for bed when the phone rang. Rosie, I thought, but it was a man's voice.

"Are you Inspector Priest?" it asked, barely audible over the background noise. There was a hubbub of conversation overlaid by a strangled tenor murdering *Will you go, lassie, go?*

"Who's calling?" I replied.

There was a long silence, and I'd have thought the connection had been broken if it hadn't been for the background noise. Eventually he said: "It's not important who I am. I read about you in the paper. You're conducting the enquiry into Tony Krabbe's murder."

"That's right. Do you have some information?"

"I... um, I'm not sure. I might have."

"Can I have your name, please?"

"No. My name doesn't matter."

"OK. So what do you want to tell me?"

"I'm not talking on the phone. I want to see you."

"Tonight?"

"No, tomorrow."

"Right. Where are you?"

"I'll be at Nine Standards Rigg at about one o'clock."

"Where?" I asked.

"Nine Standards Rigg."

"I can't hear you." His voice was soft and hesitant, and Pavarotti in the background wasn't helping.

"I said Nine Standards Rigg."

"Where's that?"

"It's, um, up near Kirkby Stephen."

"*That* Nine Standards Rigg. It's miles away."

"It's not that far. Tomorrow, one o'clock."

"How do I know...?"

"You don't," he said, and put the phone down.

Tomorrow was Saturday, so I rose early, called in the office to deploy any troops who turned up, and sneaked away. It was over a two-hour drive, right up to the northern-most outpost of the county, and then along roads designed for nothing wider or faster than a horse-drawn hay cart. That, however, doesn't stop the locals driving their four-by-fours at breakneck speeds. It had occurred that it might be a hoax, or that somebody wanted me out of the way, but if I hadn't gone I'd have never learned what it was all about. It might have been dangerous, too, but I doubted it, and a little danger never hurt anyone. What the heck, it was an excuse for a day out, and I needed a day out.

I stopped in Keld, which is an ancient Viking name meaning place-where-the-ground-is-soggy-and-the-clouds-perpetually-sit-on-the-earth-where-the-people-are-as-morose-as-the-sheep, to check the map, then took it slowly until I reached a turnoff signposted to Ravenseat.

The last stretch was on an unfenced strip of tarmac laid across the moor like a discarded bootlace for two miles until it ended in a farmyard. There was a stream with an ancient bridge that had been widened in years gone by, but still wasn't wide enough for modern agricultural vehicles. A ford next to the bridge catered for them. I parked outside the farm, next to a rusting cattle trailer, and took stock.

We were in a slight depression and it was raining hard, so all I could see in every direction was moor that faded away into the mist. Nothing stirred at the farm, although a newish Landrover was parked outside. I looked at it and wondered about the people who lived there. This was the stuff of gothic novels: remote and isolated; washed by perpetual rains and racked by the mother of all thunderstorms every Halloween.

I pulled on my boots and full waterproofs and checked the compass. A path was visible, snaking off into the gloom, and in the distance I could see a waymark. I locked the doors and set off. The waymark told me that I was on the Coast-to-Coast path, and a notice nailed to it advised on various routes to take to spread the erosive effects of the thousands of boots whose wearers had chosen to spend two weeks of their lives tramping across the breadth of the land. I pulled up my hood and followed their trail.

It was three miles to Nine Standards Rigg, and I made it in under an hour, which put me just a few minutes early, as intended. I don't know how it gets its name, but I was impressed. Just as you begin to worry if you've missed it, several tall columns of stones appear in front of you, in a line, but of various sizes. It's a good path, and you wonder if your eyes are playing tricks as the wind swirls the rain and the Riggs loom in and out of focus. Some are giants, standing as high as three or four men; some are mere striplings and some have collapsed under their own weight. None of them have any cement bonding the stones. They stand there day and night, through all the seasons, sentinels over nothing, their origins lost in antiquity.

There are more than nine of them, the exact number depending on at what size you start counting. Several upstarts, probably made by energetic school parties, have sprouted between the bigger constructions. One of them was a good representation of a Stone Age throne.

A man with a beard was sitting in it, looking like something from a Tolkein story, only the banana he was eating casting a discordant note. He looked round as he heard me approach and threw me a friendly wave.

"That looks a good seat," I said.

"It is, and most welcome. Are you doing the Coast-to-Coast?"

He was, and for the next ten minutes he told me all about it. He'd just retired after umpteen years as a schoolteacher, and this was a treat he'd promised himself for years. He was enjoying it immensely and he'd resolved to do other walks of a similar nature, but earlier in the year. This was his new beginning and I almost felt envious.

Except, I thought, after seven days on the road he's craving human company. He asked what I did and I admitted to being a cop. This triggered him off about problems he was having with his pension, but I wasn't listening. I decided that this was one of the most remote places I'd ever been. In every direction there wasn't a sign of civilisation, just rolling moorland that merged into a monochrome sky.

I wandered off to the far end of the line and had a pee. When I looked again the man had packed his sack and was hooking it over his shoulders. I gave him a wave as he turned to go. There's a happy man, I thought.

I saw the runner when he was only about 300 yards away, heading towards me, head down into the driving rain. He was tall, as tall as me, and even skinnier. He had a headband tying his long hair back, a waterproof top and his legs were enclosed in black Lycra. His trainers were chunky and looked expensive, even at that distance.

He chugged up the hill, bursts of vapour from his mouth indicating his exertions. I'd walked back to the throne and was sitting on it when he saw me and slowed to a walk. When he was ten yards away he said: "Are you Priest?"

"I might be. Who are you?" He was about 30, I reckoned, and when it came to fitness and fiddles he was in the Stradivarius class. He tilted his head warily, and walked across the front of me in an arc, not coming too near.

"Nobody," he replied. "Doesn't matter." He had a tiny, streamlined rucksack on his back and runnels of water were dribbling down his clothes.

"Sit down," I invited, indicating a pile of stones, "and tell me what you know."

"No, I'll stand. And don't try to grab me."

"I've no intention of trying to grab you," I told him. "I give you my word on that. What is it you wanted to tell me?"

"Have you caught Krabbe's murderer?"

"No. I was hoping you'd tell me who it was."

"I don't know. But I can tell you about, um, about Jeremy."

"Jeremy Quigley?"

"Yes."

"Go on, then."

"He was on Everest with Krabbe when he... when he was... when he was k-killed." The word *killed* stuck in his gullet until he spat it out.

"So I understand. What can you tell me about it?"

"There was a notebook and a camera. Jeremy kept a diary. It was found on his body by some Austrian climbers who gave it and the camera to... to... somebody else."

Steam was rising from him but he seemed oblivious of the weather. I said: "Look, you're going to catch your death in this. Why don't we meet at the pub in Keld in say, an hour? Or at my car in Ravenseat?"

He shook his head. "No. I'm OK."

"Fair enough. So what did the diary say, and where is it now?"

"Jeremy wrote it at camp IV on the last day, before they pushed for the summit. He said that Krabbe had been first to wake and had made a drink for them, which was unusual, but he was eager to go. It was dark, of course, but they had head torches. Jeremy said that Krabbe had put the wrong crampons on. He'd put them on in the tent, and shredded the floor. He was in a hurry to get out and have a look at the Hillary step. He didn't come back so Jeremy put Krabbe's crampons on and followed him. That was the last entry."

"Where's the diary now?" I asked.

"Krabbe stole it. Destroyed it."

"Why would he do that?"

"Because it proves he took Jeremy's crampons. His own were useless. He stole it and destroyed it."

"What was wrong with his crampons?"

"They were his own make. Krabbe Klaws he called them. They were both wearing them, and climbing Everest was going to be good advertising. They were OK, gripped well, but Krabbe had modified his. He'd cut more teeth into them and drilled some holes, to make them lighter. Mark two, he said they were when he showed us them. But he must have cut too much off them, made them weaker, because the front points broke off. He must have known what was happening. Maybe he saw they were cracked. You couldn't get up there without points on your crampons. It's a knife edge, with an 8,000 foot drop on either side."

When he showed us them, he'd said. Was that a slip of the tongue? Was my mystery witness there with them, on Everest?

"Is that it?" I asked.

"There are some photographs," he replied. "The Austrians took them. That's what they do, when somebody dies. For the insurance people. They prove what I'm telling you."

Great, I thought, except that I wasn't sure what he was telling me. That Krabbe wasn't the hero we all thought, but was driven by ambition to the extent that he'd jeopardise – sacrifice – a colleague's life? "Why haven't you told all this before?" I asked.

"Because, um, because nobody would listen. I tried to, but they wouldn't publish it."

"So why are you telling me now?"

"Because…"

"Because what?"

"I don't know. It's the truth. Perhaps I want to help the murderer, understand him. Because I want the world to know what sort of a person Krabbe was."

"Who has the photos?" I asked.

"The Austrians gave the film to Krabbe, because he was the expedition leader. Krabbe gave it to Jeremy's girlfriend, Gabi N-Naylor, so she could do all the legal stuff."

"Before it was developed?"

"Yes."

"So he didn't realise it might incriminate him?"

"No."

"I see. Anything else?"

He stood there, swaying slightly, looking at me. The wind had pushed his hair to one side so it clung to his cheek and covered an eye. He'd been standing slightly sideways-on to me, ready to bolt like a rabbit should I try to grab him, but now he turned to face me and came a step nearer. "Do you know about the d-death zone?" he asked.

I shrugged my shoulders. "A little."

"You're OK up to about 17,000 feet," he told me. "No problem. But after that some people get mountain sickness. So you acclimatise. You go up, then come back down again. You do that for three of four days and then move your camp higher. Base camp is at 17,700 feet. But above 26,000 feet acclimatisation doesn't work. The air is too thin. Above that height your brain cells start to die and your lungs fill with fluid from pulmonary oedema. Down here, at sea level, life expectancy is about 75 years. Above 26,000 feet, in the death zone, life expectancy is two days. Two days maximum. Everybody is dying. Nobody can help you. Helicopters can't go that high. At midnight you start out for the summit, and if you don't make it by two in the afternoon you turn around and come back. If you don't you'll be stranded. You rest every two paces. *Two* paces. There's no way you'll make it through another night, up there. The blood vessels in your lungs and your brain are leaking and you're hallucinating, and you don't know which way is up and which is down. That's when you need somebody like you've never needed anybody in your life. They leave the bodies. You can't do anything about them. There are about 200 frozen in the ice, including Jeremy's."

Rain was running down his face and there were tears mixed in with it.

"Funny, isn't it," he continued. "It's the highest point on Earth, and it's right at the limit we can exist at. Who dare say that we weren't designed to live on this planet?"

Yeah, I thought. Hilarious.

Wallenberg's briefs didn't complain to the chief constable. No doubt he ordered them to forget the whole thing. His wife was mixed up with some shady characters when she was young and struggling to make her mark on the modelling scene, he'll have told them, and the conviction was all a big mistake. She was in the wrong place at the wrong time. Mr Wood wanted a full review of progress so I spent most of Monday morning in his office.

Dave had left a note on my desk about the crash that cost Sonia Thornton a place at the Olympics. I read it, rang High Adventure to confirm that she was working, and drove over to see her. Robert had been hard at work at a VDU. Before I left I asked him if he wanted to come, but he said he was busy and he wasn't keen on ice maidens.

She was standing at the foot of the climbing wall, holding a rope. Belaying, I believe, is the proper term. A little girl, aged about ten, was just starting to climb. She moved like a monkey, stretching and reaching for grips, shifting her weight, moving higher all the time. Sonia pulled spare rope through the belay and it coiled at her feet. Unfortunately the little girl was wearing low-cut pants, which were highly fashionable but impractical for climbing, so we were treated to a view of her bottom as she moved up the wall. After every move she reached back and tried to hitch the pants higher.

I was grinning as I said hello to Sonia. She turned and returned the smile, almost as if she were pleased to see me.

"She's a natural," I said, nodding towards the little girl.

"A natural what, though," she laughed, then, seeing the photo album under my arm, added: "Oh, you've brought my pictures back."

I said: "I'm not saying anything until that young lady is firmly on the ground again. If it were me up there I'd expect you to give it 100 percent attention."

"Well done," Sonia called up to her as she reached the top. "Lean back and let go." She paid out the rope and the girl came down in a series of jerks, her feet dancing against the wall.

"Want to try the blue route?" Sonia asked.

"No thanks, my dad's waiting," the girl replied.

"That was brilliant," I told her, but she just adjusted her jeans and dashed off to hand in her harness.

I tapped the book and looked at Sonia. "I'd like to hang on to this and the other a little longer, if you don't mind, but there's a couple of questions I need to ask you."

"OK," she replied. "Let's go in the office."

The office was just a partitioned off area behind the wall, but there were four desks each with a VDU. I placed the album on a desk and opened it a couple of pages from the end. "Who is that?" I asked.

"Hum, that's Chris," she replied. "Chris Quigley."

"Jeremy's brother?"

"That's the man."

"Tell me about him, please."

"Oh, let me see. I'd never met him until after the Everest expedition. Like with Gabi, I met him at the memorial service. It was at Selby Abbey. I think they'd both been choirboys there. Afterwards he came to visit a couple of times. He took his brother's death badly. His big brother's death. Apparently he hero-worshipped him, couldn't believe he was dead. He just wanted to talk."

"Was he on the expedition?"

"Yes, but I don't think he was in a summit team. He paid his way, just for the experience. According to Tony he cracked up, became a liability."

I said: "Those crampons we saw in your attic. Were they the ones Tony wore to the summit?"

"Yes. That's why he wanted them saving. They'd been on top of Everest."

"Can you remember what colour the straps are?"

"The straps? Hm, they're blue, aren't they? Why?"

I opened the album at the last page and placed my hand over the bottom of the picture. "Which one is Tony?" I asked.

Sonia placed a finger on one of the grinning faces, saying: "He is. That's Tony."

"And the other one is Jeremy?"

"Yes."

"Are you certain?"

"Of course I'm certain. What's this all about?"

I moved my hand away. "I'm not sure," I lied. "Look at the shadows. They're long, so the sun must have been low. I'd guess that this was taken at Camp IV the evening before they pushed to the summit. They'd grab a few hours rest and set off, I'm told, around midnight."

"Yes," she agreed. "That's how I understand it."

"If you look carefully," I said, "you'll see that in this photo Jeremy is wearing the crampons with blue straps. Tony's straps

144

are black." The climbers' feet were thrust towards the camera, the wide-angle lens making them look disproportionately large.

"Oh!" she exclaimed. "So they are. No wonder you're a detective. What do you make of that?"

"Nothing," I declared, untruthfully, and shut the book. "Nothing at all. It just seemed curious. In this job you look for little things like that. That's all."

"Right," she said. "So do you want a go up the wall while you're here. On the house?"

"M-me?" I spluttered, suddenly developing a pain in my stomach and a twitchy eye.

"Mmm, why not," she replied. "What size shoes do you take?"

"Umm, there's something else I want to ask you," I remembered. Panic is a wonderful memory-jogger.

"What's that?"

I suddenly felt better. I was on safe ground again. "I've had a word with our traffic people about your accident," I said. "Apparently when they arrived on the scene the car was halfway up a tree just round a bend and you and Tony were attempting to walk down the road. He was assisting you. They asked which of you was driving and you said you were, so they breathalysed you. It's standard procedure after an RTA. Needless to say, you didn't register."

"I hardly drink," she replied, "and it was only three days before I was due to fly to Atlanta, so I'd been on the mineral water."

"Fair enough," I said. "Tony, they reckoned, was well under the influence but he wasn't breathalysed. After they sent you off in the ambulance they went to have a look at the car. You had a badly cut leg, but the only blood was at the passenger side, and there was a dent in the glove box just about where your knee would have been."

Her face had turned pink and she studied her hand. Her forefinger was polishing a little patch of desktop but she didn't say anything. It moved side to side, then back and forth, over the same little square of desk.

"They were called away," I continued, "to an accident on the bypass. It made no difference to them who was driving so they didn't pursue it. You said you'd been forced off the road but the other car didn't stop and there were no witnesses. You were both well known and you'd sorted it out between yourselves. Case closed. And it doesn't make any difference to me, Sonia. I'm conducting a murder enquiry, so all I'm interested in is the truth. Who was driving the car?"

"You're right, he was," she whispered.

"Why did you lie for him?"

"He persuaded me to. It was obvious my Olympics were over, and I was sober, so I'd nothing to lose. I thought he'd been drinking low-alcohol beer all night. He said he was and they'd just offered him some sponsorship, so I believed him. When he saw the police car he panicked, told me he'd be well over the limit. He'd spent years building up the expedition to Everest. It was his dream, he said. If he were prosecuted for drunk driving it would have ruined him. He'd never find another sponsor and his career would collapse. He begged and pleaded for me to say I was driving. The policeman looked at us and asked the question. We stood there for a few seconds and I could feel Tony's eyes boring into the side of my face. 'Me' I said, and that was that."

"I suppose you were being loyal," I said. "Thanks for telling me the truth."

"Is it relevant, Inspector? Does it make me even more of a suspect?"

"Did you kill Tony Krabbe?" I asked.

"No, of course not."

"There you are, then. That's the question most murderers dread us asking. Others are just waiting for us to ask it. They want to confess, get it off their chests."

Sonia looked down at herself, then back at me. "I've nothing on my chest," she said, and suddenly it was my turn to blush.

I opened my mouth to speak, shut it again and flapped a hand at her, "Um, no comment," I said.

"You never told me what size shoe you took."

So there I was, five minutes later, tied into a harness that Madam Cyn would have had raptures over, with climbing shoes on feet, hardhat on head, looking up at 60-odd vertical feet of papier-mâché cliff and feeling like one of the Village People.

I took my watch off and handed it to Sonia. "There's just one thing," I said to her. "If anything happens to me, my name is Charlie."

"Right, Charlie," she replied. "Off you go."

There was this saint, never knew his name, who walked across Europe with his head under his arm. Paris to Moscow, something like that. When he was asked how he did it he said that the first step was the hardest.

I was six inches off the ground looking for the next foothold. Sonia told me to go for the green one on the left but I could hardly make it. The little girl I'd watched was about half my height but she'd had no trouble reaching the holds. I stretched some more and wedged my toes against the pitifully small block of brown plastic. Well, at least I wasn't showing my bum. I reached up with my left hand, then my right, and brought my feet up one at a time. Repeat at will. A quick glance down and I was shocked to see how far I was above Sonia, which was strange because the top didn't look any closer.

"You're doing fine," she called, encouragingly.

Most of the holds were big and comforting, cut away at the back to make them easy to grip. They were in different colours but these didn't seem relative to the shape of the hold. I reached out for a green one, tested it for security and heaved myself higher. There was a blue one nicely placed just above my left foot, except that my left foot was bearing all my weight. I wondered if a quick hop from one foot to the other was a manoeuvre in the climbers' repertoire but Sonia read my mind.

"Go for the green to the right," she advised.

It was miles away. I reached towards it, couldn't make it and retreated.

"Stretch!" she called up to me.

I stretched, reached the hold and moved over to the right. After that I deserved a rest, I decided. Sonia was a different person to the ice maiden I'd first met. I supposed she had every right to be wary when I came knocking on her door: I was investigating a murder; she was the deceased's ex-partner. Admitting to being the driver had been stupid, but understandable, and she'd been in a state of shock at the time. She'd paid for it, though. If she'd won the gold at the Olympics she would have earned herself contracts worth hundreds of thousands. Millions if she'd kept on winning. She couldn't blame Krabbe for that, though. The accident hadn't been his fault. A couple of yobs take a corner on the wrong side and cause an accident. They drive on, laughing, unaware of the heartache they've caused. It's a regular story; we hear it all the time. Krabbe was unlucky, that's all.

I looked down and nearly wet myself. Sonia looked about as big as an ant. The rope I was on stretched upwards to a karabiner through a ring bolt in the wall and then down to the belay plate on the front of her harness. I was surprised how secure it felt, how much confidence it gave you. I reached for a yellow and pulled myself higher.

There was a slight overhang near the top. My right leg was carrying all my weight and it started to twitch. I transferred onto my left and wagged the right in the air, flexing my knee to keep the circulation going. After a second or two it stopped twitching and I placed it back on the block.

A lot of people would kill for a million, I thought. Or would kill for revenge if a million had been lost. I was nearly there. Foot, foot, then hand, hand, and I was within touching distance of the top. No, it wasn't Krabbe who lost her the money. It was the little scrotes in the other car. They were the ones who she should have held responsible. Except...

Except I was wrong: it was Krabbe who lost her the money, and that was good enough reason for wanting him dead. I knew it, and she probably realised I knew it. I was 60 feet above the ground.

And she was holding the rope.

11

"Well done," she called up to me. "Plant the flag and come down."

I twisted round and grinned down at her. "I forgot the flag."

"Lean back and kick off."

I did as I was told and enjoyed a relaxing ride as she lowered me to safety. I was at the bottom quicker than expected and suddenly found myself stumbling to stay upright. Sonia grabbed my arm and steadied me.

"Phew! That was fun," I declared, buzzing with enough adrenalin to power a small village.

"Slightly unorthodox style," she told me, "but effective. I'd keep the day job if I were you."

I unclipped myself from the rope and stepped out of the harness. "I might bring the troops over for a climb, sometime," I said. "Male bonding, all that stuff. Do you have concessionary rates for parties?"

"Oh, I think we could work something out, Inspector."

The High Adventure complex houses restaurants, cinemas and retail outlets as well as the climbing wall and ski slope. It was Monday morning, but there was an intermittent procession of people of all ages carrying skis and snowboards, heading for the real-snow slope. It was amazing how many citizens of Oldfield were apparently competent skiers.

Straight across the foyer from the wall was a Starbucks coffee lounge. I said: "Let's have a coffee, I need to talk to you." When we were seated behind two regular lattes I said: "The kids in the other car ruined your career. You must me angry with them."

"Yes, Inspector," she replied. She picked up her coffee, decided it was too hot and put it down again. A couple with two children walked by carrying snowboards in nylon bags. The boards looked much bigger than I thought they'd be.

Sonia watched them go by, avoiding looking at me. In her day she was one of the finest athletes in the world, but she was a lousy liar.

"Charlie," I said.

"Char-lee. O-Kay."

"But it wasn't just the Olympics, was it? The honour and the glory and all that. It must have hit you financially."

"You can say that again."

"Can you put a sum on it?"

"Not exactly, but the numbers were big. I'd done the fastest time of the year, so I was in with a chance. If I reached the final I had contracts that would have brought me a quarter of a million. Guaranteed. If I won, I was looking at a million over the next couple of years."

"Except," I began, "it wasn't really those kids who lost you the money, was it? Apparently you didn't get a good look at them."

She heaved a sigh and placed both hands on the table. She twisted in her seat, looking across the large open area towards the climbing wall. There was a Frankie and Benny's off to our left and a Burger King the other side. Her cheeks were tinged with pink when she looked at me again.

"Was there another car?" I asked.

She shook her head. "No. Tony just came out with it when we were talking to the police. He'd been driving like a maniac. He always drove like a maniac. They all do. I just nodded and went along with it."

"All do?"

"Climbers. They're adrenalin junkies. If there's no risk it's not worth doing."

"And Tony was one of the worst."

"Yes."

"So it was just Krabbe and yourself. When he begged you to say you were driving he talked you out of a fortune. And you went along with him."

She nodded her head, studying the plastic coffee container she was holding. I went on: "If you'd told the truth, that

Krabbe was driving, you'd have been eligible for a third party insurance claim. You could have sued him, in effect. It's routine, happens all the time. Put your contracts on the table and you might have received your money without having to break into a sweat for it."

"Yep," she said. "You sussed it right, Charlie. Five seconds' stupidity, protecting the man I thought I loved, and that was the cost. He went to his precious Everest with his reputation intact, came home the conquering hero, and I ended up working here for peanuts. He wanted me to make a claim against the non-existent youths in the non-existent other car. Apparently the insurance companies have some sort of contingency fund for uninsured cases, but I couldn't do anything like that. We had some colossal rows about it."

I took a sip of the hot milky liquid and placed the beaker back on the counter. She looked at me, made a "huh" noise and gave me a wry smile. Her hair was short and fair and she had tiny diamond studs in her ears. I said: "You made a balls of it, Sonia."

"Yes," she agreed with a nod. "I think that's an accurate assessment. I made a balls of it."

I'd had a good day. The search for Krabbe's killer had progressed not one jot, but Sonia Thornton had turned out to be something other than the cold, aloof figure I'd first encountered. She'd been warm and charming, and we'd even shared a joke. Sitting in a queue of traffic on the M62 I remembered the first time I saw her on television. It was the AAA championships and several guest runners from overseas were competing in the 5,000 metres. In the preliminaries the young Yorkshire lass, Sonia Thornton, was hardly mentioned, but by the end of the race we had a new golden girl. She took the lead with a lap and a half to go and elegantly eased away from her rivals. She had a high, prancing style of running, her head held high, and the tabloids quickly dubbed her The Gazelle.

After supper I decided to ring Rosie and tell her about my adventures on the climbing wall.

"It's me," I said, when she answered the phone. "How's things?"

"Oh, um, I'm alright, thank you."

"Are you sure? You sound doubtful."

"Of course I'm sure."

"Good. What sort of a day have you had?"

"Charlie…"

"Mmm."

"I'm not in the mood for small-talk. Can we just… call the whole thing off, please?"

"Oh. What do you mean by the whole thing?"

"Me and you. Us. Except there is no us."

"OK, if that's what you want. I'm sorry if I've been a nuisance. It's just that I'm fond of you and care about you. I worry about you."

"I know you mean well but I don't want you to be fond of me or worry about me. I just want some time to myself. Don't you see?"

"You're going through a bad patch, Rosie," I said. "It'll pass, but you mustn't give in to it. How did the class go today?"

"What if it's not a bad patch, Charlie. What if this is the real bit?"

"Happiness is a natural state," I argued. "Think about good things; all that travelling you have to do."

"I don't want to do any travelling. I want to be left alone. Don't you ever wonder what the purpose of it all is, why we bother?"

"No, not really," I said, although it was a feeling I knew all too well.

"Well I do. Goodbye, Charlie."

"Right, well, there's nothing more to say, is there?"

"No, there's nothing more to say."

"If that's what you want…"

"It is."

"Goodbye, then."

I'm not sure which of us put the receiver down first, but it didn't matter. What was certain was that I'd been dumped. I'd been dumped before, but never quite like that. I wondered which part of the cycle of moods that ruled her life she was on, or if she was under the influence of medication, but dumped is dumped, whatever the provocation. I could take it, but I was still concerned about her.

"You must be mad," Dave declared when I told him of my exploits. "How did you know it wasn't a set-up?"

"He rang from a Dales pub," I said. "Live music on a Friday night. You could hear the crunch of sawdust underfoot and the slurp of hand-pulled Black Sheep being poured. It was obviously one of the outdoor fraternity who rang me, not one of Wallenberg's cronies."

"You still should have told me."

"I thought about it, decided not to bother you."

"So he's a suspect, this brother?"

"He's got the motive. Could've worked an opportunity. But I can't see it."

"And what about Miss Thornton?"

"The climbing wall's terrific," I said. "We'll all have to go, sometime. It's great fun."

"And the instructress?"

"Well, since you've asked, she was a little more responsive than on my first visit."

"Is she a suspect?"

"Motive by the bucketful; and like Quigley, she could have arranged an opportunity. But nah, she didn't do it. Neither of them did."

"This is the famous Charlie Priest intuition at work, is it?"

"They both had feelings towards him bordering on hatred, that's for sure."

There's a well-known adage that the first two days are the most important in a murder enquiry. After that, if you haven't caught your man – or woman – it could be a long haul. We'd had seventeen days and questions were being asked.

But I don't wake up every day and wonder if we'll catch

the culprit today. I believe in gathering evidence, talking to people, studying relationships and, sometimes, stirring things up. Then, when we've gathered all we can, I stick it in the computer called my brain and start asking it questions. Sometimes, hopefully, one name keeps popping up more than any other. Statistics are important but not gospel. One says that in 80 percent of murders the killer is known to us in seven days. It's just a matter of eliminating all the others.

The path round the house where Krabbe had lived was made of gravel. We'd returned to it several times, in all weathers, and it was impossible to sneak up behind someone on it. Of that we were sure. We'd checked, and there was nothing wrong with his hearing, so Krabbe, it would appear, knew his assailant. He died from a single blow, but a fine spray of blood and brain was ejected from the wound and deposited on the ground around him. And, we hoped, on his killer's clothes.

The phone rang and Dave picked it up. He listened for a moment, pulled a face at me that suggested it could be interesting and started making notes. "Is he talking?" I heard him say. "Any form?" He wrote the answer down. "Keep hold of him. We'll be straight over." I didn't say anything, just spun my chair round and waited for him to fill me in.

"They've arrested someone in Halifax for attempted car theft. He tried to hijack a Jaguar XK8, but came unstuck. The computer has thrown up a match: a similar Jag was stolen from a house in Bradford last week."

Since the crash involving the Golf, which we believed had been racing another Golf, and the apparent race between the two MGs, we'd had the DVLA computer looking for thefts of matching sports cars anywhere in West Yorkshire and Greater Manchester, and it looked as if it had come up with the goods.

"What are we waiting for?" I said, reaching for my jacket.

The Jag belonged to a female estate agent whose name graced boards dotted randomly all over the district. It was a symbol of her success, a talisman for an ever-burgeoning property market. Mess with it at your peril.

"She does three hours at the Halifax office every morning," the arresting officer told us, "then leaves at eleven-thirty, regular as clockwork, to go to the Elland office."

"A creature of habit," I said.

"That's right. But ever since the Sally Wilcox case she's carried a pepper spray with her. Laddo got into the car alongside her as she started the engine and told her to drive. She pulled the spray from her bag and gave him a dose. He rolled out on to the ground. She jumped out, ran round the car and emptied the lot in his face. Nearly blinded the poor sod."

"Is he alright now?"

"Just about. We've given him a pair of shades."

"And he says he's called Douglas Jones?"

"Yep. Aged 28, hails from Leeds and his form is longer than a self-assessment tax return. Nearly all car related. He was twocking at thirteen and has appeared in the dock more times than the QE2. He was done for GBH on a punter whilst working as a nightclub bouncer, did fifteen months, but has been clean for the last two years." He handed me the sheaf of photocopies listing all the previous convictions, and took us to meet him.

They clone them, I'm sure they do. Nightclub bouncers. Somewhere there's a factory turning them out. I'm not certain if they are born to a woman in the normal way, or if they fertilize the cell in a test tube and all the development takes place in a tank of proteins, but there's definitely a set procedure. Then it's years of workouts in a stuffy gym, with ample doses of steroids between meals rich in red meat. The Victorians put miscreants in the treadmill; nowadays their descendants pay a health club £30 a month for the privilege. The lack of oxygen in the gymnasium gives them brain damage, and the steroids cause them to develop buttresses on their shoulders, to hold their shaven heads in position.

Douglas Jones was the Mark I, standard issue model, but without the optional skull decorations. I wasn't sure that the shades were a good idea: they gave him a certain cachet. The tapes were running and I was in the chair.

"How are your eyes?" I asked.

"Sore. 'Ow do you fink they are?"

Correction. He was the Mark II model, with the inbuilt speech impediment.

"Has the doctor seen you?"

"You know 'e has."

"And he gave you those drops."

"Yeah." Jones was holding a tiny plastic bottle of Optrex.

"You're entitled to have a solicitor present."

"Don't want no s'licitor."

"OK. And you've been given a copy of your rights under the Police and Criminal Evidence Act."

"Yeah, yeah. I know."

"So why were you trying to steal the Jaguar?"

"Why do you fink?"

"I'm asking you."

"It's a nice motor, innit."

"What were you going to do with it?"

"Dunno. Just 'ave a drive, that's all."

Dave was sitting alongside me, casually perusing Jones's record. "Who did you steal it for?" I asked.

"Myself."

"I don't think you did."

No answer.

"Where were you going to take it?"

"For a ride. That's all."

"A car like that's worth, what, about five or six thousand on the black market, wouldn't you say?"

"Don't know, Guv. You know more about it than me."

"What did you do with the other one? The one you stole in Leeds?"

"Don't know what you're talking about."

Had there been the slightest hesitation before he answered? I wasn't sure. "Tell me about the racing," I said.

"What racing?"

"You know what racing."

Out of the corner of my eye I saw Dave sit up. I didn't hear

Jones's reply because Dave had taken the top off his pen and was underlining something on the list of papers he was holding. He passed it to me.

The paper was the top sheet of Jones's record of offences. I've read thousands of them. Sometimes they make you angry, sometimes they're sad, and often they're funny. Dave had underlined the words *Painted Pony*, which I knew to be the nightclub Wallenberg had supposedly bought from Joe Crozier's partners. I read the rest of the summary and saw that Jones was working there when he assaulted the customer.

"A word," Dave said to me when I'd finished reading, and rose to his feet. We left a big PC babysitting Jones while we went for a walk towards the front desk. There was the drinks machine blinking in the corner and Dave fed coins into it and handed me a can of Fanta. It gave a satisfying *psssst* when I lifted the pull, and aggravated my fillings when I took a swig.

"So he may have worked for Crozier," I said, not really knowing what to make of it. It was unlikely to be a coincidence but the nightclub world is a small one.

"You haven't twigged, have you?" Dave commented.

"No."

"C'mon, think about it. It's an unforgettable face. Looks like it's been set on fire and put out with a shovel"

"I've seen a thousand like him."

"If I said Dale Dobson's funeral?"

"God, you're right!" I exclaimed. "He read the eulogy, that poem. *I am not dead, just sleeping*, or something. Jesus, where does that leave us?"

We sat on the bench normally reserved for anxious parents and cantankerous girlfriends and sipped our drinks. I took out my diary and found a clean page. "Let's get the timing sorted," I suggested. "It's not very clear to me what came first." I found the calendar at the front, next to the other essential information like lighting up times and phases of the moon, and held the place with a finger.

"Crozier went into the river in the early hours of the 21st of October," Dave told me, and I wrote it down. "So when was the Dale Dobson crash?"

I turned a few pages. "Here we are," I said. "Thursday morning, the 23rd. That's two days later."

"And Dobson's funeral was on bonfire night, the fifth of November, nearly two weeks later."

"So that's what the fireworks were for."

"How do you want to play it?" Dave asked.

"Let's go look at the photos," I suggested. "See what they tell us, and then have another go at him."

We collected sandwiches from Greggs and ate them in the incident room. Jones featured in several of the photographs, we were pleased to find, and Wallenberg was often in the same frame. When we looked at the pictures of Wallenberg, Jones was usually hovering in the background.

"He's Wallenberg's minder," Dave declared.

"Chauffeur handyman," I said.

"Doer of dirty work."

"Mmm. I wonder if that extends to murder?"

"I think you'd better tell Nigel."

"I think you're right."

"So he used to work for Crozier and now he appears to work for Wallenberg," Nigel summarised, after we'd filled him in. We were sitting in the canteen of Halifax nick, awaiting the duty solicitor to arrive. When the message came through that he was waiting for us we trooped off to the interview room again.

This time Dave didn't sit in. Nigel and myself were seated at one side of the table, Jones and the solicitor at the other. The uniformed PC detailed to prevent us administering lighted matches under the prisoner's fingernails started the tape and I did the introductions. Jones was reminded that he was still under caution.

"Joe Crozier spoke very highly of you, Duggie," Nigel said.

"Did he?"

Good one, I thought. He's admitted knowing Crozier, straight off.

"Very highly. It must have been a shock when you heard that he'd died."

"Yeah, it was."

"When did you hear?"

"'Bout free weeks ago. Heard it on Radio Leeds, didn't I."

"And when did you last see him?"

"God, I don't know. About a munf earlier."

"What do you think happened to him?"

"Fell in the river, didn't he."

"How often did you speak to him?"

"Not very often. Just said goodnight, that sort of fing."

"So what was your job?"

"Doorman. I was on the door at the *Painted Pony*."

"And that's all?"

"Yeah."

"That's not what I've heard. According to Mr Crozier's business partners you were his right-hand man."

"Nah, not me. I just drove 'im, sometimes. That's all."

"Ah! So you were a little more than just a doorman?"

"No, not really. If he'd had a drop too much he might ring me and ask me to pick 'im up. That's all. I wasn't no right-hand man or noffing."

"You were his driver?"

"Yeah. I suppose so. Sometimes."

"You like driving?"

"Yeah. Love it."

"What sort of car did he have?"

"A Lexus. Lovely motor."

"Did you drive Mr Crozier over to Heckley on Monday the twentieth of October?"

He thought about it, or pretended to, although pretending to think could have been beyond his intellectual capabilities. Duggie's problem was that he was thick. Nigel was teasing some good stuff from him, and we still had Dobson and Wallenberg to hit him with. I decided that we'd keep the

Wallenberg connection under wraps for a while longer. Duggie was digging a hole for himself and we were at the top, looking down, so as long as those shovelfuls of soil kept landing on our feet we'd let him keep going.

"No, I don't fink so," he eventually decided.

"You didn't take him to a restaurant called *L'Autre Place*, in the town square?"

"No, not me."

"Let me try to jog your memory: this was the night Mr Crozier died. Does that help?"

He shuffled in his seat, looking uncomfortable, and glanced at the duty solicitor, but he found no help there. "No, I don't know noffing about that," he replied. "I never took 'im to Heckley. Not ever."

The duty solicitor came to the rescue. "It's been a long day," he said. "Any chance of a cup of tea?"

We used the break to good advantage, too. Nigel said he was prepared to release news about the tape around Crozier's hands and feet, I confirmed that I wanted the Wallenberg connection keeping quiet. Jones and his brief had a picnic in the interview room, we scoffed a quick sausage roll and a milky coffee in the canteen. It was nearly five o'clock when we resumed the interview.

"You read a poem at Dale Dobson's funeral," I began.

He blinked like an owl in a spotlight, not sure which direction I was coming from.

"Yeah," he replied.

"It was very moving. Did you write it yourself?" And did the Spice Girls compose the Brandenburg Concertos?

"No, not me," he confirmed, as if any of us were in doubt, but he swelled, ever so slightly, with pride.

"How long had you known Dale?"

"Years."

"How many?"

"Dunno."

"Where did you meet him?"

161

"At Forpe Arch, when we was doing time."

"The young offenders institute?"

"That's right."

"You were both twockers."

"Yeah."

"In Leeds."

"Yeah."

"So you had something in common."

"Yeah…" he hesitated, as if to say something else, then clammed up.

"Go on," I encouraged.

"Dale was clever," he said. "We was banged up together. He knew all sorts of stuff, like animals' names and astronomy. An' he was good for a laugh. He used to make up poems, just little ones, about the screws. An' we was bofe mad about cars. He was worse than me. That's all he lived for."

"Did you stay in touch?"

"Yeah, for a bit. Then I got time and lost 'is address. He moved. I fink he worked in Manchester for a few years, then 'e landed a job in Heckley."

"How do you know this?"

"We met. Accidentally, like. He was working for this guy and Mr Crozier asked me to take 'im to a meeting one night. I was told to wait in the KFC and call for 'im in an hour. Dale was already in there. He'd brought the other guy. He said they were planning somefing."

"Any ideas what?"

"No. He didn't say."

"What did you think?" Nigel asked. "Something like a bank robbery, a bullion hold-up?"

"No, I don't fink so. Mr Crozier didn't do business like that. I fink it must have been to do wiv buying an' selling, or houses. He did a lot about houses. Not proper criminal stuff."

I said: "Who did Dale land the job with in Heckley?"

He wriggled about on the plastic chair and wiped his neck with a hand. The temperature was about 80° and the room

162

was windowless. I caught the PC's eye and asked him to open the door for a minute or two.

"The job in Heckley," I reminded Duggie. "Who was it with?"

"Don't know. He never said."

"And you never asked?"

"No."

"So now we'll never know."

"Don't s'pose we will." He looked relieved, but it may have been the cool draught that made him feel more comfortable.

"Tell me about the racing," I said.

And now he didn't look so comfortable. "Racing?" he echoed.

"Mmm. Racing. In the cars. The MGs and then the Golfs. It was in all the papers that he'd been killed in an illegal car race."

"I don't know noffing about no car racing."

"I don't believe you."

The brief sat up at that comment, jolted from his nap, but he wasn't sure what he'd missed so he decided not to say anything.

I looked across at Nigel, who said: "So you admit that you were working for Crozier at the time of his death."

"Yeah, I s'pose so, but I don't know noffing about it."

"Your boss went to Heckley, drank enough wine to render a horse comatose, and didn't call on his trusted driver to collect him."

"No."

"So how did he get there and back?"

"I dunno. It's a myst'ry to me."

"Where were you at the time?"

"Dunno. Out wiv some mates, I fink."

"Was Dale Dobson one of them?"

"Umm, yeah, I fink he might have been."

Nigel leaned forward. "So you weren't with Mr Crozier when he rolled into the river?" he asked.

"No. Nowhere near. I swear it."

"And you weren't there when his hands and feet were wrapped in masking tape, before he was pushed in the river?"

His face turned the colour of catshit and a vein high on his temple started to pulse like a worm burrowing under his skin. I said: "Good stuff, masking tape. Guaranteed not to come off in water. But it's great for holding fingerprints. When it sticks to your fingers you always leave a print behind. The SOCOs sometimes use it for lifting them." I wagged my hand as if trying to dislodge something sticky.

Jones said: "I don't know noffing about it," but his demeanour indicated otherwise. He was a bully. There was no way of knowing how many people he'd terrorised in his 28 years, or how many he'd crippled or killed, how many women he'd raped. Sometimes, when I have someone squirming, I have to remind myself of these things.

"But you know about the car racing," I said. "Were you part of it?"

"No."

"Did you have a bet?"

"Yeah."

"How much?"

"I had a couple of 'undred on Dale."

"At what odds?"

"Nine to eleven."

"Who was he racing?"

"A kid from Manchester. Works for someone over there. Don't know 'is name."

"Was Dale good?"

"Yeah. Brilliant."

I thought of all those flowers at the roadside, and the messages from the Wallenbergs. "Who was Dale working for?" I asked.

"I dunno."

And then of the photographs at the church, with Duggie hovering around the Wallenbergs. "And who are you working for?"

"Nobody."

He got ten out of ten for loyalty, that was for sure, but we'd soon crack it.

Nigel said: "Let's go back to the moment when Mr Crozier, your boss, rolled off the dockside into the water. We think you were there, Duggie. You're looking at a murder rap but we know you weren't alone, and why would you want Crozier dead? That's what we don't understand."

"No, I wasn't there," he protested.

"Who was driving the Range Rover, Duggie? Was that you?"

But before he could reply the solicitor announced that he'd like a consultation with his client. I said: "The interview is being halted at the request of the accused's solicitor," and read the time from the clock on the wall behind them. The PC stopped the tape and I stood up and hooked my jacket over my shoulder.

I went for a walk outside and sat on the wall for a few minutes. The streets were busy with workers scurrying for their buses and trains, or back to their vehicles in the multi-storey. Christmas decorations, thankfully still un-illuminated, had started to sprout from all the street furniture, and the stores were advertising their pre-Christmas sales.

When we reconvened the solicitor presented us with a hand-written statement. The story was that on the night of the twentieth, Dale had phoned Duggie in an agitated state. Duggie went to meet him and was told that Dale and Crozier had quarrelled. Dale had hit Crozier and killed him, and now he wanted Duggie to help him dispose of the body. First thoughts were to bury it on the moors, but then they decided to put it in the river, near where Crozier lived. The tape was Dale's idea. He said it would confuse things.

Nigel read the statement into the tape recorder and asked us all to sign it. "You'll appear before a magistrate in the morning," he told Jones, "on the charge of aggravated theft of a motor vehicle. Bail will be opposed on the grounds of more serious charges pending."

165

I treated Nigel to pizza and we talked about other things for a while, but inevitably came back to the case. Jones was now happy to point the finger at his dead friend, but was still protecting Wallenberg. We knew that Crozier was alive when he went in the water, contradicting Jones's story, because if he'd been dead he wouldn't have drawn river water, with its unique microscopic wildlife, into his windpipe. It was no help though, he'd just say that they must have made a mistake: Crozier hadn't been as dead as they thought.

I made a detour on the way home, past Rosie's house, but it was in darkness and her car wasn't outside. I took it as a good sign.

Jones was charged with attempting to pervert the course of justice and being an accessory to a murder. I interviewed him twice in the next couple of days, but he didn't change his story and now he had a clued-up brief at his side. I didn't talk about Crozier – that was Nigel's case – and Wallenberg wasn't mentioned. Jones had attempted to steal the Jaguar, he claimed, for his own use. He was bored, wanted a joyride, that's all. It was an opportunist theft. He hadn't spent hours watching the car until he knew exactly when the owner would be climbing into it with the keys in her hand. When I'd suggested that he was going to take part in the next car race himself, maybe to avenge his pal's death, the expression on his face contradicted his shake of the head. The brief accused me of fabricating the story.

Two days later the fire brigade were called to a burning car in a lay-by up on the tops. It was the Jag stolen earlier from a house in Bradford. It looked as if the car-racing season was over.

In the north of the county the moors are based on limestone and have a unique assortment of plant life growing on them. The ground is stony and breaks the ploughs of farmers unlucky enough to have inherited it. As you come south the geography changes. The underlying strata become sandstone and millstone grit, good for shedding rainfall and therefore the ideal place to build the reservoirs that feed the surrounding conurbations. Further south still, heading into Derbyshire, we have peat moors which are criss-crossed with deep cloughs and virtually sterile. Only cotton grass struggles to maintain a root-hold in the soft, shifting ground.

The long dry summer had caused the peat to shrink and crack, so when the autumn storms came the rain found new gullies to wash down, filling in old streambeds and scouring out new ones. Sometimes, ancient tree trunks, thousands of years old but preserved in the acidic, oxygen-free ground, are brought to the surface.

And sometimes it's bodies.

The walkers on Bleak Tor found the first one, a police dog found the second a few yards away. I was in the office, Saturday morning, when the call came. Dave had just waved me a goodbye but I caught him before he left the building. We collected his Wellington boots from his car and headed out of town, up onto the tops.

They looked as if they'd been desiccated rather than decomposed, which was marginally more pleasant. They didn't smell and weren't buzzing with flies. We stood at a respectful distance, ignoring the east wind whipping at our clothes, as the stone-faced SOCO picked and scraped the soil from around the nearest body with scalpel and paint brush. If they'd been the embalmed bodies of the Boy King's wives he couldn't have treated them more carefully.

He stood up to stretch his back and I said: "You're doing a great job, Steve."

"Yeah, well, Charlie," he replied. "With luck this will be my last case. Mind you, I thought the last one would be."

I was standing on a stepping plate, trying not to lose my balance. The legs of the plate were sinking into the ground and it wasn't level. It was an easy place to bury something if you were in a hurry. Dave rang me on my mobile, from the roadside about 50 yards away.

"I've asked for a tent," he told me. "It looks like rain and I doubt if we'll finish today. The professor says he'll be about an hour and I've asked for task force assistance. Anything to report?"

I glanced at the sky. Ragged clouds were churning up on the horizon and the temperature had dropped a couple of degrees. "Both appear to be female," I said. "God knows how long they've been here. Couple of years, maybe. I'll be with you in a minute or two. I'm sure a flask of coffee would be appreciated."

Steve, the SOCO, looked up at me and nodded his approval. "Come and look," he said.

The face of the one he'd done most work on was simply a skull with skin stretched across it and remnants of blonde hair clinging to the sides. The eye sockets were filled with peat and there was a gap where one of the canine teeth should have been. Her arms were crossed in front of her and she was wearing a knitted cardigan with embroidery on it. Yellow flowers with green leaves on a red background. Flashes of brightness on a cheerless day. Denim jeans completed the ensemble, and her feet were bare.

"Earrings," Steve said, pointing with his little trowel. "An upper canine missing, thin gold chain around her neck."

My phone rang again. "Entomologist's here," Dave told me.

"I'm coming out," I said. "Send him in."

Who and when are the burning questions. Until we know those answers we can't start an investigation. We have a caravan that we sometimes use as a mobile incident room, and office space was running out, so I decided to use it for this case, standing in the nick car park. Sunday morning I had a look in and checked the installation of all the paraphernalia we needed. After that I drove to the place where the bodies were discovered. Task force were doing a fingertip search of the area but hadn't found much. It was about 50 yards from the road, which fitted in with the normal pattern. Bodies are heavy and awkward to carry. Chances were that the person who buried them would know the area well and live not too far away.

A Home Office pathologist came up from Oxford to do the post mortems, and I sat in on the first one. Monday afternoon I had a meeting with Gilbert and my sergeants.

"Body One has been there about a year," I reported. "Entomological evidence confirms that it's been in the ground for one summer. Body Two is in a greater state of decomposition, has been there for about a year longer. We'll know more about Body Two in a while. Body One is of a young woman, white, aged 18 to 22. Approximately five feet four high and of slim build. In fact, according to the professor, her bones indicated that she was undernourished and had gone through a period of malnutrition. Several of her teeth were missing and she'd had a certain amount of low quality dental work done."

"What do you mean by missing?" Jeff Caton asked.

"Extracted," I replied. "Not knocked out. Her front teeth are OK."

"She didn't look after her teeth."

"No. Her clothing is of particular interest. Her cardigan is hand-knitted, in what we'd call an ethnic design, and her jeans are of an obscure manufacture but have been decorated with embroidery. The label on them is in a so-far unidentified language with some characters in Cyrillic script. Her blouse and underwear are from Marks and Sparks. She had four small gold studs in each ear and a tiny gold crucifix of an unusual design on a chain around her neck."

"Cause of death?" Gilbert enquired.

"Hyoid bone fractured," I said, "indicating that she was strangled. Any suggestions?"

"Illegal immigrant," Jeff stated.

Pete Goodfellow turned on him. "How do you know she was illegal?" he demanded.

"Because she hasn't been reported missing."

I jumped in with: "We don't know if she's been reported missing or not. When we have more on the second body we'll ask missing persons." I went on: "Body One's jewellery has

169

gone for analysis. The gold content can indicate where it comes from, and casts are being made of her dental work, or lack of it. Somebody might recognise their handiwork. Initial thoughts are that she is of East European origin. Oh, and she was pregnant. Probably about three months gone. Any questions?"

"When will we know about the second body?"

"This afternoon. There's just one other thing: Body One's head has been removed and will be taken down to Oxford for a cranio-facial reconstruction, so then we'll know what she looked like. The bad news is that it could take a fortnight."

Gilbert walked into the main building with me. "Do you want some help from HQ?" he asked.

"Not yet," I replied. "We won't be spending much time on these two until we have an idea who they are. Makes you wonder how many more bodies are buried up there."

"Nine-nine will find them, if there are any." Nine-nine was the helicopter, which we had quartering the moor, scanning the ground with its thermal imaging camera. "So what's the latest on Krabbe?" Gilbert asked.

A youth was banging the drinks machine with the flat of his hand. He latched on to us, complaining: "Hey! It's kept my money."

"Now you know how it feels," I said as we walked by. "We'll give it a reprimand. Krabbe?" I repeated. "We're making slow progress. Indications are that he had lots of enemies in the climbing fraternity. He's not the golden boy we all thought he was. He'd suddenly jumped on the conservation bandwagon and was upsetting some of his former climbing friends by campaigning against the way anyone with sufficient money can be taken up Everest. Some of them earn their livings that way. Unfortunately they're all spread far and wide, but we're getting there."

"And what's happening with Wallenberg? Any progress in that quarter?"

"Nigel thinks he had Crozier killed, and I'd agree, but Jones is keeping schtum on that one. We know Wallenberg was involved in the car racing, through his connection with Dale Dobson. Apparently he likes a flutter, so they were probably gambling big sums on them. It looks as if Duggie Jones was going to be his new ace driver."

"Anything to be gained by leaning on Jones?"

"Everything, but he has a good brief. I'd rather wait until I had something to feed him that would make him reconsider his position. If he knew he was looking at a murder rap he might suddenly begin to see things more clearly."

"Well, try to keep it within the guidelines, Charlie," Gilbert advocated.

"Of course, Gilbert. Of course," I assured him.

12

Ludmilla brushed at the creases in the dress she was wearing and looked at herself in the bathroom mirror. Too much lipstick, she thought, and wiped it off with a tissue. Five minutes later it was as she wanted. She combed her hair to one side, half off her face, half on, as she'd worn it at the village dances when she was small, and fixed it with the clasp she'd worn on the journey here. Everybody said it suited her that way. She brushed her teeth and dabbed the cheap perfume on her neck. This was the third time today that she'd made these preparations, but she was determined to look her best when he came. Her sexiest, most alluring best. Last night she hadn't looked good, and she hadn't given value for money, of that she was certain. Phone-calls will have been made, complaints passed along the line. He was sure to come.

She was dozing when she heard the key in the door, and sat up with a start. What was it she was going to say? She'd learned more English in the three weeks she'd been here but still felt awkward using it. And what if it was Duggie who came? She was no match for him. He'd beat her and rape her, probably bring a friend or two, and she'd have planned all this for nothing. She jumped to her feet and stood at the far side of the bed, one hand clutched to her breast and her mouth and eyes wide with fear.

The door was flung back against the wall and Wallenberg was standing there, the long package containing his *little electric friend* in one hand.

"What the fuck do you think you're playing at?" he demanded, striding into the room and locking the door behind him. He threw his coat and jacket on the floor and flicked the plastic bag off the prod.

"I explain," Ludmilla protested. "I explain."

But he wasn't listening. He switched the prod on and jabbed it against her outstretched hand. Ludmilla screamed as the electricity pulsed through her. "Please please!" she whimpered. "I explain. Please let me explain."

"Explain what?" he shouted at her. "There's nothing to explain. You're costing me a fortune; you know that? Duggie says you can't be trusted, so we have to keep you locked up and fed. And now this. Do you know how much he was paying, last night? And for what? An evening with a frigid little cow like you. I'd have thought you'd learned your lesson, but it looks like you didn't. We'll have to teach you some manners, young lady, and then Duggie will want to give you a lesson of his own. He jabbed the prod against her neck and it felt as if her head had been blown off.

"No! No!" she screamed, clutching her throat. "Not your little friend. Ludmilla not know what he wanted. I try, please, I try. Me not used to this. I work hard for you. But he difficult. He an old man. I not know what to do."

"Well you should have used your imagination, shouldn't you?" He pointed the prod at her, waving the end around, avoiding her hands held up defensively as he tried to touch it against her body.

"Ludmilla not have imagination. Why you not show me? I work hard for you. I do my best. But I am young. I need lessons. I learn very quickly. Why you not show me, then I earn lots of money? You pay me, one day, maybe, if I do well? I earn lots of money for you. For us."

"Show you?" he repeated, suddenly interested. The straps of her dress had slipped down her arms and her hair was pinned to one side, making her look more sophisticated than any of his other girls. Sophistication was a quality he didn't normally expect from them.

"Ludmilla a good girl," she said. "You show me what to do. Please." She stood helplessly in front of him, tears running down her cheeks. "Ludmilla only want to please you."

He grabbed her shoulders and slid the dress down. She put her hands on his waist and started to pull his shirt from his pants. Soon her hands were on the small of his back and his were fondling her breasts. She turned her lips to his and their mouths fused together. Wallenberg was filled with amazement. Prostitutes don't normally kiss their clients. It was an unwritten rule, and this was beyond anything he'd experienced before with one. He pushed her back on to the bed and they rolled into the middle. She came out on top, astride him, and began to unbutton his shirt.

She hated every second of it. She hated the smell of him and his bristly chin and the ripple of his ribs down his chest. She hated the greasy hair and the curve of his spine. She hated his fingers probing and exploring her, and the thick wet lips as they chewed at hers. Most of all she hated herself for making him believe, for just a few minutes, that she could ever enjoy this.

Her left hand fell on the fly of his trousers and she could feel his hardness inside them. She fumbled with the top button as her tongue slid alongside his, until she withdrew it, teasing him, prolonging the pleasure, and allowed the tip to follow the curve of his jaw towards his ear. He turned his head to accommodate her, wondering what other delights she held for him, turned away from the electric cattle prod he'd left leaning against the bed, oblivious of her right hand as it slowly walked across the sheets, towards it.

Wednesday morning Dave was holding court when I entered the big office, with the others showing varying degrees of interest. He was just coming to the punch line of one of his stories. "And the gynaecologist handed the woman the box of chocolates and said: 'These are from Brian in the burns unit, to say thank you for his new ears.'"

Some laughed, most shook their heads and turned back to their desks. I said: "Is this all you have to do?"

"Raising morale, Chas," he replied. "Something that's lacking from your style of leadership."

"I'll bear it in mind. Put the kettle on, please. Anybody any biscuits?"

A manila envelope that I'd been waiting for was on my desk. I dialled Heckley Grammar School, jammed the phone between my chin and shoulder like I'd seen busy people do on TV, and tore the envelope open..

"Could you tell me if Miss Barraclough is working?" I asked the school secretary when she answered. I think it was the school secretary, but from her attitude and accent it could have been the Minister for Education on a state visit.

"I'm sorry, but I'm not at liberty to release any information on staff members."

Jesus Christ, I thought. I want to know if she's working, not where she banks and her PIN number. "This is Heckley CID," I said. "My name is Inspector Priest. If she is working would you be good enough to ask her to ring me?"

"Oh, the police," she stumbled. "Um, I suppose it's alright, then. Miss Barraclough rang in on Monday, said she was sick."

The envelope contained a summary of the post mortems on the two bodies. I'd driven past Rosie's a couple of times, but there was no sign of either her or her car, and she hadn't answered the phone when I rang.

There was little in the reports that the Home Office patholo-gist hadn't told us at the time. Both girls were about the same age and had died approximately one year apart. The earlier corpse was wearing all British clothing but her trainers were of continental origin. The later one was wearing a mixture of makes but no shoes. Both had undergone some dental reme-dial work with amalgam fillings and several extractions. The earlier corpse had a freshly healed broken left ulna and an old fracture of the right fibula that had healed badly. Causes of death were uncertain, but the broken hyoid bones indicted strangulation.

It's what a report doesn't say that is most eloquent. I rang the professor at the General who had assisted at the post mortems and caught him between jobs. "Would I be right in thinking East European, or ex-Soviet Bloc," I asked.

"I'd say so, Charlie," he replied. "The dental details have gone to the forensic odontologist for his comments, and we should get something from the jewellery, but it's looking like it. Interpol might be able to tell you about the trainers and those jeans."

"I'll prepare a submission to them, and ask if they fit the profiles of any missing persons. Is there anything else, off the record, that occurs to you?"

"Not directly, but they'd both had hard lives and knew what it meant to go hungry. They'd be easy to lure over here and force into a life of prostitution. Perhaps the toxicology report will tell us something."

"The West was hardly the Land of Opportunity for them, was it?" I said.

"No, I'm afraid it wasn't," he replied.

At lunchtime I went for a walk into the town centre. A ridge of high pressure had parked itself above Heckley, so it was cold in spite of the bright sun. The town was bustling with shoppers looking for bargains in the run-up to Christmas and office workers collecting their sandwiches or sneaking into the pub for a quick uplifter. I walked towards the mall and gave the *Big Issue* seller a pound coin, told him I didn't need the magazine. A beggar was sitting in the door-way with his dog, a handwritten cardboard sign saying he was homeless, God bless. They all drive BMWs, according to popular belief, but I don't know where his was parked.

I strolled up into the food court, using the stairs instead of the escalator because I needed the exercise. The choice was Chinese, KFC, Burger King, Massarella's, fish and chips, pizza, jacket potato or Yorkshire pudding with a filling. Nearly all the tables were taken, mainly by young women with babies in buggies and toddlers bearing names straight out of the celebrity trash magazines. A snotty-nosed infant called Timberlake was doing his best to destroy his portion of the planet while his mother spoon-fed a baby with goo from a jar. I committed his face to memory, then decided I'd be long-gone before he was old enough to be deemed responsible for his deeds. The place was buzzing with conversation and reprimands and the scrape of chairs on the hard floor. I hesitated outside

Massarella's then decided not to bother. I'd take a sandwich into the office.

Art of Asia was still closed, "Until further notice" according to the signs in each window. We'd got the keys and the place was preserved as evidence, but for what we had yet to decide. Wallenberg had not declared himself the owner, and the rent had been paid, so nothing was spoiling. Jeff Caton came down every morning and checked the mail but nothing of interest had turned up. I peered through a window and a big fat Buddha smiled back at me. A lithe Indian lady was sitting on his lap in what might be termed a compromising position, so his smile was well justified.

I strolled out of the mall into the town square. Some of the office workers were wearing sunglasses and a hardy few had shed their jackets. Everybody walked purposefully, cramming as much as possible into their hour of freedom. Two girls in identical skirts and blouses were huddled in the doorway of HSBC, pulling on cigarettes like drowning sailors, while two more, in fishnet tights and grammar school blazers, drew on their cigs more furtively. The travel agents were offering short breaks in Malta for the price of a pair of designer jeans, and Specsavers would give you two-for-one.

L'Autre Place was busy. There was a lunchtime menu in a frame in the doorway, listing two courses for £9.99 or three for £11.99, and they weren't short of takers. They weren't policemen, of that I was sure. The Malta offer was tempting. I could go in and book it, get myself to the airport Saturday morning and have a week of sunshine, cheap wine and relaxation. I bought a chicken tikka sandwich at Greggs and took it back to the office, content that Heckley was functioning normally and a safe place for women and children.

I was hovering over the kettle, waiting for it to boil, when Gilbert came in. "Can I have a word, Charlie," he said, "in my office?"

I wondered what was wrong with the phone and followed him up the stairs. Jones's brief had complained about me, I decided. So what? I was fireproof. The worst that could happen was that they'd pay me to go quietly, on full pension. It'd be a wrench, I told myself, but I'd survive. Maybe I'd be going to Malta after all. Or Marrakesh. I'd always wanted to go to Marrakech.

It wasn't until he was in his seat and I was facing him that I noticed how white his face was. He glanced towards the window, then down at his blotter, which he decided needed moving a couple of inches to the right. He looked anywhere but at me. Gilbert always looks grave, but this was something extra. "What is it?" I asked as I lowered myself into the chair.

"I've some bad news, Charlie," he said, finally facing me. "It's your friend Rosie. Rosie Barraclough. I'm afraid she's been found dead."

13

She couldn't be. That was my first reaction. It was impossible. She was vibrant and beautiful and bubbling with life. She always wore red, highlighting her silver hair, and pictures of her flashed up before me: Rosie the first time I saw her, sitting behind a desk at the grammar school; Rosie waving her geologist's hammer at me deep in a quarry in the Dales; Rosie at the football match, shouting for the referee to put his spectacles on. She couldn't be dead. It was impossible.

But that was the visible Rosie. There were other times, when she wouldn't see me, when her demons came, and I knew it wasn't impossible at all.

Gilbert was talking but I hadn't heard a word. "I'm sorry, Gilbert. What was that?"

"I was just saying that Graham Myers, Superintendent Myers from Scarborough, has been on the phone. Rosie was found this morning in a bed-and-breakfast in Scarborough. First indications are that she'd taken an overdose of paracetamol. There was a note, addressed to you. Graham would like you to go over and do the necessary."

"Identify her?"

"Mmm."

"Right." I rose to my feet and looked around. What did I need? I wanted to get over there, see for myself. I didn't believe it, wouldn't believe it, until I saw her lying there. "I'll go now," I said, "if that's all right?"

Gilbert jumped up. "I'll tell one of the DCs to take you. Go collect your jacket and I'll be down in a minute."

"No," I protested. "I'll be OK. I'll manage on my own."

"It's too far to go on your own," he insisted. "And you'll be in the wrong frame of mind. I'll see you downstairs; that's an order."

Poor old Robert drew the short straw, mainly because he holidayed with his kids in Scarborough. We drove most of the way in silence, passing the occasional comment about other drivers and briefly talking about the job. People from Yorkshire divide into groups according to which seaside resort they prefer: Scarborough, Filey, Whitby or Bridlington, with Scarborough devotees considering themselves to be a cut above the others. They refer to the place as the Queen of Watering Holes, and acknowledge no rivals. All it meant to me was that he knew where to find the police station.

Graham Myers could not have been more considerate. He shook my hand and told me how sorry he was. Robert said he'd see me tomorrow and turned to go.

"Aren't you waiting for me?" I asked. "It won't take long, will it?"

They'd obviously worked it out between themselves. Robert brought me, I'd stay overnight, somebody would deliver me back home. I was incapable of straight thinking, was being blown along by events, so I just accepted what they said. I thanked Rob for bringing me and he said it was a sad business.

"Will you tell the others, please," I said before he left. I didn't want embarrassed glances and everybody avoiding me when I was back in the office.

She was at the hospital. I'd expected her to be in a funeral home, but I should have realised that there'd have to be a PM, so she was at the hospital. I've been through the procedure dozens of times, and it's never easy, but this was the first time I'd been the person doing the identification.

The attendant lifted the sheet back and there was Rosie, her face framed in silver and red, looking blissfully unaware of the grief she was causing. Her eyes were closed and I swear there was a hint of a smile on her lips as she lay there, deep in the peaceful oblivion she'd craved for so long.

"Do you want leaving for a while, Charlie?" Superintendent Myers asked.

I shook my head. "No." I touched the side of her face with the back of my fingers, then stooped to kiss her forehead.

"No," I repeated, adding: "This is the woman I know as Rosie Barraclough."

The note Rosie had left was in the super's office. "It's only a photocopy, I'm afraid," he told me. "The original has gone for tests. We were playing safe, as we knew nothing about her, but I'll get it for you in the morning."

He produced the photocopies from his drawer. The first was of the envelope, addressed to *Detective Inspector Charles Priest, Heckley CID* in a small, neat script. The next sheet was the note.

Dearest Charlie, I read. *This is the hardest thing I've ever done in my life. Not the pills. That's the easy bit. That's the bit I've been drawn towards for years. No, it's the writing of this note to you that is troubling me.*

I warned you that I came with baggage, but I didn't tell you how much. I once told you about my husband, said he was a waster. He wasn't. He was kind and considerate and had the patience of a saint. I drove him to drink and gambling, drove him away from me. I didn't want to do that to you. You deserve better.

The football match was fun. One of my happier memories. Your face when I came back from the Ladies was a picture. I hope you catch all the criminals, whoever they are. If anyone can do it it's Charlie Priest.

I can't put this off any longer. It's calling to me. When you read this I'll be part of yesterday's ten thousand years. Thanks for trying, Charlie. Thanks for making me happy during our brief friendship, and please forgive me for doing this to you. I hope you find someone who deserves you more than I did.

All my love
Rosie

Graham Myers had left the room, left me alone with Rosie's final message. I looked around and saw the usual trappings of office: the staff college photos; his uniform cap hanging on a hook; the law books that he'd never read. On the wall to the side of his desk was a picture of the Skye Coulins, torn from a calendar and pinned up because it had special meaning for him. He was a man of the hills and I warmed to him. No doubt he'd turn to it when he was bogged down with NIMs and SARA and income generation and benchmarking, and off he'd go to where the only problem was to get back to safety before nightfall, before the pub closed.

I was looking out of his window when I heard the click of the door catch as he came back into the room.

"You all right, Charlie?" he asked.

"Yeah, fine, thanks," I replied, moving back to the chair I'd been sitting on. "Can I keep this?"

"Yes, of course, and I'll have the originals returned to you, as soon as I can. What did you make of the message on the back?"

"On the back?" I hadn't seen a message on the back. I turned the page over but the reverse side was blank, then I realised that there were two sheets.

The writing was much different on the second sheet. It was drawn out and had lost its neatness and precision. It was a drunken scrawl, and a shiver ran through me as I realised that she'd been far-gone as she'd struggled to write her final message. Oh, Rosie, Rosie, I thought. Why did you put yourself through this?

The words were difficult to decipher, each one tapering off as if the exertion were too much for her. The first one was particularly obscure.

Shahtoosh, I read. "What's that supposed to mean?"

"Is that an S or is it a G?" Graham asked, pointing with a finger.

"It looks like an S to me, but a G doesn't help much, either, does it?"

"No, It doesn't."

It just came to me, the note continued. *It's a nasty business. Ros*

That was all. "It doesn't mean anything to me," I said.

"She was probably hallucinating," he suggested. "Like

182

when you're dreaming and have these enlightening thoughts on how to attain world peace. They turn out to be gibberish."

"I suppose so."

"How long had you known her, Charlie?"

"Not long, about six months," I replied, although four months was probably nearer the mark. "We weren't, you know, an item. Just good friends. I wanted it to be more than that, but Rosie fought shy of it, as you'll have gathered from the note. I went to a geology class, and Rosie was the teacher..." I left it hanging, left it for him to imagine how the hotshot detective had been smitten by the slim-shouldered tomboy with the shock of silver hair.

"What about her next of kin?"

Poor old Superintendent Myers, I thought. Lumbered with me but still having to play the policeman. "Her mother is in a nursing home in Norfolk," I told him. "She has dementia or something. Rosie reverted to her maiden name, so her mother will be called Barraclough, too. And there's a brother... somewhere, but he's... they don't talk, he's disowned her. And the ex-husband, of course. I don't know his name. Her father committed suicide. He hanged himself."

"That fits," he said. "These things often run in the family."

I stood up and glanced towards the window. Darkness had crept up on us and the sky was yellow with the glow of sodium lamps. "Thanks for everything, Graham," I said. "I'll look for somewhere to stay and see you in the morning."

"Nonsense," he replied. "I've told my wife to set an extra place and air the bed in the spare room. You're staying with us tonight."

I didn't have any choice. The meal was excellent but I wasn't hungry. We sat and talked, sometimes about the world we lived in, sometimes about the job and a little bit about Rosie. Graham had never handled a murder case – which is the norm, most senior officers haven't – so his wife was interested to learn what I did. I think she was a little disappointed that he'd become a desk pilot, but I laid it on about the irregular hours and she was pacified. They originated from

Birmingham, so Scarborough was a culture shock, but they were loving it. She'd bought season tickets for the Stephen Joseph theatre and he was negotiating a share in a fishing boat.

Next morning I spoke to the coroner on the phone and he was happy to release the body, on condition that the post mortem findings concurred with the belief that she'd taken her own life. Rosie had left another envelope containing a will, although it was unwitnessed and not strictly legal. She appointed me as executor and, it could be argued, full beneficiary. I was to take what I wanted and sell the rest, the proceeds going to charity. I went down to the CPS office and had a word with one of the solicitors, but he had no experience in this field. He rang the Federation solicitor who was more familiar with civil law and in a better position to give advice. I took the phone and he made sucking noises through his teeth as I explained the circumstances to him. When I told him that I'd be happy with a small, valueless memento, he said we might get away with it, subject to no other will being found and the relatives not objecting.

Dave arrived at about ten o'clock and brought me home. When he turned off the high street I said: "Where are you going?"

"Your house," he replied. "Where do you think?"

"I want to go to the office."

"Mr Wood said I've to take you home. He doesn't want to see you until Monday."

I'd had enough. Everybody, starting with Rosie, was deciding what was best for me. I said: "Listen, Dave. I'll say this once and once only. I'll take the rest of the day off and come in tomorrow. Tell everyone that I want no messages of sympathy, no hugs and no understanding looks. It's back to business. I'm upset, Dave," I told him. "Of course I'm upset. I was fond of Rosie, wanted her in my life. But I'm angry, too. Suicide is a selfish act and I refuse to feel guilty. Rosie was ill. How ill we'll never know, but it was her decision and I'm not letting her take me down with her. I wanted to help her but she wouldn't let me. I tried, believe me, I tried." I looked out of the window at my house as he pulled up and reversed into the drive. "Sorry for sounding off, Dave," I said, "but that's how I feel."

He pulled on the handbrake and tugged at his door handle. "C'mon," he said, "I'll let you make me a pot of tea."

When he'd gone I put on my Gore-Tex coat, slung an old rucksack over one shoulder and walked all the way to Wicks DIY store, three miles away. I bought six tins of enamel paint in primary and secondary colours and put them in the sack. On the way home I purchased a salmon fillet, some ready-scraped new potatoes and a tin of peas. There was probably a tin in the cupboard but I wasn't sure. It rained all the way back but I didn't mind. I left the potatoes simmering while I had a shower, and grilled the fish in lashings of margarine. After that I watched one of the Kennedy videos that Dave had loaned me.

At about nine o'clock I went into the garage and spread the two sheets of board on the floor. One was already white, so I painted the second one bright blue. I found an old half-inch brush that was worn out, dipped it in the yellow and started flicking.

It pays to have a rough idea of what you are trying to achieve before you start. I wanted a blue focal point somewhere on the white board, and a green one, or possibly two, on the blue board. Or perhaps a green one and a red one. I'd see how it developed. You have to be prepared to adjust your vision of the finished product, go where the paint leads you.

When both boards had an even distribution of yellow squiggles, splodges and dashes on them I switched to green and did it all again. Then it was black followed by red. I stood the boards against the wall, sat on my heels squinting at them for ten or fifteen minutes, then dipped into the yellow again and started all over. It's not as easy as it looks. All the time you are making decisions: more emphasis here, less there, not too much of that colour. It's all done by design and nothing is left to accident. Your mind is fully engaged, assessing the effects you are creating, balancing the colours and the depth of the coverage. And progress is painfully slow. You kneel next to the canvas, flicking paint, and as it goes from your hand to the painting it takes a little bit of you with it. It's you on display with the finished work, not merely a pattern of colours and shapes. The final work has no subject, not even a focal point. It's all about emotion and spirituality. The artist tears his soul out and puts it on the wall for all to see. That's what the critics claim. Me? I just like doing them and think they look good.

A single human cell is small. Ten of them could stand on the sharp end of a pin and still leave room for a viruses picnic. But packed into every one of those cells, crushed and contorted, is over a metre of DNA. It must look a bit like a Jackson Pollock painting inside there, I thought.

At midnight I made myself a mug of coffee and took the Rasta blaster into the garage, with Vaughan Williams on the CD deck. At half-past three I declared the paintings finished and went to bed.

We do follow-up interviews. Not always, but we say we do. It's a good excuse to go back and let a fresh pair of eyes and ears assess a witness. Or a suspect. Lloyd Lloyd Atkins were a firm of accountants with swish offices in Leeds. Atkins was long gone, but the two Lloyds were Crozier's partners who had owned the Painted Pony nightclub. Nigel had spoken to them – they were associated with his case, not mine – but had learned nothing, except that they were streetwise when it came to answering questions from a policeman. They were helpfulness itself, and answered his questions fulsomely, until it mattered. Then the shutters came down.

The 1944 Education Act has a lot to answer for. Before then we had the criminal classes. After it, when education became a universal right and not the privilege of the wealthy, the top villains could recite Milton or large chunks of the periodic table, while the children of the aristocracy slowly sank into comfortable dottiness, where they belonged. The ones with criminal genes, the clever ones, got themselves an education and moved into the professions where the pickings were easy. They went where the money was.

Two hundred years ago they'd have been highwaymen. A hundred years ago they might have stalked the streets of wherever armed with knobkerries to stun their unlucky victims. Nowadays their methods are less violent, more subtle and infinitely more rewarding. Paul and Desmond Lloyd said they could fit me in between clients on Saturday morning.

Where once were factories for the making of locomotives and printing presses that moved the world, literally and emotionally, there are now shiny new brick and glass office blocks advertising millions of square feet of floorspace for today's movers and shakers. Leeds has changed from being a manufacturing city into a centre for the service industries, whatever they are. I found Agincourt House, home of the headquarters of Lloyd Lloyd Atkins, and pressed the number I'd been given into the keypad. Normally there's a front desk with a person manning it, but service industries don't run to working Saturday mornings. I introduced myself to the voice coming from the hole in the wall and the gate slid back. "We're on the third floor," the voice told me.

They were good-looking lads, of about half my age. Identical twins, I realised, and they did nothing to allay the confusion that their similar appearances created: similar modest hairstyles; designer spectacles; blue suits and shirts; big cufflinks and identical tans. No doubt there were matching Porsches somewhere, with adjacent registration plates, and a pair of wives like glamorous animated bookends.

After the introductions Desmond, or was it Paul, said: "Would it hurt, Inspector, if I left you in the capable hands of my brother? I've been invited for a game of squash and it's so damn difficult to book a court on a Saturday. He knows everything I know."

I said: "To be honest, Mr Lloyd, it might even simplify things for me."

"Good show. I'll be off then. See you tonight, Bro."

"I'll bring the wine," his brother called after him.

The office was all light oak, stainless steel and pot plants. The workstations were by DELL and everything matched and was cordless. Flat screens. They had flat screens, and they were big ones, too. We were in the inner sanctum, where the brothers worked. Outside, I'd hesitated for about a minute in a small waiting area adjacent to the receptionist's office, furnished by Habitat and with a supply of up-market magazines. *Yorkshire Life* right through to *Forbes* magazine. OK, so the *Forbes* was six months old, probably picked up on an airliner by one of the twins, but it gave an insight into what life could be like for potential customers. I was sorry the receptionist wasn't there. Receptionists can be a fertile source of information and gossip. Another door probably led to the office where any other staff worked. I assumed there would be other staff; I couldn't imagine the Lloyd brothers toiling over balance sheets and cashflows at this stage in their careers.

"Coffee, Inspector," Paul Lloyd asked. Or was it Desmond?

"Um, no thanks. It's Paul, isn't it?"

"That's right, but I might deny it if pressed." He was smiling as he said it.

"That could lead to an interesting point of law," I replied, returning the smile.

We sat down at either side of his desk and he extracted a cellphone from a pocket. He inspected the display for a couple of seconds before switching the phone off and placing it back in the pocket. "Sorry about that," he said. "Now, how can I help you?"

"You were business partners of Joe Crozier," I began.

"Poor old Joe. Yes, I suppose you could say that. Desmond and I held shares in a nightclub with Joe. The Painted Pony."

"How did that come about?"

"We were his accountants. He opened this club in the old Alexander cinema, but it didn't take off. It looked as if Joe might go bankrupt, but he had a good product, we thought. So we worked out a rescue package and put some capital into it. Eventually, when the Alexander was demolished, the opportunity arose to relocate to the Waterside Heights building. Joe lived there, so it was a great opportunity. We held equal shares and changed the name to Painted Pony. My wife thought of that one."

I remembered the Alex with affection. When I lived in Leeds I occasionally took a girlfriend there. We'd grab a double seat on the back row, and if my luck was in I wouldn't see much of the film. That's why I remembered reading about it, four or five years ago, when it burned down. I wondered if arson was part of the rescue package that they'd worked out. It certainly looked like it.

"What happens to Joe's share?" I asked.

"It's part of his estate. Depends who he's left it to."

"I believe you've sold the club, haven't you."

"That's right. It was Joe's baby, really. He lived on the job, got a kick out of sitting in the sound box at night, watching the chicks, as he called them. Desmond and I didn't have much to do with it."

"But it was lucrative?"

"It certainly was, but an offer came in and we decided to accept it. We weren't looking forward to working with a new partner, whoever it was, and all the aggro that might ensue, so this way sewed things up neatly."

"Was it a good offer?"

He sucked his cheeks in before answering. "It was a substantial sum, Inspector, but we could have done better. We just wanted it out of the way."

Interesting answer. They'd sold it for peanuts, at a guess, and he was torn between pretending he was happy with the price and having a little grumble about it.

"So who is the new owner of the Painted Pony?"

"A man called Peter Wallenberg. Do you know him?"

"Yes. He's just bought Heckley football club."

Lloyd looked puzzled, then pointed a finger at me. "I knew I'd seen you before," he declared. "You were at the do there three weeks ago."

"That's right, but I didn't see you."

"Well, it was a bit of a scrum." Enlightenment spread across his face like sunrise across the Serengeti. "You won the raffle," he recalled. "And your wife went up to collect the prize. Now I remember – my wife commented on how attractive she was, and I agreed. You won the signed shirt – you're a lucky man, all round" He threw his head back and laughed. "Ha ha! What has she done with it? Used it to polish the kitchen floor?"

No, she's dead, I wanted to say. The beautiful, vivacious lady you saw me with is lying in a refrigerated drawer in Scarborough hospital mortuary. Instead, I said: "Weren't you rather hasty in selling the club?"

"I don't think so. Wallenberg had made us several offers, and we'd discussed them between ourselves. It was usually Joe who didn't want to sell, and although we out-voted him we were content to keep the club. As I said, it was Joe's baby."

"His final offer," I began. "Was it made after Joe died?"

"No."

"Are you sure?"

"Positive."

"How do you think Joe died?"

"He fell in the river. He was drunk, went for a wander in the dark."

"Are you scared of Wallenberg?"

"Scared of him? No."

"Are you sure he didn't make you *an offer you couldn't refuse*, as they say in films?"

"Absolutely."

It was like Nigel had said: the shutters were down. Up to now he'd been chatty and cooperative, but when his answers counted he was evasive. He could have said: "Scared of Wallenberg? Why should I be scared of him? We have a drink together sometimes, have a laugh. Old Pete's a business acquaintance, wouldn't hurt a fly." But he didn't. He just said no. And the same with Joe and the river. He could have told me how dangerous it was, how Joe was in the habit of going

190

for a midnight stroll, or feeding the ducks, or sailing model yachts on the tainted waters of the River Aire, but, again, he just said the bare minimum. Joe was drunk, end of story.

I said: "Have you ever met Tony Krabbe?"

He jumped to his feet, saying: "Would you like to change your mind about that coffee, Inspector?"

"Not for me, thanks."

"Do you mind if I have one?" He disappeared into the reception area, leaving me alone with all those computers and filing cabinets. I should have leapt up and rifled through them, opening drawers, playing tunes on the mouse, until, a split second before he reappeared, the exact document I was looking for, the one that incriminated the villains, fell into my hands. That's what I should have done. Instead, I sat and watched the pigeons wheeling over the glistening rooftops of south Leeds.

"Tony Krabbe," he reminded me, as he returned carrying a steaming mug. "A terrible tragedy, don't you think? Ironic. All the dangers he's faced in his career, and then some punk with an ice axe murders him on his own doorstep. Yes, I knew him. Fact is, we did his accounts for him, but Desmond handled them, not me."

He'd had a think, decided that he'd better own up to doing Krabbe's accounts, because we could have discovered it via other sources.

"Did you handle Wallenberg's affairs?" I asked.

The same logic applied. He thought about it for a second before admitting that they did. "Well, some of them," he added, defensively. "Mr Wallenberg's affairs cover a wide spectrum of activities. We've handled some of his property transactions."

"Do you meet him socially?"

"No, not if I can help it."

That came from the heart, I thought. "You don't like him?"

"Well, let's just say that we don't see eye-to-eye about certain things."

"What things?"

191

"I've said too much."

"So tell me more."

He shook his head, but added: "Have you spoken to his wife?"

"The lovely Selina? No."

"Perhaps you should."

I made the short drive to the Royal Armouries car park and walked along the embankment towards the Waterside Heights block where Joe had lived, where we believe he was dumped in the river. It used to be the gay quarter along there, long before most cities had a gay quarter. It wasn't a pleasant way to go but I didn't feel sorry for him. Joe Crozier didn't become the owner of a nightclub and a string of betting shops by driving a tram or standing alongside a lathe for ten hours a day. More than a few old men, and one or two widows, will have settled in their armchairs a little more comfortably after they read about his body being dragged from the river.

I walked back to the car and pointed it towards Heckley, wondering how I'd get to Selina without her husband knowing.

Sunday I visited Rosie's house and had a good look around. One bedroom was lined with bookshelves, and there still wasn't room for them all. I let my eyes run along the spines, hardly taking in the titles or authors. One section was on geology and there was a whole series of travel books, from Bill Bryson to Eric Newby and Paul Theroux. Then there were dozens of English classics: what must have been complete sets of Jane Austen; the Brontes; Trollope and so on; but in varying editions. She'd gone through various phases: Tolstoy; Dostoevsky and Pasternak sat comfortably alongside Fitzgerald, Hemingway and Steinbeck. As I looked I realised how much cleverer than me she was; how much of a waste her death had been. Two complete shelves were filled with feminist literature: Germaine Greer; Naomi Wolf; Helena Kennedy's *Eve Was Framed*.

We shared similar tastes in music so her CD collection was

less humbling. I even found a couple of Dylans down at the bottom, just above the freebies from the Sunday papers and the lemons we all have that we've bought, played once, and abandoned.

Her bed was made and all her clothes put away. I wanted to open a drawer, take up a handful of her clothes and bury my face in them, but I didn't. I tiptoed through the other rooms, feeling like an intruder, carefully turning the door handles as I closed them, as if not to disturb somebody sleeping in one of the rooms.

I shouldn't have been there, but I was, and I wasn't stealing anything. I had a quick look round the garden and then drove to B&Q. I came back with an incinerator in the back of the car and a couple of big plastic boxes. The incinerator was really a galvanised dustbin with holes in the bottom, but it would do.

Rosie had masses of photographs. I sat at the kitchen table and went through them all. One in a silver frame was of her with the man I presume to be her husband, sitting on some rocks in what could have been Scotland. I put it in one of the plastic boxes, together with one of Rosie posing with two schoolgirls. The sun was shining and they looked as if they were sharing a joke. Hubby might turn up one day, and I'd be able to give him the photo in the frame. The other one was for me. I stuffed all the others in a bin liner and left it standing by the kitchen door.

Her bank statements and salary slips were in the drawer of a writing desk. I put them in envelopes with her latest utility bills and her chequebook stubs. For some reason I wasn't sure of I read the gas and electricity meters and wrote the figures on one of the envelopes. Her address book was in the same drawer, and I wondered if I ought to write to everybody in it. It was full of names and addresses, telephone numbers and email addresses, all in her precise handwriting. I found my entry, probably the last one she'd made, and saw that she'd put a little Smiley face next to my name.

Rosie's car wasn't in the garage – she'd left it parked in front of the boarding house in Scarborough – but hanging on a hook I found her geologist's hammer. That would do as my memento of her. I carefully took it down and ran my fingertips along the rubber shaft and over the chrome-plated head. And two of her roses. She grew roses, old-fashioned varieties. Those with floppy heads that smelled nice but lost all their petals overnight. Irresponsible and ephemeral, I thought, like her. I unhooked a spade and went round the front to dig two up.

It was well dark when I finished in the house. I carried the bin liners into the back garden and lit a fire in the incinerator, and for the next hour I fed the remnants of Rosie's life into it. The sparks spiralled out of chimney and up towards the sky, back towards the stars whence we all came, and I smiled at that thought, content that Rosie would have liked it. Before I left I turned the central heating down low and locked the door.

My hands smelled of perfume and ashes. At home I had a bowl of cornflakes and a can of lager, and fell asleep on the settee with the lights out, watching the gas fire cast patterns of light on the ceiling in an endless, tedious pavan.

Gilbert was growing annoyed with the lack of progress in the Krabbe case and I wasn't too pleased about it myself. Questions were coming down the chain of command and the newspapers weren't slow to ask where our enquiries were leading. Monday morning I told him about my interview with the Lloyd twins and their suggestion that we talk to Selina Wallenberg.

"Haven't you spoken to her before now?" he demanded.

"Well, no."

"Why not?"

"Because we haven't had reason to."

"Well get on with it, then."

I went back to my office and spent a couple of minutes talking to directory enquiries. Then I rang the vicar of Uley. Uley is a picture postcard village in the county of Gloucestershire, in an area more familiarly known as the Cotswolds. It's a beautiful place, on a hillside facing the sun, overlooked by the church and surrounded by ancient woodland. When the sun is low the walls of the houses glow like buttermilk. There are two graveyards in Uley. The churchyard filled up a hundred years ago, so since then the corpses of deceased villagers have been buried over the road, in a field that once grazed cattle. But in the deepest corner of the old graveyard, lost beneath giant yew trees where the sun never shines, is the burial place of Abraham Barraclough, Rosie's father.

I introduced myself to the vicar, reminded him about Rosie, and asked if it would be possible for her ashes to be buried next to her father.

"Of course it will be," he replied.

And that was that. All that remained was to have the house and its contents valued, sell her car to a garage in Scarborough and arrange the cremation that she'd asked for. Her books could go to the school and her clothes to a charity shop. Then I'd take her remains on the long drive south and pick up the pieces of my own life.

Dave came in bearing two mugs of tea. "How's it going, Squire?" he asked.

"Gilbert's getting a bit ratty," I replied. "We need some action," and told him about my meeting with Paul Lloyd.

"Selina Wallenberg," he said when I'd finished. "What's she like?"

"Glamorous," I told him. "Dark haired, good figure, likes to flaunt it."

"And she's had a conviction for running a house of ill-repute."

"Yep."

"Sounds like your type. Want me to fix something up?"

"Let me try. Go listen on your phone."

Dave went to his own desk and set us up for a three-way conversation. I nodded to him through the window and dialled Wallenberg's mansion.

The man's secretary answered the phone. "Could I speak to Peter, please?" I said.

"I'm afraid Mr Wallenberg isn't in today."

"Oh. In that case, could I speak to Selina?"

"Who wants her?"

"My name's Choulianskovitch; I'm an old friend."

"Oh, um, I'll put you through."

I winked at Dave through the glass that surrounds my little enclave.

"Hello," a female voice said.

"Is that Mrs Wallenberg?"

"Yes it is. Who's calling?"

"My name's Priest," I told her. "Detective Inspector Priest from Heckley CID. I was wondering if I could have a word with your husband, but I understand he's not available."

"No, I'm afraid he's not."

"Do you know when he'll be back?"

"No."

"In that case, could I come and have a word with you?"

"I don't see how I can help you with anything, Inspector."

"Oh, you never know. Shall we say in half an hour?"

"Um, no, that's not possible. I'm seeing a friend in town at ten. Will it wait until this afternoon?"

"I suppose so. Will two o'clock be convenient?"

Two o'clock was fine. I put the phone down and relaxed.

Dave came back and took a sip of coffee. "I suppose you'll want to handle this one yourself," he said.

"Nah," I replied. "We'll both go. Two heads are better than one, even if they're sheep's heads."

"There is an alternative," he suggested.

"Go on."

"We could see who the mystery friend is she's meeting."

"Your deviousness never ceases to amaze me," I remarked. "Get your coat."

14

We went in Dave's car and parked about 50 yards from Wallenberg's security gates. The house was on the outskirts of Huddersfield, heading up on to the moors, and had once probably been the home of a mill owner or slave dealer, or both. There was a wall all round the small estate so we couldn't see much other than the roof, but a couple of the lads had taken a peak over the wall, strictly off the record, and reported that it had been extensively modernised and extended. The stable block was now garages, and an indoor swimming pool was appended on the side.

"I bet those chimneys are a bugger to sweep," Dave commented, nodding towards the roof.

"They probably send a small boy up," I said.

"There's smoke coming out of one of them. Is this a clean air zone?"

"I don't know, but I'll check. The yanks did Al Capone for tax evasion, so I don't see why we shouldn't do Wallenberg for having a coal fire."

"That would please Gilbert."

"True."

"He's an ugly little toad, isn't he."

"Who? Gilbert?"

"Nooah! Wallenberg."

"Mmm, but I've heard women describe men like him as being ugly in a handsome sort of way. There's no accounting for taste, or the pulling power of money."

"It certainly worked on Selina."

"I suspect that was the money."

"I suppose so. I sometimes wish that I'd been born rich instead of handsome."

I turned to look at him and he wasn't smiling.

A red Mazda MX5 poked its nose out of the gateway like a rat seeing if the coast was clear, then emerged on to the road and accelerated away. Dave spun the engine and followed her, all the way back to Heckley. She parked in the pay-and-display and headed towards the town centre, her high heels clacking on the block paving. I felt sure she'd go to *L'Autre Place*, but she turned off and entered an Italian restaurant in the pedestrianised quarter.

We followed her in. She didn't wait to be seated but walked straight past the desk towards a table where another woman was sitting.

"Table for two, gentlemen?" a waiter was asking.

"Yes please," Dave replied.

The two women exchanged big smiles and brief kisses and sat facing each other. I said: "On second thoughts, I don't think we'll bother, thank you."

The waiter shrugged and replaced the manhole-cover sized menus back on his pile and we left.

We had a cup of coffee in another place but it wasn't possible to see the restaurant door, so we didn't stay too long. Then we sat in the car for an hour but she didn't come back to hers. First Dave went for a walk and confirmed that they were still in the restaurant, and I did the same.

"Whose crackpot idea was this?" I complained.

"Did you know that there's a club called the Three Hour Lunch club," he said.

"Is there? Looks as if we've stumbled upon the founder members."

We were standing in a doorway over the road when they came out. They exchanged air kisses again and wandered off in opposite directions. As I didn't have a car I followed the mystery friend.

She was looking in the window of a jewellers shop when I caught up with her. "Excuse me," I said, showing her my ID card. "I'm Detective Inspector Priest. I couldn't help noticing that you were just talking to Selina Wallenberg. I wonder if I could have a word with you?"

She was dark haired, like Selina, wearing a woollen coat with a fur collar. Perhaps a few pounds overweight, according to the standards set by the fashion victims, but nothing that a normal man would complain about. She turned to face me and I looked straight into two huge brown eyes framed by what could have been a pair of crushed tarantulas.

"I'm sorry," she said, making it sound like an accusation.

I held the ID in front of her nose. "I'd like a word." We were standing across the road from Sainbury's, and I could see people in their cafeteria. "Let's go in there," I said, "where we can sit down."

I gestured for her to lead the way and she looked around as we entered the café. Whether she was taking in the unfamiliar surroundings or hoping none of her friends were watching I had no way of knowing.

"Did you say you know Selina?" she asked when we were seated just inside, after I'd asked her name.

"I'm seeing her this afternoon," I said. "Didn't she mention it?"

"Well, yes, she did. She said she'd had this mystery call from a policeman and he'd been ever-so assertive." She giggled and I caught a whiff of her scent.

"How long have you known her?"

"About, oh, ten or fifteen years." She looked downcast, as if the memory of all that time passed by was a shock to her.

"Where did you meet?"

"Hm, Holland, I think. Yes, we met in Holland."

I didn't push it. They probably went over there as teenagers, looking to break into something or other. They'd survived, and that was all that mattered. If it doesn't kill us it makes us stronger, as my dad used to say before he threw me out of the rowing boat. Getting out of the sack was the hardest bit.

"So you go back a long way."

"Thanks for reminding me, Inspector. What exactly is it you want to know?"

"Tell me about Peter Wallenberg."

"Hopalong? What's to tell?"

"Where did they meet?"

199

"I don't know. You'll have to ask Selina."

She'd gone on the defensive, and I sensed her hackles rise at the mention of his name. "Do you like him?" I asked.

A couple of workmen from the building site next door sat down near us, their plates heaped high with cholesterol-bearing goodies; all the tasty stuff we're told not to eat. They were wearing thick woollen shirts, torn jeans and riggers' boots. She stared at them as they poured ketchup over the piled-up plates.

"Peter," I reminded her.

"Um, er, no, I don't like him."

"Why not?"

"Have you seen him?"

"Yes, once or twice."

"Then you know why."

"Appearance isn't everything," I said, "which is fortunate for some of us. Beneath that unprepossessing exterior there might beat a heart of pure gold."

"Beneath that unprepossessing exterior, as you call it, there beats a vicious, scheming animal. Why she stays with him I'll never know. Well... well, never mind."

But I did mind. "He claims they have an open marriage," I said. "Is that true?"

"Uh!" she snorted. "By open, he means that he can do what he likes. Go with his... his girl friends. It's different for Selina."

"But she did have a boyfriend," I stated. She looked at me warily, wondering how much I knew. I went on: "Wasn't he killed in a car crash?"

"You know about that?"

"Yes. Did you know him?"

"No, it was her big secret. She called him her bit of rough, her toyboy." She glanced across at the workmen again, wondering if he'd been like them.

"And Peter never knew about him?"

"Good heavens, no. He'd have killed her if he'd found out. He was insanely jealous. They had a big row about six months ago and he beat her up. He accused her of having a boyfriend and went berserk. She's his property, and nobody touches his property."

"Right. I'll have to have another talk with Mr Wallenberg. Can I walk you back to your car? I'm not in mine so I can't offer you a lift."

"That's all right, Inspector. I've some shopping to do."

It was a ten-minute walk back to the office, and Dave's car was back in its place when I arrived. "Thanks for coming to collect me," I said. "I didn't get very wet."

"It's stopped raining. How did it go?"

"OK." I told him all about it. "How about you?"

"She filled up with gas – £27.72 – called in the garden centre for a bunch of flowers – gladioli, £4.99 – and drove home."

"How many flowers in the bunch?"

"Five."

"That's interesting. I saw five magpies this morning."

"Five for luck, isn't it?"

"I doubt it: two of them were squashed on the road."

"Maybe I'm wrong about the luck. Want me to come with you?"

"To see Mrs Wallenberg? Yeah, why not. We'll go in my car, this time, then you can walk back."

But she wasn't in. We parked outside the gates and pushed the bell, but nothing happened, and nobody answered when we telephoned. The secretary had probably gone home and Mrs W was otherwise engaged.

We could see more of the house through the railings, but nothing moved larger than a blackbird, pulling worms out of the lawn. The leaves were falling and they'd been brushed into soggy piles at intervals along the edges of the drive. The lawn had received its final cut of the year but the borders were matted with dead flowers and drooping stalks. I took hold of the gate and shook it impotently, willing the electric circuit to make contact and pull the gate back, but it didn't.

"Let's have a walk round," Dave suggested, and I followed him.

The wall is about seven feet high and difficult to climb when you're wearing leather shoes and it's drizzling with rain. About halfway round we stood on the low branch of a tree that gave us a view of the rear of the building, which was about as interesting as watching cows graze. There was a covered wood store, piled high with logs, and a greenhouse that was falling into disrepair. An outside light was left burning but all the windows were tightly closed.

"We could climb that wall if we were really determined," Dave declared.

"No," I said. "When we go in it will be through the gates." My feet were wet and the first trickle of rain had penetrated my collar.

"If you say so."

"I do." I was cold and frustrated and didn't know what to suggest next. I'd have liked to climb the wall and have a good fossick around, but it would have been counter-productive. Anything we found would be inadmissible, not passing the continuity test. Getting down from the branch Dave slipped and sat down in the wet grass, which made me feel better.

We had egg, chips and beans in the canteen, next to a radiator. I was deciding between a sausage roll and a custard tart when the phone rang and the canteen manageress waved to me.

"Are you answering the phone to women these days, Charlie?" the desk sergeant asked when I took the handset. "She said it's personal."

"Put her on."

It was a voice I didn't recognise. "I'm sorry, I didn't catch your name," I said.

"Lorraine."

"Lorraine what?"

"It doesn't matter. I'd like to talk to you about something that's going off under your noses and you don't do anything about it."

"So tell me."

"Not on the phone."

"OK. Come to the police station and I'll be happy to listen to you."

"I'm not sure. Can't we meet on neutral ground?"

I said: "Listen, Lorraine. I'm up to my eyeballs in work. I've been out in the rain all morning and I'm trying to grab a bite to eat. If you want to speak to me about something that is bothering you, I am willing to listen, but not on your so-called neutral ground. If you haven't broken the law, this is neutral ground."

"You sound pissed off."

"Got it in one."

"It's like this, Mr Priest. I run a hostel for women who are at risk, and it's necessary for me to maintain a degree of secrecy. Do you understand?"

"Perfectly, Lorraine. So come to the station. We can talk in an interview room and then you can be on your way. If any action needs to be taken, we'll take it. You're Lorraine, I'm Charlie, that's all we need to know at this stage, unless, of course, we're talking about serious crime, then you have a duty to help us."

"I am talking serious crime."

"I think you'd better come in, don't you?"

"Will fifteen minutes be alright?"

"Fine."

I made it the custard tart and finished my mug of tea. Dave went off to commit this morning's escapade to the computer and I put my socks back on. I was reading reports in my office when the summons to the front desk came.

At first I didn't think it was her. There was a figure wearing motorcycle waterproofs and holding a crash helmet that I assumed was a youth bringing his papers in for inspection, but when she moved forward I realised it was a woman.

"You must be Lorraine," I said. "I'm Charlie," and we shook hands.

"Charlie Priest," she replied.

"That's right. Now you have me at a disadvantage."

"Let's just say that we have a mutual acquaintance who said you were a sympathetic listener."

More like a soft touch, I thought, but I accepted it as a compliment. The desk sergeant shrugged his shoulders when I glanced at him, telling me to take any of the interview rooms. When we were seated I said: "So what's it all about, Lorraine?"

She placed the skidlid on the table and unzipped the top of her jacket. Rain glistened on her waterproofs and dripped into a dirty puddle on the floor, and a sticker on the front of the helmet said she was a member of the Women's International Motorcycle Association.

"Like I told you on the phone," she began, "I'm involved with a hostel for women who have abusive partners. We've just had this young woman come to us who has been forced into prostitution. I'll be honest with you, Charlie: she entered the country under false pretences."

"An illegal immigrant?"

"Not quite. She thought she was coming to a job, for only a few weeks, but she said it was for a holiday. Slightly illegal but her intentions were good."

"Where's she from?"

"I'd rather not say."

"OK. Go on."

"A man met her at the airport, as arranged, and took her to a flat somewhere. There, he beat her up, tortured her with an electric cattle prod, and raped her."

I flinched at the thought of it. "Was this in Heckley?" I asked.

"Um… I'm not sure."

"So did she escape?"

"There's more. She was kept prisoner in the flat. The following night two men came and subjected her to a serious sexual assault. I believe that's the sanitised way of putting it. The following night they came back with a group of friends and some beer and had a party. She was the entertainment. They raped her repeatedly, all through the night, and performed various acts with her. What that poor girl went through doesn't bear thinking about. After something like that you don't have a shred of self-respect left. The humiliation is total. Working as a prostitute after something like that is easy."

We hear stories about these things and wonder if they are true. We've all read about snuff movies and baby farms. We retreat from them, hoping that it's another urban myth launched by the tabloid press, but there's always a kernel of truth there. There must be. It's like the atom bomb: once you've invented the genie, you can't keep him in his box.

"She escaped?" I asked again.

"Yes. She ran out of the flat and into the road. She was in a state, to put it mildly. The first shop she came to was an Asian mini-market. Fortunately for her all the menfolk were out. The owner's wife knew about us and gave her shelter until we could collect her. We do a great deal of work with Asian girls who are being forced into marriages against their will."

"Where is she now?"

"In a safe house. I can't tell you where. Young girls who won't marry the chosen husband, or who are reckless enough to have boyfriends of a different religion, are murdered for family honour, as they dare to call it, so we have to be careful."

"What did she tell you about the men?" I asked.

"Not much. They were big, with shaven heads. Typical thugs."

"Any names? Did any of them use anybody's name?"

"Just one. She pronounced it Doo-gie. I think she meant Duggie."

"Duggie!" I echoed. "Are you sure she meant Duggie?"

"I think so."

"What about a description? Did she describe this Duggie?"

"No."

"And the man at the airport? Did you get a description of the man who picked her up at the airport?"

"No. She'd been through enough without us raking everything up again. We've had a friendly doctor see to her and she's under sedation. She'll never get over this."

"I have to see her, Lorraine," I said. "I must insist. I don't care how we do it, but I give you my word we won't harass her or your organisation. If you want this stamping out we have to have your cooperation."

"I... I don't know."

"I insist. Otherwise, there'll be another young woman taking her place in the next few days. It's up to you."

"I'll have to speak to some people."

"OK. Speak to anybody you want. You know where to find me."

I didn't tell her that Duggie, if it was the same person, was safely behind bars. Duggie had barely mastered tying his own shoelaces; it was the person who wound him up and set him off that we wanted. But there was satisfaction in knowing that adding kidnapping and rape to the charge of accessory to a murder would keep him off the streets for another eight or ten years.

I was in the garage, seeing how the paintings had dried, when the phone rang. It was Graham Myers from Scarborough.

"Hello, Graham," I said. "How are you?"

"I'm fine, Charlie, but what about you?"

"OK. Being busy helps keep your mind off things."

"Any nearer catching Krabbe's killer?"

"I suppose we must be, but we're still baffled."

"I've had the original of the note put in the post to your home address. Thought I better tell you to expect it."

"Thanks. That's thoughtful of you."

"And the post mortem confirmed that it was a paracetamol overdose."

"Right. I had no doubt it was, but we have to do these things."

"We've had a word with her – Rosie's, that is – Rosie's GP. She'd been seeing him recently. He diagnosed that she was suffering from what he calls bipolar depression. Apparently there's major depression, where you feel bad, and then there's bipolar depression. That's where you go through

206

cycles of feeling low and having a high for a while. It's a terrible illness, can strike at anyone. They don't know if it's biological in origin or a chemical imbalance in the brain."

"So I believe." I'd looked it up, had discussed it with the police doctor.

"She was also worried about her mother. Apparently she's been diagnosed as schizophrenic, and Rosie thought that she was showing the first symptoms herself. That's probably what tipped her over the edge."

"I didn't know that. Poor old Rosie."

"It's a sad case, Charlie. If there's anything else we can do, don't be afraid to ask."

I decided that the blue painting needed a bit more work. One of the highlights was a bit lost but it could wait. I needed two frames for them. A PC who's a dab hand at woodwork knocks them up for me at cost price. I'd ring him in the morning. Then I'd let the gallery know that they were ready and they'd send a van for them. After that I'd have to find something else to pass away the dog hours.

I watched television until after midnight and went to bed. I ran through the case in my mind, concentrating on the women. Go where the money is, and then the women. That's what I was taught. Krabbe knew how to pick them, that was for sure. He'd lived with Sonia Thornton for several years and then hitched up with Gabi Naylor, ex-fiancée of the man he'd possibly sent to his death. They were both still attractive women, and Sonia had been a celebrity.

I still hadn't seen the photos that Chris Quigley said Gabi had of his brother's body. If she still had them. She'd have sent copies to the insurance company, or to the local registrar of deaths to obtain a certificate, but she may have kept copies. Perhaps I'd ring her in the morning.

It was 30 days since Krabbe was killed. When a murder is unsolved after 30 days it starts to appear near the top of a list on the assistant chief constable's desk. When it's still there after another couple of days he familiarises himself with the case and suddenly appears at a briefing, asking questions, making suggestions, showing off his knowledge. I was treading water. Krabbe had enemies and one of them killed him, but I didn't know which one. Murder is a heavy burden to bear, and not many people can carry it off. They crack under the strain, have to share it with someone. Sometimes it's somebody close, but not too close, who notices the change in them and has a word with a friendly policeman. It's unscientific, but I was relying on it.

My mind kept returning to Rosie. Graham Myers meant well but his call had upset me. I thought about her, how scared she must have been when she thought her mother's illnesses were about to descend on her, how alone she must have felt. I'd opened the envelope with her note and the faintest remnant of her perfume still lingered on the paper. I read it again and turned the page over to the final scrawled message she'd struggled to write on the back. It must have felt like the most important thing in the world to her, her life's work.

I got out of bed and retrieved my dressing gown from the bathroom. The sky was clear outside and a half moon was riding high, white as a ghost. I watched it for several minutes until a taxi came down the street and deposited one of my neighbours outside his house. He shouted a goodnight to the driver and slammed the taxi door.

I went into the spare bedroom and sat down at the computer. When the screen was filled with soaring seagulls I double-clicked on *Internet*, and waited to go online. It was the hour of the geeks, when they all come out from under their stones, so the lines were busy. Then it was *Favorites* and *Google*. I typed *shahtoosh* into the box and clicked *Go*.

The search took less than half a second and found over 3,000 references. It's going to be a long night, I thought, but it wasn't. In fifteen minutes I knew all there was to know about shahtoosh.

15

I decided that Gabi Naylor was more likely to open up to me if I were alone. I rang her, just to confirm she'd be there, and headed east, squinting into the bright sun. The changeable fronts had passed, as the weatherman promised they would, and we were due for a more settled period. There was a queue of slow-moving traffic near the A1 junction, but once we were past that it was a straight blast to the Humber Bridge.

Landscapes always look better when the sun shines, and north Lincolnshire was suddenly a more inviting place. Santiago was still gazing lugubriously over the hedge and Pedro and the dogs came to greet me at the gate. Gabi herself came close behind them. We shook hands and she asked where my *colleague* was.

"Dave?" I said. "Oh, it's his turn to mind the shop. I should have brought some carrots, shouldn't I?"

"That's OK." she replied. "They're cheap enough at the moment. I'll sell you some Christmas cards, though. I'm sorry, but I've forgotten your name." She led me into the kitchen and beckoned for me to sit down. As before, she put the kettle on and spooned coffee into mugs without asking if I wanted one.

"DI Priest," I reminded her, "but Charlie will do." We talked about the animals enjoying the sunshine and she told me that they'd just taken in a python that some youth in Hull had kept in his bedroom until it gave him a near-death experience.

"I can't keep it," she said. "but we'll find a home for it in a zoo somewhere."

"Do you ever turn anything away?"

"Not so far, but these days… It's weird what some people keep as pets. I don't suppose you want a Vietnamese pot-bellied pig, do you?"

"No thanks," I replied, "unless it's cut up and jointed." She placed a mug of coffee in front of me and pulled out a chair. "Sorry," I said. "Are you a vegetarian?"

She gave me a big smile. "Only on Fridays. No milk, isn't it?"

"That's right." There was something about that kitchen, with the Aga gently clicking and hissing against the wall and the sun casting patches of brightness on all the surfaces. My eyes were heavy and I remembered that I'd had a sleepless night. The paperwork was still on the table, untouched, but now there was a tiny blue vase containing pansies next to it, and cyclamen were blooming in pots on the windowsill. I took a sip of coffee and wondered if Gabi had found what most of us are looking for.

"I've seen Chris Quigley," I said.

"Chris? You've seen Chris? How is he?"

"I'm not sure. He was a bit upset."

"That sounds like Chris."

"Tell me about him, please."

She looked at the steam rising from her coffee for nearly a minute, as if she were trying to conjure up his image, swirling in the mist, and I remembered him appearing almost out of nowhere when I met him.

"He's a strange man," she said, eventually. "But he's a gentle soul. He wouldn't hurt a fly. He was devastated when Jeremy died. I didn't realise he was in this country. Where did you see him?"

"At Nine Standards Rigg, up in Arkengarthdale. Where did you think he was?"

"In Nepal, or possibly Tibet. He was caught up in the whole mysticism thing. He wanted to join a Buddhist monastery, but I don't know if he did. I doubt it. Chris wasn't as single-minded as Jeremy. He's a butterfly, flitters from one thing to another."

"How well did you know him?"

"Quite well. Then, after the expedition, when he came back, he started coming round more frequently. I think... I think..."

210

"What?"

"Oh, I don't know. Who was it in the Bible who married his brother's wife? I think Chris thought that because Jerry was dead he and I would automatically become a couple. I had to spell it out to him that I wasn't looking for anybody else."

"But you were seeing Krabbe at the time?"

She looked uncomfortable, picked up a spoon and slowly stirred her coffee.

"I know," she replied. "It was awkward."

"Did you know that Chris blames Krabbe for Jeremy's death," I asked.

"Yes."

"What's your take on it?"

She shook her head. "Tony was ambitious," she replied after a pause. "He wanted Everest more than anything. Jerry was more happy-go-lucky. He climbed for the fun of it. He wasn't expected to be in the first summit team, but he proved to be stronger than the others. They'd climbed together before but weren't friends. If they didn't make the top it was no big deal to Jerry, but it was everything to Tony." She looked down at the table and said, very quietly: "Knowing what I know now, I believe he'd have done anything to get to the summit."

She stood up and walked over to the window. Pedro was outside, hoping for scraps to eat. Gabi pushed the window open and threw him a crust.

I said: "Chris told me that Jeremy left a diary. Do you know anything about that?"

"Well," she began. "It's true that he always kept a diary or journal on all his climbs, so there must have been one."

"What happened to it?"

"I only know what Chris told me. He claims two Austrian climbers took it from Jerry's body and gave it to him, but he lost it. He reckons that Tony stole it."

"Did he tell you what it said?"

"About the crampons? Yes."

"Do you believe it?"

"Yes, but it could have been accidental. I don't know what

to believe. All I know is that Jerry's still up there, frozen in the ice, with other climbers passing him by and barely sparing him a glance." She'd been standing with her back to the window, facing me, but she turned away and I heard her sobbing. I stood up and offered her a tissue, my other hand in the small of her back. She turned to me, put her arms on my waist and I felt the shudders of grief passing through her body.

"I'm sorry," I said, and wrapped one arm around her shoulders.

After a moment I made her sit down and I put the kettle on again. Gabi dried her eyes and apologised.

"It's me who should be apologising," I said. "This must be unpleasant for you. I've some more questions but I could always come back."

"No, Charlie. I'm all right. Honest I am."

"If you're sure."

"I am."

"Chris said that the Austrian climbers took some photographs, for insurance purposes."

"That's right."

"Do you have copies?"

She said she had and went to fetch them. I stepped over to the window where Pedro was still looking in. There was a bunch of celery on the drainer so I broke a stick off, had a bite and passed the remainder out to the donkey.

Gabi came back with a manila envelope. "They're here."

I looked into the envelope and saw about four ten-by-eight colour prints. I said: "Why don't you go feed the animals for a couple of minutes while I look at these?" She thought it was a good idea and left.

I spread the prints on the table and stood so that they were in the shadow of my body. When I saw the first one I was glad that Gabi wasn't looking over my shoulder. It was of the dead man's face, in close up and full colour. His eyes were closed and his lips were slightly parted. He'd died cold and alone and feeling betrayed, and it showed in his expression. Clods of snow were stuck to his skin and a film of ice covered his features as pitilessly as if he were a rock.

The next one was a general one of his body. It was snowing and out of focus. I thought about the Austrian climber who took the pictures. He'd have to remove his mitts, find the camera and fumble with the controls. And all the time his chances of making the summit, or returning safely, were diminishing. Photo three was the one I wanted. It was a close-up of Jeremy's legs, taken to give a reason for his predicament. One was twisted, looked broken. He'd died trying to crawl back to camp, up there in the death zone. The left boot was thrust towards the camera, and the front two points of the crampon were missing. No doubt about it. I remembered how prominent, how vicious, they'd looked in the photo that Sonia Thornton loaned me, but I couldn't see the colour of the fixing straps now because his ankles were caked in snow.

The final shot was entirely different. It was of the Himalayas, the roof of the world, stretching out for what looked like infinity. Hundreds of peaks, many unclimbed and unnamed, all the way to the Karakorams. The left corner of the picture was lost in cloud as a storm moved across, and the mountains in the foreground were shivering in the shadows while the distant ones were bathed in *alpenglow*. It was a view in a million, and you had to brave the death zone to see it. Again, I wondered about the photographer. Had he taken this shot to show where the body lay, or was he trying to tell us much more than that? Was he saying that this was the last view the dead man saw? That this was what it was all about? Don't ask me, I'm only a cop.

I put the photos back in the envelope and went outside. Gabi was sitting on a garden seat, rubbing Pedro's nose.

"Did you find what you wanted?" she asked.

"Yes. Thank you for letting me see them. The crampons look broken, but it wouldn't stand in a court of law. There's no overlap of the photos, so the one of the legs couldn't be proved to be of the same body. It could've been faked. It obviously wasn't, but I doubt if CPS would let it through in a murder case. That's not what they had in mind when they took the pictures."

"Is Chris a suspect?" she asked.

"Yes, as much as we have any suspects. Do you think he could have done it?"

"I don't know. I doubt it, but somebody did it."

"He was at base camp, wasn't he?"

"Yes. I think he went to pieces. He tried to go up there, into the death zone, to find the body. An American team brought him down."

"Can we go inside," I said. It might have been a bright day but the wind was from the east and I didn't have my porridge for breakfast. She followed me in and I closed the door behind her. "Sit down, please," I said.

I moved the envelope containing the photographs to one side and looked at her. I'd raked up events that she'd tried to forget, and it showed on her face. The counsellors believe we should face up to our problems and talk about them, but I'm not so sure. Some things are best left undisturbed.

"What do you know about Krabbe's business interests?" I asked.

She shrugged her shoulders. "Not much. He spent a lot of effort over there meeting people, looking for products, chasing contracts. I didn't know anything about it, except for…" She let the sentence tail off.

"Except for what, Gabi?" I prompted.

"Nothing. It doesn't matter. Like with the crampons, there's no proof."

I picked up my coffee mug, now cold and empty, looked at it and replaced it on the table. "I'll make some more," Gabi said, half rising to her feet.

"No, it's OK," I insisted. "I was just fidgeting." When she was seated again I asked: "Did you ever hear Tony mention a man called Peter Wallenberg?"

She looked thoughtful before saying she'd never heard of him. "Who is he?" she asked.

"Peter Wallenberg? He's a businessman in Heckley. He

214

sponsored Krabbe for the Everest expedition, and they have business connections. I went to a charity function that he organised, about a month ago, and Wallenberg's wife was there, as you might expect. She was wearing a sexy dress that left little to the imagination, with a rather nice shawl to protect her modesty and keep her shoulders warm. The person I was with asked her about it. The shawl, that is. Apparently it was called a shahtoosh, and they're very expensive. What can you tell me about shahtoosh, Gabi?"

She sat back, her hands still on the table, and I noticed the missing pinky for the first time. Her face coloured up and her shoulders rose and fell as she breathed. "Is it true," she asked, "about the shahtoosh?"

"I don't know," I replied. "You tell me what you know."

It took her a full minute to gather her thoughts. "I was working with this film company," she began in a very soft voice. "It was a dream job. Tony helped me get it, pulled some strings. It was just what I wanted to make me forget Jerry. Not forget him. I'll never forget him. To help me build my life again without him. We were making a film for TV about the Silk Road through west China and the Changtang region of the Tibetan plateau, into Nepal and then Kashmir. I fell in love with the land; I could understand for the first time what it was that kept drawing Jerry back there. It's probably due to the altitude and the thinness of the air, but you feel slightly high…" She smiled at the pun. "Light-headed, I think that's a better explanation. You feel slightly drunk, all the time. Well, I did."

And then the smile fled from her face. "We saw the birds first," she said. "Dozens of them wheeling in the sky. One of the technicians said: 'I wonder what they've found?' so we had a drive over.

"They were eagles and vultures. Lammergeiers and black vultures. Griffons, too. You could see them thousands of feet up, like little black flies, homing in on the place. They have territories that they patrol, way up high, watching the ground, endlessly circling. Out of the corners of their eyes they can see

215

their neighbour tens of miles away, patrolling his domain. If he suddenly vanishes they turn that way to see what he's found. In minutes, birds from hundreds of miles around converge on the spot."

"And what had they found?" I asked, although I knew the answer.

"The ground was black with birds in a feeding frenzy. I should have been thrilled to bits, seeing those great birds for the first time, and so close, but it was frightening. Carcasses were spread all around with these big black monsters tearing and pulling at them. We could see by the horns that they were some sort of mountain goat, but they'd been skinned. Everyone of them had been skinned. We watched these great birds gorging themselves until they were too heavy to fly, reducing the carcasses to skeletons before our eyes. It was sickening. It was obscene."

"How many dead goats did you estimate there were?"

"Between 40 and 50. I found out later that they are called chiru, or Tibetan antelope. They live at about 15,000 feet and have the finest wool in the world. It's used to make shawls which are considered high-fashion items in America and parts of Europe, even though it's against the law to possess one. The antelope can't be farmed. The only way to gather the wool is to kill them. It's illegal in China, but there's a ready market in the West for the shawls, which can sell for over £10,000. The poachers use high-powered rifles, and kill the animals as they migrate. The females are pregnant, but that makes no difference. They skin them where they fall and smuggle the skins through Tibet or Nepal into Kashmir, where the wool is plucked from them and woven into shawls. What we saw would make four, possibly five, shawls."

"So what did you do?" I asked.

"I wanted to expose the whole racket. We met up with Tony in Kathmandu, as we'd arranged, and told I him all about it. He tried to persuade me to forget the whole thing. He said that if we caused trouble we wouldn't get filming or climbing permits; the government was corrupt – they turned a blind eye to the trade; I could jeopardise the contracts he'd negotiated; and so on. Then he said that if we did report it to the authorities, all we would succeed in doing was force the price even higher, and make the trade more lucrative for the poachers. I'm ashamed to say I fell for that one. I did nothing, held my silence."

"Do you think Krabbe was involved in the trade?"

"I didn't, but later I learned that he was buying and selling pashminas. These are shawls made from the wool of another goat that lives high in the Himalayas, but one that can be farmed. They're still expensive – I couldn't afford one – but the trade is legal. When I learned that Tony was importing pashminas I was convinced that he was involved in the shahtoosh trade, too."

"But you never saw anything to prove it?"

"No."

"Is that why you fell out with him?"

"It was the final straw. He wasn't the person I thought he was. I saw a side of him that wasn't very nice, and started to believe what Chris had said about the crampons."

I stood up and carried my coffee mug to the sink. Pedro was standing several yards away, watching the geese. I rinsed the mug and left it standing on the drainer.

"Thanks for seeing me, Gabi," I said. "And for being so frank. I'm sorry about the circumstances."

She walked with me to the gate. As she opened it she asked if I had any suspects for Tony's murder.

I said: " Suspects, but nobody really stands out."

"Have you ever seen the film *Spartacus*?" she asked.

"Only on TV," I replied.

"You know the scene at the end where the Romans are looking for him amongst all the prisoners and one of his soldiers stands up and says: 'I am Spartacus'?"

"I remember it."

"Well, if you gathered everyone together who knew Tony Krabbe, and asked which of them had killed him, I hope that

I'd be first on my feet to say I did, and one by one all the others would join me."

"You feel that strongly about him?"

"I learned to hate him, Charlie. I hated him."

Gabi hadn't told me anything about shahtoosh that I hadn't learned from the internet. The wool, which is six times finer than human hair, is plucked by hand from the pelts in Kashmir, where it's not against the law, and woven into the shawls by traditional methods. They are the world's experts at that sort of thing. Shahtoosh became a high-fashion item in the late 80's, after fur coats fell out of favour. For some reason wealthy women feel more pampered when their clothes have a savage origin. There's a paper there for some psychiatrist, I thought. It probably went right back to when we lived in caves and the boss hunter was the man to be seen with. In the late 90's the Tibetan antelope became endangered, rapidly approaching extinction, and adverse publicity caused the shawls to go out of fashion, but the market still exists.

There's a parking place in the nick car park, right next to the door. It's marked *Chief Constable* and stands empty for approximately 99 percent of the time. Today, though, when I returned from my visit with Gabi Naylor, the Assistant Chief Constable (Operations)'s Jaguar was standing in it. I did a quick circuit, parked in the road outside and dialled my own number.

"DI Priest's office," I heard Jeff Caton say.

"It's me," I said. "I've a job for you."

"Where are you? The boss is looking for you."

"I'm miles away. Is Dave in?"

"Yeah."

"OK. I want you both to meet me across the road from the nick, and bring the keys for Tony Krabbe's shop in the mall. Quick as you can."

"How long will you be?"

"I'm already there."

218

A figure appeared at the second floor window. "Hey, I can see you."

The figure waved and I flashed my headlights. "Quick as you can," I urged. A minute later Dave and Jeff came running across the road. "Did you bring the keys?" I asked, and Dave waved them in my face.

On the short drive I gave them a brief history of the shahtoosh. We parked in the pedestrian precinct and marched purposefully towards the mall, Dave leading. I'd hung back, hoping to see a parking warden and explain what I was doing there, but you can never find one when you want one. I strode out to catch up with the other two.

The Salvation Army brass band was playing a Susa march, soon to be replaced by their Christmas repertoire, and the *Big Issue* seller was in his usual spot. I shook my head slightly as he started to proffer the latest issue, and he nodded an acknowledgement. The beggar and his dog weren't there. Probably having the BMW serviced, I thought.

The mall was buzzing with shoppers. Unfortunately for the traders it was mainly of the window kind. Wandering around displays of goods we can't afford or don't want is the new national obsession. Touchers and feelers, the shopkeepers call them. People with money to spend are like the chiru antelope – an endangered species.

A woman was peering through the window of Art of Asia. As Dave unlocked the door she stood behind us, expecting to be let in. "We're not opening, love," I said to her.

"How much is that Buddha?" she asked.

I stooped to read the label. "Three hundred pounds," I told her, and she nodded her thanks and wandered off. "Lock us in," I said, "before we have a rush."

"What are we looking for?"

I led them through into the back room and retrieved the flat cardboard box from the shelf where I'd placed it when we first turned the shop over. "These," I said.

I cleared the table that stood in the middle of the room and placed the box at one end. As I removed the lid and several sheets of tissue paper Dave said: "So are these shah-whatsits?"

"No," I told him. "These are pashminas, and perfectly legal. Well, I think they are. Feel the softness." They both took hold of a corner and rubbed the material between fingers and thumb.

"Colours are nice," Jeff said.

"They are, aren't they." They were earth colours, but these were from the more exotic corners of the planet: browns merging into purples; oranges that lay comfortably alongside reds; and greens that tied them all together. No palate I'd ever seen could match them for perfection. I lifted the top shawl out and tried to spread it over the table. Jeff saw what I was doing and started to help. Dave watched.

We'd lifted six out and the cold fingers of doubt were starting to clutch at my nether regions when we found the first shahtoosh. It was simply laid on a pashmina and folded up with it. The extra weight and thickness were negligible and we'd never have found it without fully spreading them out. It was just that bit finer, the colours slightly more muted, that much more expensive feeling.

"How did we miss these, first time?" Dave asked, but I'd seen him nudge Jeff.

"Don't ask me." I replied.

We found three more straight off and then I called a halt to the search. There were another fifteen pashminas in the box that we didn't unfold. "Let's pack them back up," I said, "and take them to the station for safe keeping. Tomorrow we'll hand them over to customs and excise. This is their baby."

The ACC had gone and I hadn't eaten all day, so I collected a ham sandwich in the canteen and had it at my desk. I was catching up with the whereabouts of everybody else when Nigel Newley rang.

"What's happened to Wallenberg?" he asked.

"No idea. Why?" I replied.

"We were keeping him under surveillance, nothing heavy, just normal hours, but he seems to have vanished."

"On my patch," I protested with feigned indignance. "You mounted a covert operation on my patch without telling me?"

"I know. Scandalous, isn't it? So where is he? You haven't arrested him, have you?"

"No. How long has he been missing?"

"Well, he hasn't been home for four days, or to the Painted Pony or any of his haunts that we know about."

I thought about things for a few seconds. "OK," I said. "You're invited. Tomorrow morning we're going to raid his house. It's a big place so we need all the help we can get. Meet here at seven a.m. for a briefing. We'll supply the forced entry party, you bring along a couple of searchers."

It was a murder case, so I didn't need a warrant, although I wasn't sure if I had enough information to obtain one. Mrs Wallenberg would be there, hopefully, and I wanted a substantive interview with her. Also I was confident we'd find at least one shahtoosh on the premises. That would do for starters.

At the briefing I outlined the cases and tried to identify what we were looking for. The sawn-off end of the ice axe was number one target, followed by photographs of his parents posing with the axes. I described the shawls as best I could and suggested that the two women officers in the party might be best qualified to look through Mrs Wallenberg's wardrobes. Their eyes gleamed at the prospect. Then they could empty all his jacket pockets to see if the napkin with the address that I'd seen him write at the football club was still there.

There were ten of us, plus two customs and excise officers I'd managed to find and the audio visual unit. We drove to Wallenberg's in five vehicles and parked in the lane at the front of the house. Two officers went round the back and radioed when they were in position.

I dialled the only number I had for the house but nobody answered. Pressing the bell on the imposing gatepost brought a similar result. I nodded to the two most agile officers I'd brought along and within a second or three they were over the gate.

They hammered on the door with their fists and eventually Mrs Wallenberg came and shouted at them through the glass. She let them in after they'd explained who they were and threatened to break the door down. The big gates slid sideways and the rest of us drove up the short driveway.

Selina was my objective. Tough, but I believe in leading from the front. Never ask the troops to do something you're not prepared to do yourself, with the possible exception of facing armed men and going up ladders. I showed her my ID and said we were investigating the smuggling of the products of endangered species. Nothing heavy. Nothing about murder. She was wearing a long bathrobe and her hair was a mess. I suggested she dress and asked where we could talk.

Half an hour later she joined me in a room on the ground floor lined with books and CD racks. There was a huge TV at one end, with a B&O hi-fi system and all the latest gismos for watching and listening. The material available was depressing: Readers' Digest editions that looked untouched; CDs of classical and pop compilations, plus plenty of Elvis; and DVDs of all the *Lethal Weapon* and *Rocky* series. Selina was wearing trousers and blouse when she reappeared, but hadn't had time to apply the normal half-pound of makeup. Her face was pale but her expression defiant.

"Who's the Elvis fan?" I asked, replacing the CD I was holding as she came into the room.

"I am. How long are your people going to be?"

"How many staff do you employ?" I asked, ignoring her question.

"Three, all part-time. A secretary, a cleaner and a gardener. They just work mornings. I asked how long you would be."

"It depends what they find."

"They won't find anything. I hope you'll pay for any damage they do."

"Sit down," I told her, and pulled an easy chair round to face the one I'd indicated for her to take. "We had an appointment on Monday," I said, "but you weren't at home."

"I lead a busy life."

222

"So do I. Where were you?"

"I met a friend for lunch. We over-ran."

"You left your friend at one o'clock and went home. Our appointment was at two."

"Was it? Well, let's just say that I decided I didn't want to see you."

"What have you to hide?"

"Nothing. I couldn't be bothered."

"Where is your husband?"

"I don't know. Am I under arrest?"

"Of course not."

"Should I have a solicitor present?"

"If you think you need one. Do you?"

"No."

"So where's Peter?"

"I don't know."

"When did you last see him?"

She thought about it for a few seconds, then said: "Saturday lunchtime."

"Does he often leave home without saying where he's going?"

"Sometimes."

"For four days?"

"No. Not usually for this long, but sometimes he's gone for a day or two."

"Did he say anything before he left?"

"He said he had some business to attend to, that's all."

"Have you any idea where he might be?"

"No."

"What was he wearing when he left?"

"His normal clothing. Black suit and overcoat."

"He likes his black clothes, doesn't he? How many black overcoats does he own?"

"Four or five, I think."

"He met you in Amsterdam, I believe."

"Yes."

"When you were working there?"

"What did she tell you?"

"Your lunch friend? She just said you were working there. I take it she rang you."

"Yes. She couldn't wait. It was in a club. Peter thinks he rescued me. What else did she tell you?"

The door burst open and one of Nigel's detectives stood there, looking awkward. "Sorry, boss," he said. "Thought it was empty."

"Ten minutes," I told him and he closed the door again. "She told me that Peter is a violent man. Is he?"

"No. No, he isn't. She's wrong."

"Then why are you scared of him?"

"I'm not."

"I think you are. Tell me about the time he beat you up."

"Beat me up?"

"Mmm."

"Which time?"

"The first time."

"It was nothing. A misunderstanding."

"Did he use his fists?"

She shook her head. "No, it was nothing."

"Tell me about Dale, then," I said. "You were fond of him, weren't you?"

"Dale!" she exclaimed. "What do you know about Dale?"

"A lot. Were you having an affair with him?"

She nodded her head and bit her lip, close to tears. I waited a minute until she recovered then asked: "Did Peter know about it?"

"No, of course not. He'd have killed me. Dale was everything Peter wasn't. He was funny, and generous, and…"

"And what?"

"And he was good in bed."

"So why didn't you leave Peter?" As if I didn't know.

"We talked about it. We were trying to work out a way of doing it. A way that would hurt Peter financially."

That was one way of putting it, I thought.

"And then," she continued, "Peter found out."

"About you and Dale?"

"No. About me and someone. We were seen by one of his so-called friends, but he didn't recognise Dale. That's when he beat me up. One of the times. He wanted to know who I was with. Said he'd have them killed. I couldn't tell him. I couldn't. Then he went out and came back with this… this… thing. It was like a long gun. He touched me with it and it gave me an electric shock. It was terrible. After that I'd have told him anything. He was yelling names at me. Is it so-and-so he'd shout, and I'd shake my head. They were all his business friends. All the people he suspected I was having an affair with were his business friends. He'd have killed me there and then if I'd said it was his driver. 'Is it Krabbe,' he shouted at me and jabbed me with the thing. 'Yes,' I screamed. I had to, to make him stop. 'Yes,' I said. 'It's Krabbe,' and he stopped."

Mrs Wallenberg was sobbing like a jilted bride. When some composure was restored I said: "Tony Krabbe was murdered on the night of the eighth of November. A Saturday. Do you remember where you were on that night?"

"Yes," she replied without hesitation. "I was here, at home."

"And was your husband with you?"

"Yes." She fidgeted with the cuff of her blouse then added: "At first."

"So he wasn't with you all the evening?"

Another long hesitation, but she'd made up her mind that she'd had enough. The time had come to make the break. "No, he wasn't."

"Where was he?"

"I don't know."

"But he definitely wasn't here with you?"

"Not… not later."

"So he was here at home with you for the early part of the evening and he went out later?"

"Yes."

"Did he go in the car?"

"Yes."

"Driving himself?"

"No. Duggie came for him."

"Duggie? Who's Duggie?" As if I didn't know.

"He works for Peter, as his driver. He was an old friend of Dale's, apparently, and he worked for an acquaintance of Peter's. When his employer died Dale asked Peter to give him a job. When Dale died he started driving Peter. He's a bit of a thug. I don't like him."

"Would that employer happen to be Joe Crozier?"

"Yes, it was."

"Hmm, that's interesting," I said, although I already knew it. "So where were we? Duggie came and picked up Peter. What time would this be?"

"I'm not sure. Fairly late."

"Nine? Ten?"

"About then." She stood up and walked over to a reproduction sideboard that was doubling as a video cabinet and found a box of tissues in one of the cupboards.

When she was seated again I said: "And what time did he come back?"

"Not much later. He was only gone about an hour, an hour and a half. I hadn't gone to bed. I was surprised to see him so early."

"Did he say where he'd been?"

"No... he... he didn't say."

"What did he say, Selina. Tell me what he did say."

She wiped her eyes and blew her nose. "He said... he said that I was to forget he'd been out. He'd stayed in all night. He was tense, excitable. I thought they'd had too much to drink and crashed the car or something. Next day I learned about Tony Krabbe."

"And you put two and two together?"

"No. I... I don't know."

I went over to the door and stood with it open, waiting for someone to come by. It was Robert. "Ask one of the WDCs to come here, Bob, please," I said to him.

Maggie appeared and I asked her to take Mrs Wallenberg

226

up to one of the bedrooms and take care of her. Maggie gave me a look that my mother would have called old-fashioned and off they went.

Jeff had set up station in the hallway, with a fresh notebook to catalogue everything we were taking away. The WDCs had found Mrs Wallenberg's shahtoosh hanging in her wardrobe, with another one like it, and a box containing ten brand new ones was found tucked away in one of his wardrobes. There was no sign of the napkin with the address that I'd seen him put in his pocket at the charity bash. I gave instructions for his collection of long black coats to be seized and placed in evidence bags.

Nigel appeared. "Found these for you," he said, and handed me a pair of black and white photographs that were creased and tattered at the edges. One showed two figures, male and female. He was wearing plus fours and she a long skirt, with tweed jackets and snow goggles. They were each leaning on an ice axe. The other photo showed just the woman, sitting on a rock with an ice axe leaning against her leg. She looked like Grace Wallenberg.

"That's brilliant, Nigel," I said. "That's brilliant."

I had a wander around, taking my first decent look at the house where two generations of crooks had lived. The impression was that the old man and his wife had a certain amount of taste, but little of it had passed down to their only child. The place was desperately in need of a makeover. Modern tat sat uncomfortably with several decent pieces of furniture that looked as if they belonged there. Most of the rooms had real fireplaces, and the ones in the lounge and kitchen had the embers of log fires still smouldering in them. Neat piles of kindling and logs were stacked in the fireplaces. Very nice, I thought, when you had someone to do the dirty work.

A team was going through a room upstairs where they kept all the stuff of memories. Every house has somewhere like that. There were bicycles with upright handlebars and wicker baskets, wooden skis that must have weighed a ton, boxes of *Beano* and *Film Fun* annuals. Everything was piled up in the order that it had ceased to be of interest, like an archaeological site dedicated to amusement. I reminded the troops what to look for and resumed my wanderings.

The audiovisual team took video footage of everything. Their role is two-fold. They are part of the evidence-gathering process but they also protect our backs against accusations of wrecking the place.

"The staff arrived at nine," Jeff told me, next time I passed through the hallway, "so I sent them home. There's a secretary, a housekeeper and a gardener who looks about 90. I've taken their names and addresses."

Two DCs came down the stairs carrying bulging evidence bags. "Three overcoats, as requested," one of them said, and Jeff wrote the details in his book and labelled the bags.

Maggie arrived back from ministering to Selina. "Another one you left sobbing, Charlie," she said, and then coloured up and looked embarrassed.

"Is she OK?" I asked.

"Yeah. I made her a cup of tea. I'm… sorry. I wasn't thinking."

"Don't worry about it. C'mon, show me where the fixings are and we'll make a cup for the troops."

We were standing in the kitchen, checking on the strength of the brew before allowing it to be distributed, when Dave knocked at the window. I held up my steaming mug and mouthed: "I'm busy," at him, but he shook his head and gestured for me to come outside. I gestured for him to join us but he was adamant.

"It's important," I heard him shout, his voice reduced to a murmur by the double-glazing.

"I'd better see what he wants," I said, standing my hardly-touched mug of tea on the counter. Maggie did the same and followed me outside.

He was round the back of the house, where the sun rarely shines. The ground was still wet and the brief dry spell had not been enough to drive off the air of decay and dereliction that lay around there. The grass was long and the hedge overgrown with brambles. Dave was standing outside the woodshed.

"In there," he said, nodding towards the lean-to building.

I went in very slowly, looking all around me, allowing my eyes to adjust to the gloom. Down at the floor, up at the tiled roof, forward at the wall which was whitewashed and hung with various tools. One end was piled to the roof with neatly sawn logs, and at the other end an ancient circular saw stood, its motor caked in sawdust, only the gleaming blade indicating that it was in working order. I took a deep breath and enjoyed the smell of the wood. It conjured up memories of childhood bonfires and school camps. I was looking for the sawn-off end of the ice axe used to kill Krabbe, but it wasn't there. Between the saw and the logs was a pile of kindling, each piece cut to precisely the same size as its companions. It was a big pile, enough, I imagined, to see them through the winter.

I turned back to Dave and shrugged my shoulders. "What?"

"Keep looking," he said.

The sawdust in the air was making my eyes water. The tools on the wall were old carpenters' tools. Giant brace and bits, several clamps and a spare saw blade with teeth the size of chocolate Hobnobs. I looked up at the roof. Big hooks were screwed into some of the beams. An ancient hurricane lamp hung from one, and various threaded components, caked in rust and dust, from some of the others. They looked as if they might be for screwing through fenceposts, or be gate-hinges, but I was guessing.

I turned round. "C'mon, sunshine," I said. "What have you found?"

Dave broke away from the conversation he was having with Maggie and joined me in the shed. He stood in front of the pile of kindling and pointed. "Down there."

16

I followed his pointing finger. Hooked over a nail, half-hidden by the pile of sticks, was the implement used to chop them. It was the head of another ice axe, but with a different handle. A short one designed for a hammer, at a guess, and suitably modified. I wondered about fingerprints, decided we had nothing to learn from them, and carefully picked it up. Cast into the side of the pointed blade was the manufacturer's name: *Scheidegger*. Dave had found the twin of the axe that had killed Krabbe. For 50 years, unknown to Wallenberg, it had been used by the gardener to chop kindling to keep the home fires burning. Now it was going to put the head of the household in jail for the rest of his life.

"Well done, kid!" I said. "Blinking well done!"

We'd had a good day. We were taking three overcoats back for forensic examination, plus photographs showing that Wallenberg's parents had owned two ice axes similar to the ones in question, plus the actual blade of one of them. Wallenberg had a motive for killing Krabbe, his alibi was shot to pieces and Duggie was incriminated, which meant I'd be able to play one off against the other. And then there was Selina. She'd signed Krabbe's death warrant to save her boyfriend and herself, but that wasn't against the law.

First thing I did when we were back at the nick was put out an APW for the arrest of Peter Wallenberg. If he tried to leave the country we'd have him. Then we had a debriefing.

The Customs and Excise people took the shahtoosh. They'd send samples to the Textile Technology group to confirm that they were what we thought and raise their own prosecution of Wallenberg. The overcoats went to our lab for examination.

One team had looked in the triple garages at the house. Mrs W's Mazda was in there but not her husband's Range

Rover. The garages were well-equipped with tools, they reported, and we wondered if this was where they prepared the cars used in the races. I asked for details of the Range Rover to be circulated and arranged for Mrs Wallenberg to be given protection.

The prison service likes to flex its muscles occasionally and let us know that it is an independent entity, beholden to no one. They shelter their charges jealously. If we need to see one of them we have to go through their visits office and take our turn with the wives and mothers and girlfriends that most of them attract like carpets attract the side of your toast with butter on. There is another way, of course. I rang Bentley prison and asked to speak to the governor. It helps when you're old friends, and everybody is susceptible to a bit of flirting. She's no fool – you don't get to be governor of one of the toughest jails in the country by falling for smooth talk – but when I explained that Duggie Jones was facing a murder charge and his co-conspirator was still on the loose, she agreed to cut a few corners for me. I thanked her and said I'd arrange transport to bring him to Heckley in the morning.

I filled in the diary and started to think about a submission to the CPS, but before that we had to find Walleneberg. When I felt myself nodding off seated at my desk I decided to call it a day and went home. I collected a rogan josh from the Last Viceroy and after a shower I fell asleep in bed and dreamed about log fires – which was understandable – and those traffic cones that have a flashing yellow light on top, which was weird. I had to count them, but they were moving around all the time and if one flashed I had to start again and my hat kept falling over my eyes. I only thought about Rosie after the alarm insisted another day had begun.

They found Wallenberg's Range Rover Vogue in Heckley multi-storey car park. I was in Gilbert's office, giving him a positive update for once, when the message came through. I asked for it to be handed over to Forensics for a thorough examination, and told them to let me know if they came across an electric cattle prod. One hadn't surfaced during the search of his house.

That meant that Wallenberg was either still in Heckley or had an accomplice who had spirited him away.

"Or he's travelling by public transport," Gilbert suggested.

I pulled a face at him.

"Taxi to the airport?" he explained.

"Possible," I conceded.

There was a message on my desk when I returned to my office. A woman called Lorraine rang, it said. She wouldn't leave a surname but she'd try again later.

The convoy bearing Duggie Jones arrived and he was ushered into the station. I grabbed a mug of tea, two sausage rolls and a Kit Kat while he familiarised himself with his solicitor and his story. When we were good and ready Dave and I joined them in interview room number one.

It was laid out ready with notepads and pens for each of us, and four new tapes still in their cellophane wrappings sat in the middle of the Formica table. Dave fumbled with them until he found a loose corner and set the recorder going. I did the introductions.

"We're talking about fresh charges, Duggie," I said, "so I have to caution you again and remind you of your rights under the Police and Criminal Evidence Act. Do you understand?"

"Yeah," he mumbled.

"Have you had some breakfast?"

"Yeah."

"A full English?" I couldn't resist asking.

"What?"

"Never mind." I recited the caution and went through the procedure, reminding him of his rights. It always sticks in the craw that we have a *criminal* justice service and not a *victim* justice service. He nodded to say he understood and the solicitor stifled a yawn.

"You are currently on remand charged with being an accessory to the murder of Joe Crozier," I said.

"Yeah, I know."

232

The brief sat forward. "We will be petitioning for the charge to be reduced to assisting in the disposal of a dead body," he stated. "My client was under the belief that the victim was already dead."

Don't bother, I thought. That was only for starters. I said: "Tell us about the car racing, Duggie."

" I don't know noffing about it," he replied.

"You knew Dale was involved, though, didn't you."

"Yeah, I told you that before."

"So you did, but you didn't say that he was working for Peter Wallenberg."

"Didn't know, did I?"

"Or that you'd taken over Dale's job after he died."

He looked uncomfortable. "Yeah, well…"

"Is that what the Jaguars were stolen for? Another race?"

"No."

"Organised by Wallenberg? Mr Wallenberg enjoys sport, he says. Even bought himself a football club. You knew he gambled heavily on the races, didn't you."

"If you say so."

"Did you know he had a little side bet on the last race? £10,000 that said one of the drivers would be killed. Did you know that?" I sensed Dave looking across at me. Sometimes, I improvise.

He didn't answer. It was all too much for him, overloading his puny brain with information. The top of a tattoo was visible poking out from the neck of his prison shirt and I wondered how close to the carotid artery the needle went when you had a tattoo like that. Not close enough. We'd named Wallenberg, but now Duggie was desperately trying to remember if he'd ever acknowledged knowing him. Being a liar is difficult when your brain cells are outnumbered by your fingers and toes.

Dave said: "Who did you prefer working for: Crozier or Wallenberg?"

"Oh, come on!" the brief protested. "Mr Jones has never said that he worked for this Mr Wallenberg, whoever he might be."

He's the person who's picking up your bill, I thought.

"Do you know Wallenberg?" Dave persisted.

"Yer, a bit," Duggie admitted.

"You know him a bit?"

"Yeah."

"Do you work for him?"

"No, not proper. Just a bit."

"You drive him, now and again?"

"Yeah."

"Run errands for him?"

"Yeah."

"Do odd jobs for him?"

"Yeah. Sort of."

"Like rolling bodies into rivers?"

"No. I didn't know about that. I did that for Dale. It was noffing to do wiv Mr Wallenberg."

"Where were you on the night Tony Krabbe was murdered?"

"I dunno."

"It was Saturday, the eighth of November. Five weeks ago."

"I dunno."

I leaned forward. "Let me jog your memory, Duggie," I said. "You picked up Mr Wallenberg at his house at about half-past nine, and you returned him home about half-past ten or eleven o'clock. Does that help?"

"No."

"We have a witness who will swear to that."

The brief said: "Can I ask who your witness is?"

"All in good time," I said. "Duggie?"

"I don't remember."

"I think you do, Duggie. I think you'll probably remember that night for as long as you live. The night you took Mr Wallenberg to kill Tony Krabbe."

"I must object to the degree of supposition you are inserting into this interview, Inspector," his brief said.

"Then it's up to Duggie to remove the supposition," I

replied. "Tell us how Krabbe died, Duggie. He was killed by someone who knew him, and there were most likely two people present: one to walk alongside him, engaging him in conversation; one to deliver the blow from directly behind him."

"I dunno, do I?"

"Wallenberg thought his wife was having an affair with Krabbe, didn't he? But it was Dale she'd been having an affair with. Did you know that? Did it make you smile when you learned that Krabbe was taking the blame. Did you think: Good old Dale, even when he's dead he manages to wriggle out of trouble. Is that what you thought?"

"No."

The brief said he'd like to consult his client and Dave stopped the tape.

We went up to the office for a quick coffee. Duggie's solicitor had a conflict of interests: he could hardly defend Duggie by laying the blame on Wallenberg, his paymaster; but if he sacrificed Duggie, then Duggie might sing like a love-sick tomcat. The CPS had recently opened an office in the nick, so we went down to see them. I outlined the evidence pointing to Wallenberg, but added that the most likely scenario was that Wallenberg walked alongside Krabbe while Duggie hit him from behind. The CPS lawyer agreed to Duggie being charged with murder.

We reconvened in the interview room and Duggie's brief said that they would strenuously deny any involvement with the murder of Tony Krabbe.

I said: "OK, Duggie, so tell us about the foreign girl."

"What foreign girl?"

"The one you raped. The one that you introduced all your friends to. The one that's just dying to point you out in a line-up."

"Don't know what you mean," he replied, but his body language said otherwise. It was all too much for him. Murder, murder again, and now rape. Where had it all started to go wrong? Things had been looking good. He'd had a sweet little number: plenty of sex; money; fast cars and booze. What more could your average neighbourhood hoodlum ask for? But now it had all gone pear-shaped. He buried his head in his arms and sobbed. He was sorry. Sorrier than he'd ever felt in his life. If the truth were known it was the first time in that life that he'd ever experienced the emotion. But his tears of grief were reserved for one person, and one person only: himself.

The solicitor looked at him and his lip curled back in disgust. I nodded at Dave and he stood up.

"Douglas Jones," he said, "I'm arresting you for the murder of Anthony Turnbull Krabbe…"

He appeared before a magistrate the following morning and was remanded in custody. We issued a press release saying that a 28-year-old man had been arrested for Krabbe's murder and I started the paperwork. When I returned to my office after the morning prayer meeting there was an envelope with an Oxford postmark waiting for me. I sliced it open with my paperknife and retrieved the contents: three photographs and a letter. They were the reconstructions of the skull found on Bleak Tor. Body One, as we'd unimaginatively called her.

It was a good face. It looked like someone; someone you thought you'd seen somewhere. When an amateur artist draws a face it always has the right components – two eyes, nose, mouth, etcetera – in all the right places, but it doesn't necessarily look like anyone. This one did. I don't know why I was surprised but I was. There was, I had to remind myself, a real skull under all that plasticine. A skull that had once belonged to a real live girl. She'd had her hardships, life hadn't been kind to her, but the face that gazed blankly at me could have been anyone that I'd seen window shopping in the mall or waiting at the checkout in Sainsbury's. Except that if we'd ever met, if I'd collided with her and she'd dropped her groceries, I'd have apologised to her but wouldn't have recognised the language she spoke back to me in. I placed the profile pictures behind the frontal one and leaned them against the wall, facing me.

Lorraine rang shortly after. "I was just thinking about you," I said.

"In what context?"

"What you told me. Wondering where we were with it."

"She said she'll talk to you. She didn't want to, but we've persuaded her."

"Will she be free from the tranquillisers?"

"Yes, she's managing without them. She's a remarkable girl."

"OK, when can I see her, and where?"

"It's not that easy."

"It is to me. You arrange something and I'll be there."

"She's in a safe house. It wouldn't be safe any more if the police knew about it."

"So choose a neutral venue."

"How do we know you wouldn't alert your colleagues and have her arrested?"

I said: "Perhaps you don't know, but there's something called trust, Lorraine. It would be a bleak world if we didn't have any trust in anyone. I thought that was why you chose to ring me."

"The people we deal with, Inspector, have had all the trust knocked out of them. I can take you to meet her but you'll have to be blindfolded."

"Blindfolded," I echoed. "That sounds drastic. How far away is she?"

"A fair way."

"And you want me to sit in a car with a blindfold around my head? Or do I have to lay in the boot?"

"We've made some spectacles for you to wear. Sunglasses. We've painted them so you can't see through them."

"How do you know I won't take them off when we get there?"

"If you do we'll come straight back."

I didn't want to go for it, but I looked at the plasticine face staring at me from the photo, I thought of the two bodies up on Bleak Tor, and I remembered the story Lorraine had told me. "OK," I said. "We'll do it your way. You don't trust me but I'll trust you. When do we do it?"

"Monday," she replied. "I'll ring you Monday morning."

We had a celebration beverage in the Bailiwick after work. It was Friday, so I stood the troops down for the weekend. When we'd had a couple of drinks, talk moved round to starting the walking club again. It always does. We all have fond memories of the walking club and the exploits we endured. The passage of time enhances the good memories, exaggerates our exploits, and dulls the recollection of the days when the sun never shone and we swished, slopped and dripped round the route in full waterproofs like North Sea fishermen washed up on an alien landscape.

"We haven't done Ingleborough for a long time," Dave said. Ingleborough isn't the highest peak in Yorkshire, but it ought to be. It broods like a sleeping lion between the Ribble and the Greta, and is the nearest place we have to a spiritual home. There are the remnants of settlements on top which we like to believe were unconquered by the Romans.

"We always do Ingleborough," Jeff protested. "It's nearly worn out. There are duckboards all the way up it. They'll be installing an escalator next. Let's go down into Derbyshire."

So on Sunday nine of us in three cars drove south and parked in Edale. Approaching Ladybower reservoir Dave began to quietly whistle the Dambusters' theme, and, dead on cue, Jeff reminded us for the seven hundredth time that they'd practised there.

We walked to Blackden Edge via Ringing Roger, then past Madwoman's Stones and down Jaggers Clough. For much of the way we were on peat like that on Bleak Tor, and I wondered how many bodies we walked over. None, probably, but it was easy to imagine they were there. We made it to the Strines Inn before closing time and were back in Heckley for tea. Dave had arranged that I eat with them, so it was a good day out.

Lorraine rang at ten o'clock, Monday morning. "Can you be at the corner of the High Street and Westland Road at half-past?" she said.

"No problem," I replied. It was a five-minute stroll away.

"And don't be followed," she stressed.

"I won't be."

I made a few notes about what I needed to know, left instructions for the troops and made neat piles of everything on my desk. The photo of the face of Body One was still staring at me. I placed all three pictures in an envelope with a couple of others and my notebook and thought about taking a tape recorder. I decided that it might be intimidating, so I abandoned the idea. I looked at my watch. I could have used a coffee but didn't know how long I'd be cooped up in the car. Stopping for a pee, whilst blindfolded, didn't appeal to me, so I abandoned the coffee idea, too. I placed three fibre-tipped pens in the envelope and pulled my jacket on.

It's a woman's privilege to be late, so they took advantage of it. Five minutes isn't too bad, I suppose. They were probably having me watched or drove by several times. A Ford Fiesta with a noisy exhaust pulled up alongside me and Lorraine jumped out of the passenger's door. She pulled the seat forward and manoeuvred herself into the back, indicating for me to sit in the front. I was looking for my seatbelt when we moved off.

The driver had a stud in her nose and spiky hair. Lorraine said: "This is Charlie Priest, this is Magda," and I said: "Hello, Magda."

Magda pulled into a lay-by at 40 miles per hour and hit the brakes. "There's some glasses in there," she said, pointing to the glovebox. "Put them on."

They were those big wrap-around ones you see advertised in the Sunday supplements, that can be worn over a pair of spectacles. They were originally designed for welders on the oilrigs, but due to an administrative cock-up too many were manufactured. They'd painted the inside with black paint to make them totally opaque. I put them on and it was almost like having my eyes closed. I turned to the driver, saying: "There we go," and she dropped the clutch and we were on our way.

I was sitting with my knees pressed against the dashboard. First thoughts were that I'd count the turns, calculate where we were going, but I soon tired of that. I'd settle for the general impression. We were heading towards the motorway. After five minutes we made a high-speed left turn and I reckoned we'd taken to the slip road, which meant we were heading west. Manchester, probably. The boom of the exhaust and the wind noise confirmed that we were on the motorway, so I rested my head on the window and snoozed.

Twenty minutes later I was leaning into the seatbelt as Magda applied the brakes, then it was another twenty minutes of stop-start motoring until she pulled the handbrake on and announced: "This is it."

I think that's what she said. Her words were drowned by the noise of the airliner passing overhead on its descent into Manchester airport. When the decibel level was down to something less damaging I said: "That sounds like the 11.45 from Dallas."

The car lurched as Magda got out. I opened the passenger door and swung my legs on to the pavement. As I stood up Magda took me by the arm and started to lead me away. I stumbled slightly, my legs stiff with cramp.

I heard the squeal of a gate's hinges and she said: "Small step up."

I felt it with my toe and in four or five strides we stopped again and I heard her knock on a door panel.

Another plane was approaching. Magda knocked again as its roar grew louder. Suddenly it was above us and I swear we could feel the heat from its engines. "Here comes the 11.49 from Australia," I announced, turning my blind gaze upwards and sticking fingers in my ears. The door opened and I was led inside.

"You can take the glasses off now," Lorraine told me.

We were in the small parlour of someone's house. The suite

was moquette in a swirling pattern and it hardly left space for anything else in the room. They'd still managed to cram a coffee table in there, though, plus a couple of hard chairs and a sideboard. A gas fire hissed against the chimney breast and the picture above it was Monet's waterlilies. The curtains were closed and the light on. An Asian woman beckoned for me to take a seat and asked if I'd like a tea or coffee. She was wearing a pale blue sari and had a long, finely chiselled face. It was a face that suggested that at some time in the past, long forgotten, it had been in a position of authority. I said "Tea, please," turning it into a smile and nodding.

"Where is she?" I asked.

"She's coming," Lorraine replied. A low rumble said the next plane was overhead, but triple-glazing reduced the noise to an acceptable level. I wondered what it did for property prices.

The Asian lady brought my tea on a tray with milk and sugar and hot water, all in matching china. I thanked her and poured myself a cup. Magda appeared with two mugs of coffee and handed one to Lorraine.

"So she's not staying here?" I said.

"No."

There were plenty more questions in my repertoire but I decided that asking them was futile. If they wanted to play it like a Le Carré novel, fair enough. I stared at the Monet and recalled the time as a student when I saw some of the originals in the Louvre. That was one of the happiest times of my life, I remembered, fuelled by French wine and the hint of revolution in the air. I even pulled the best-looking girl in the college, but then I ruined it all by marrying her.

The problem with triple-glazing is that you can't hear any of the other noises outside. Presumably a car pulled up at the gate and the hinges squealed again, but the first I knew of it was when the doorbell rang and the door opened. It's usually draughts they let in, but here it was the roar of two Rolls Royce turbofans. The door slammed and the noise was gone.

Lorraine and Magda went to welcome the newcomers.

Voices clashed and overlapped and someone laughed. I imagined the scene: lots of air-kissing and hugs. I'm not into same-sex hugs. Then they fell into a conspiratorial silence and one by one filtered into the room where I was sitting. I stood up to welcome them.

The girl was wearing a cheap anorak over a dress, with trainers. Her hair was startlingly blonde and her face drawn and tired looking. It could have been the plasticine one I had the photographs of, animated by some modern Frankenstein who'd finally mastered his science. Her head was bowed as if there were something on the carpet that demanded her attention.

"This is Detective Inspector Priest," Lorraine told her. "He's promised to help and not ask any questions about where you're staying."

The girl's eye's flicked briefly up at me and she nodded a silent hello.

I said: "You can call me Charlie. I'll not ask you your name."

We sat down, the girl in an easy chair next to the fire, me in the one adjacent to it. Lorraine and Magda were on the settee, the Asian woman and the person who brought the girl on hard chairs.

I said: "First of all, can I ask how old you are?"

"She's nineteen," Magda interrupted.

"Are you?" I asked.

"Yes," she replied, her voice barely audible.

"And you can speak English quite well?"

"She can understand what you say," Magda told me, "but sometimes has difficulty expressing herself."

I stood up and walked to the door that led into the kitchen and felt four pairs of eyes follow me. I presumed the girl's were still fixated by the carpet. It was bright and airy in there, and there was a small Formica table with matching chairs. I feel more at home talking to witnesses across a Formica table. The kettle felt full so I switched it on.

The women watched in silence as I picked up the tea tray

and carried it into the kitchen. I placed it on the table, pulled two chairs out opposite each other and placed the other two against the wall, as far way as possible, which wasn't very far. When the kettle came to the boil I refreshed the teapot and found a clean cup and saucer for the girl.

"Can you come this way, please," I asked her. She glanced in bewilderment at the women but rose to follow me. Usually we place the prisoner with the light on his or her face, but this time I did it differently. I sat her with her back to the window, and I was the one who had to blink into the brightness. I poured her a cup without asking and indicated for her to help herself to milk and sugar. She piled two big spoonfuls into her cup with a touch of milk.

"Thank you," she said.

Magda and Lorraine took the two other seats, the other women stayed in the front room.

"Let's start again," I suggested. "First of all, how old are you?"

17

"I am nineteen." Ludmilla told me.

It was less oppressive in the kitchen and now I could see how young she was. Her eyes were large and blue, giving her a slightly startled expression, but there were dark patches beneath them.

"And when did you come into this country?"

"On the tenth of November."

"Thank you. Which airport did you land at?"

"Is that relevant?" Magda demanded.

"Of course it's relevant," I snapped, which seemed to placate her.

"Leeds and Bradford," the girl replied.

I remembered the photographs. "Before we go any further," I said, "do you recognise this girl?" I slid the pictures from the envelope and passed them across the table. Magda and Lorraine came across and peered over her shoulders.

The girl studied them for a few seconds and shook her head. "No, I not recognise her."

"OK. Thanks for looking."

"Who is she?" Lorraine asked.

"One of the bodies that were found on Bleak Tor," I replied, and they shuddered with distaste. The girl handed the pictures back to me and I put them in their envelope. It had been a long-shot that hadn't come off.

"We were at the airport," I said. "Leeds and Bradford airport. I believe someone was there to meet you."

"Yes. A man."

"He had a board with your name on it?"

"Yes."

"What did he look like?"

She shrugged her shoulders.

"How tall was he?"

"Not tall."

"Stand up, please, and show me how tall he was compared to you."

She rose to her feet and indicated that he was a few inches taller than she was. About five eight, at a guess. That narrowed it down to fifteen million.

"What colour was his hair?"

"Black."

A movement outside the window caught my attention. The sky went dark as it was filled with a Boeing 747, headlights blazing, coming straight at me with its wheels hanging down like talons. I ducked involuntarily as it shot overhead.

"You're sure?"

"Yes."

"Good." That meant only five million left. "Was his hair short, long, wavy, going bald. Anything like that?"

She studied for a few seconds. "He had..." Her hands went to her head. "At the back, like a horse."

"A ponytail?"

"Yes. A pony's tail. Very short."

I felt a wave of excitement run through me. It was like painting by numbers, and the Laughing Cavalier's face was slowly being revealed. But let's not cut corners, I thought. Call it 50,000. "Can you describe his face?" I asked.

She touched her own and shook her head. "A bad face."

"Any beard or moustache? Hair...?" I stroked my chin."

"No. No hair on face."

"Fine," I said. "You're doing fine. What was he wearing?"

"Black. He wear black clothes."

"A jacket and trousers, like mine?" I fingered the material.

"No. Not like you. The same."

"A suit?"

"Yes. A suit. And a big coat."

5,000. We were getting there. "Anything else?"

"No."

"Anything at all that you remember about him?"

She thought about it but shook her head.

We try not to lead a witness but sometimes you have to. "Was there anything about the way he walked?" I asked.

Her face lit up and she nodded, but the words were outside her vocabulary. She jumped to her feet and walked across the kitchen, dragging one leg slightly.

"He walked with a limp?" I said.

"A... limp?" she repeated.

"Yes. A limp. That's what we call it. One leg is shorter than the other."

"Yes!" she agreed. "One shoe big." She lifted her own foot and tapped the side of her trainer.

One! We'd got it down to one. Something happened inside of me. I swallowed hard but it wouldn't go down. It felt as if a block of wood was stuck in my throat, and every time I swallowed it moved slightly, but the corners were snagging on the sides. My face was burning and I had difficulty breathing. Is this it, I thought? Is this what a heart attack feels like?

I leaned back in the chair and looked up at the ceiling, pulling air in through my nose, forcing it to the far-flung recesses of my lungs. Above me a child's mobile hung from a drawing pin. Fishes, six of them, in gaudy colours. A shadow filled the room as the next airliner came down, and the fishes twitched and rotated.

The girl was staring at me. "You've been very brave," I said when I could speak again. "Very brave, but now I want you to be even braver. I want you to tell me about the other man who came to visit you at the flat."

She shuddered and looked down at her knees. "Tell me about him, please," I said. "I believe you heard his name."

"Yes."

"What was it?"

"Doo-gie."

Lorraine said: "I think she means Duggie."

I ignored her. "What did Doo-gie look like?" I asked.

Her voice was a whisper, barely audible. "He was big," she said.

"And his hair?"

"Very short."

"What was he wearing?"

She looked around and stopped at Magda. "Like that," she said, pointing.

"A t-shirt," I suggested.

"Yes, t-shirt."

"What else?"

"And jeans. Sometimes." A frustrated look crossed her face. "And…" she began, and drew stripes on her leg with her fingers. "Adidas."

"A track suit," I said. "An Adidas tracksuit."

"Yes, I think so."

"Anything else?"

"Yes. He have…" Again her words ran out. She rubbed the top of her arm. "Pictures. He have pictures."

"Tattoos," I said. "Well done. Did you see what they were pictures of?"

"No. Many things. Bad things."

I picked up the envelope with the photographs and fidgeted with it, wondering whether to risk it. I decided to. "I said you'd been very brave, but now I want you to be even braver." I pulled a photo from the envelope and turned it to face her. "Do you recognise anybody on this photograph?"

She started to tremble and sob, great convulsions shaking her body. Lorraine jumped to her feet and grabbed her shoulders. The girl stood up and they walked into the other room. Magda came to look at the picture. There were four men on it, taken at the funeral. I think they were the pallbearers, and they were all similar looking. Bouncers Mark I. Magda sniffed and moved off.

When they returned the girl said: "I sorry."

"No," I said. "I'm the one who is sorry. We know who these men are, and with your help I can put them in jail for what they did to you. Now, can you point to the one that you think is Doo-gie?"

Her hand was shaking but there was no doubt about where her finger landed: straight on the fat smug face of Duggie Jones.

I didn't show her the picture of Wallenberg. As evidence, her identification was decidedly shaky, but it was worth sacrificing because I doubted if I'd ever persuade her to appear in court. Just the same, I'd keep Wallenberg in reserve. I said: "I think that will do for the moment. Can we have a short break, please?"

We went in to the other room and the women talked about fetching some food from a local takeaway. I pulled a twenty-pound note out of my wallet, decided it might not be enough and found another, and offered to treat them. You'd have thought I'd offered to give them all a rubdown with baby oil, but when I explained that I'd claim it on expenses and that it was a government body, i.e. the police, and not a member of the opposite sex who was paying, they acquiesced.

Fifteen minutes later we were tucking in to an assortment of Indian goodies: pakoras, samosas, bhajis, seekh kebabs, and lots of other things that I didn't know the names of. I hadn't realised how hungry I was until I saw the spread, and I piled my plate high. Lorraine and Magda piled theirs like the Tower of Babel while the girl just had one or two items. I asked the Asian woman for the names of everything and she told me, but her voice was very quiet and a plane was rumbling overhead. I bit into a samosa and nodded my approval.

When we'd demolished the spread I cornered the girl like some chancer at a party and asked her if she was happy to continue the interview. She said she was. I led her into the kitchen and we started again.

"Now I'd like you to tell me about the house where they kept you," I began. "Did you hear anybody mention the name of the town. Like, Heckley?"

She shook her head.

"Halifax? Huddersfield?"

More headshakes.

"Never mind," I said. "Did you see the house when he first took you there?"

"Yes."

"Was it a big house?"

She shrugged her shoulders. What is big when you spent much of your childhood living like a farm animal? I asked Lorraine if there was an A4 pad anywhere and one was found for me. I drew a house on it. A nice house, with a chimney and a front door with a path winding up to it. It took me about ten seconds. I spun the pad round and said: "Did the house look like that?"

"No."

I drew two parallel lines almost the full width of the paper, then vertical lines at brief intervals along them, dividing the space between the lines into squares. In each square I drew a front door with a couple of steps up to it, and rows of windows. "Did the house look like one of those?" I asked.

The girl became animated. "Yes," she agreed. "Like that." We were off again. There were probably about a million terrace houses in East Pennine, assuming the house was in East Pennine.

"Was there a little garden in front?" I asked. There wasn't.

"Was it at the end of the row?" She shook her head, but hesitantly this time. "What is it?" I asked.

She put one hand to her forehead, deep in thought. "It feel long ago," she said.

"It was long ago," I said. "A lot has happened to you in a few days. Try to remember."

The girl reached forward and took the pad again. She picked up my pen and studied the crude drawing. Suddenly she drew lines at the end of the row, indicating the last house and pointed to the one next to it. "That house," she declared. "Not at end; next to end."

"Well done," I said, smiling at her, but she hadn't finished.

"There," she said, pointing. "Name of street on wall. I not understand."

"What didn't you understand?"

"Name. Two names. I look in my… my book with words…"

"Dictionary?"

"Yes. My dictionary. Words mean trees. First word mean trees, second word mean trees also, but no trees anywhere."

I looked across at Lorraine and Magda. "Does that mean anything to you?"

They shook their heads.

"You're doing well…" I began, but cut the sentence short. Every time I spoke to her I stumbled over the words because I didn't know her name. My end of the conversation sounded false and awkward. I said: "I wish I knew your name."

The two chairs off to my left creaked but the occupants didn't say anything. The girl looked down at her lap and then at me.

"Ludmilla," she whispered.

"Thank you," I said.

Somebody brought us tea and I poured. Ludmilla put another two heaped spoonfuls of sugar in hers. She was entitled to a little treat, I thought.

"Was there anything else you remember about where the house was?" I asked. "We're there any sounds you heard. Like clocks chiming or church bells? Any shopkeepers shouting their wares?" Do any shopkeepers shout their wares, these days, I wondered? "Anything at all?"

"I go for walk," Ludmilla said.

"You went for a walk? I thought you were locked in."

"No. First night. Before… before he came. I have keys, to go buy food. I go for walk."

"Tell me about it. Where did you walk?"

"Not far. I show you." She took the paper again and started drawing. "I walk down here, and round here."

"What did you see? What shops did you see?"

She made agitated movements with her hands, frustrated by the lack of words. "Fruit," she said. "And…tables and chairs. And music. And big shop where I buy food."

"A big shop. Can you remember the name?"

She screwed up her face in concentration, but it wouldn't come. "I think… I think begin with…" She picked up the pen and drew the letter S on the pad.

"We want a big shop beginning with an S," I told the other two, but they were about as helpful as a spare wheel on a sledge. Even my feeble brain was capable of coming up with Sainsbury's and Safeways, but when I suggested them Ludmilla shook her head.

"That's terrific, Ludmilla," I said. "We're nearly there. Is there anything else you can tell me? What about the names of these other streets."

She shook her head again.

I pointed to the route she'd indicated on the drawing. "Which was the busiest road?"

"That one."

"Was it very busy?" "Yes. Very busy. Many people all over. Shops come out where people walk. Very busy."

"I don't understand," I said. "Do you mean that the shop-keepers bring their goods out on to the pavement?"

"Yes. On pavement. And many ladies dressed like the doctor."

"The doctor?" I queried.

"Doctor Kaur," Lorraine said. "In the next room."

"You mean Asian ladies, in saris?"

"Yes. Asian ladies."

We were getting there. It would take time, but we could probably pinpoint the flat from the information Ludmilla had given us. "OK, Ludmilla," I said. "You've gone for your walk and you're heading back to the house. Did you have a front door key?"

"No. Front door not locked."

"Was there a number on it?"

"No, but…"

"Go on."

"This house." She pointed to the house next but one. "This house number…" Again she drew it on the pad. Number 45. "Same age as my father," she said.

"Brilliant!" I said. "Well done." I did a quick calculation and came up with either 49 or 41 for the house in question. "Now," I continued. "You've entered the house. Where was your apartment? Was it upstairs?"

"Yes, up stairs."

251

"And you had a key to your apartment. What sort of key was it?" I quickly sketched a Yale key and a deadlock. She pointed to the deadlock and snatched the pen from between my fingers. "Number eight," she said, and drew an 8 on the pad. "The flat was number eight."

"That's fantastic. Now, I'd like you to tell me about the room. What it was like inside." Ideally, we'd want to prove she'd been in there.

"I go all round it," she said. "I do this, everywhere." She pressed her fingers on the table several times, then stood up and did the same thing on the wall and the door. "I think they will kill me, so I leave my fingers on everywhere, so you can tell that Ludmilla was in the room."

I couldn't believe it. I couldn't believe that this slip of a girl had been so brave, had endured so much in her brief life, and had such a fighting spirit. "We'll find the room, Ludmilla," I promised, "and we'll prove that you were there, and we'll arrest the people who put you there."

I was nearly done, had just one line of questioning remaining. I said: "Tell me how you escaped."

It hurt her, being reminded of those days. She was tortured and locked in a room, used as casually as if she'd been a disposable cup, and expected to die when they'd finished with her. She wrapped her arms around herself and rocked gently in the chair.

"He came…" she began, her voice barely audible. "He have… his little friend with him."

"Doo-gie?" I asked.

"No not Doo-gie. Pony's tail man. He attack me with little friend."

"Who was the little friend?" I asked.

"Little friend not a person. I steal little friend. I bring it for you. It is in car."

"Which car? The one that brought you here?"

"Yes."

Lorraine jumped up and left the room. A minute later she returned and placed this *thing* on the table in front of me.

Ludmilla shrank away from it, stood up and walked over to the window. A big jet was coming over, and she was probably wishing she'd never been on one. The *thing* consisted of an aluminium tube and a red plastic pistol grip. The words *Hotshot Made in the USA* were moulded into the handle. It was the cattle prod that Wallenberg had used to punish Selina and torture God-knows how many girls like Ludmilla into cowed submission. Sometimes I think that an-eye-for-an-eye would be too easy for people like him.

"How did you get this?" I asked.

She was still looking out of the window. She said: "He came. One night. He… he attack me. I pretend…" She couldn't go any further.

"It's OK, Ludmilla," I said. "I think we know what you mean. Did you grab this, his little friend?"

"Grab it?"

"Did you take it from him?"

"Yes. I take it. I go *pssst pssst* to him." She turned to face me as if holding the prod and made two stabbing motions.

I smiled at the thought of it. "You gave him some of his own medicine?"

"No! No medicine."

"I'm sorry." I picked up the prod and jabbed it to one side "You did this to him?"

"Yes. He not like it. Then I run away. Key was in door. I open door and make lock again and run away."

"You locked him in?"

"Yes."

I shook my head in disbelief. "You're an incredible girl, Ludmilla," I said. "Just incredible."

She'd run into the nearest shop and they'd looked after her. We had another cup of tea in the other room and they took turns to fire questions and lecture me on gender politics. I was seriously outnumbered and outgunned so I took it all. They muttered in amazement when I told them that I knew who the two men were, and that led to a short, eye-watering discussion on what ought to be done to them.

I used the bathroom and asked to be taken home. The Asian lady and the other woman shook my hand. Ludmilla looked hesitant. I gave her the apologetic smile and said I'd tell Lorraine what happened. She thanked me for helping her. I collected the cattle prod from the kitchen and told them I needed it for evidence. The blacked-out glasses were on the mantelshelf and as Magda opened the front door I handed them to her, saying: "I don't really think I need these, do you?" My words were blown away in the down-wash of a Delta Airlines Triple 7 as she took them from me.

"Peter Wallenberg," I said. "Top priority. I want him before the end of the day." We were in the main office, with everybody present. "He's either done a bunk or is lying low. Find out the location of every property he owns and look for him there. Talk to the neighbours and his tenants, show them his picture. Talk to his wife and lean on her. She'll shop him if she can. Fraud Squad – or should I say the Economic Crime Unit – are looking into his finances, seeing what they can freeze. We want him for murder, kidnapping and rape." As an afterthought I added: "And having a ponytail at his age." If anything would stir them into action that was it.

I wiped a clean patch on the whiteboard and picked up a pen. "One other thing before you go," I said. "I have a description of the house and locality where the foreign girl was held. Does anybody recognise this?"

I sketched a row of terrace houses. "This one is number 45," I said. "She was held in this one."

"49," somebody informed us all.

"Or 41," another added.

"That's right. The street down here leads to a main road…" I drew it, "and there are lots of shops here. The shops spread their wares out on to the pavement." I drew a few circles and squares to represent them. "One of the bigger shops that sells food begins with the letter S. Now, here's the clincher: the name of this street is to do with trees. Two words, and they are both trees, or associated with trees. Anybody any ideas."

Everybody gazed at the board, racking their brains for enlightenment. Jeff broke the silence.

"Are we talking about Heckley?" he asked.

I gave the wish-I-knew smile. "Not sure."

Somebody else said: "When you say trees, do you mean grove, or something like that?"

"I imagine so. What else is there, or do we have to go through the A to Z?"

"Avenue."

"Yep. Any more?"

"It's the Junipers," the youngest DC in the squad stated. "Juniper Avenue, just off Westerton Road. The shop beginning with an S is a Spar."

A sigh of agreement rippled through the room. "Well done," I said. "Juniper Avenue sounds like the place. I'd like to publicly congratulate that man on his diligence and observation. Will the rest of you please take note and act accordingly?"

"He only knows because he's screwing the checkout girl," someone said, and the meeting broke up with smiles all around.

"49, Juniper Avenue?" Dave asked when the scraping of chairs and rattle of conversation had faded away. He walked over to the wall map to check its location.

"I want somebody from fingerprints there, too," I said. "The girl says she left her prints on everything."

"What, deliberately?"

"Mmm. She thought they'd kill her so she wanted to leave her mark."

"Blimey."

I made the call and arranged to meet a SOCO at the flat. Twenty minutes later we were parking in Juniper Avenue. "Let's go for a walk," I said.

I tried to put myself in her place. She'd landed an hour earlier, straight from a country ravaged by war and sectarian hatred. I went through the names that had made the headlines

255

since the break-up of the Soviet Union: Serbia, Macedonia, the remainders of the Czech and Yugoslav republics, Kosova, Albania. And so on. A heartbreaking litany of hatred whipped up by a few men's craving for power. Where she came from I didn't know, but Westerton Road, with all its traffic and dust and bustling shoppers, must have felt like heaven to her. Workmen with a cherry-picker crane were lifting more Christmas decorations into place and stringing cables dripping with coloured bulbs across the road. The smells are the first thing you notice about a foreign country. To me it was just traffic fumes, but what would she smell on the breeze? The odour of wet peat blowing down from the hills, the freshly cut grass in the park and the aftershave and perfume of the boys and girls? We did the walk she'd done and found ourselves standing outside the un-numbered door, next but one from the end.

"It's flat number eight," I said. "Upstairs."

The front door wasn't locked, as she'd said. We closed it behind us and I found the push for the light. Dave led the way up the carpet-covered stairs. We'd barely reached the top when the light went out. I found another push and when the light came on again we saw that number eight stood before us.

I knocked, then tried the handle. It was locked.

"Kick it down," I said.

Dave pressed himself against the opposite wall, took a deep breath and launched himself at the door. Wood splintered and a gap appeared. Two more clinical kicks and we were in.

All rooms smell when they've been locked up for a week or so, but it doesn't usually hit you before you pass over the threshold. I sniffed, set my expression to one of distaste and gingerly stepped into the room, like a cat exploring a new home.

It was a businesslike room. Some businesses require computers and desks, or ladders and power tools. When sex is your business all you need is a bed and a bathroom. A coat was flung carelessly on the floor, with a jacket next to it. A black coat. I stepped between them and worked my way around the bed.

He was curled up in a corner, between the bed and the wall. His shirt was unbuttoned all the way down and his trousers and underpants were around his ankles. One hand was clutched over his genitals and the other was in front of his face, palm outwards, the fingers spread wide to offer maximum protection from whatever he was hiding from.

"Come and look at this," I whispered.

"Jeeezus!" Dave exclaimed as he came alongside me. We stood in silence for several seconds. "Wallenberg?" he wondered.

"Yeah, it's Wallenberg," I said. "Look at the expression on his face."

"I've heard of people being scared to death," Dave said, "but this is the first time I've seen it."

The SOCO arrived and we sent for the pathologist. Officially it was a suspicious death, so we had to set the machinery in motion again. I had the coat put in an evidence bag and whisked off to the lab.

"Right, where shall we start?" the SOCO said after the professor had given his permission.

"How about there," I said, indicating the middle of the door that led into the bathroom.

"Good as anywhere," he replied, and dipped his squirrel-hair brush into the aluminium powder. Ten seconds later he said: "Blimey. First time lucky." An hour later he ran out of lifting tape and had to send for replenishments.

18

I didn't go to Rosie's funeral. I don't know why; it didn't seem necessary. Funerals are for the living, not the dead. They're a statement of closure, I suppose, but Rosie and I had closed a week before she took the fatal dose. The funeral director we'd assigned the arrangements to rang me from Scarborough and asked what I wanted him to do with Rosie's ashes. I asked him if I could collect them after hours and he said no problem, so straight from work I dashed over to Scarborough and brought Rosie home.

I'd arranged to have Wednesday off. When I dug up the roses in Rosie's garden I noticed a freshly planted rambler with the ticket still on it. Something had jolted inside me when I read the name: it was called High Hopes. At first light I drove over to her house and dug that one up, too, and placed it in the car boot, next to her ashes. Four hours later I swung off the M5 and started looking for the signs for Uley.

The vicar is called Duncan and we'd met before. We shook hands and he said it was a sad story. He collected a spade and we went down the graveyard next to the church, to where Abraham Barraclough, Rosie's father, was buried. It was informal, which is what she would have wanted, with no prayers and no hymns, just two of us with our private thoughts. I asked Duncan if he minded me planting the rambling rose in the hedge, and he said of course not. I felt better after doing that. Like I said: funerals are for the living.

Have a day off and the work piles up, especially when you are trying to sew up two, or was it three, murders? The report I'd asked the lab to rush through for me was on my desk. The overcoat belonging to Wallenberg bore microscopic traces of blood and brain matter, all down the left-hand sleeve and shoulder. The inference was that he'd been walking to the right of Krabbe when the fatal blow was struck, which meant that Duggie Jones must have done the deed. Further tests were being done to prove the coat was Wallenberg's and the blood was Krabbe's, but there was little doubt.

Joe Crozier was Nigel's case, but I like to keep a fatherly eye on him. Jones had already confessed to helping Dale Dobson dispose of Joe's body and now we had him for murder. Without a complainant we couldn't touch him for the rape charges, but we'd confront him and he'd claim he was just the driver. Hopefully we'd learn a lot more from him about Wallenberg's empire. He'd be wearing communal underpants for the rest of his life, but if he was a good boy and cooperated with us he might be allowed to wash them for himself.

Which left us with the late Mr Wallenberg. I inspected my *In* tray and looked under all the papers on my desk, but there was no PM report from the pathologist. I don't like to harass the prof so I went down to the incident room to start on the paperwork. Jeff Caton was in there, sorting through the reports, putting to one side any that were obviously irrelevant now that we had a suspect.

"Hi Chas," he said. "Have a good day off?"

"Hello Jeff. No, not really."

"Go anywhere?"

"Mmm. I went down to Gloucestershire; took Rosie's ashes to the cemetery where her father is buried."

He looked embarrassed. "Sorry, Chas..."

"That's OK. It had to be done. It was just a long drive, that's all. What have we got?"

"These," he said, pointing to the photos of Body One. "And the other girl – Body Two. Presumably these are still ongoing."

"Hmm, I'd think so. We can try for forensic links to Wallenberg, but I doubt if we'll find any. I suspect he's involved, though, but I doubt if we'll ever know. What's the expression we use: *a police spokesman said they are not looking for anyone else.*"

"Did you see my report for yesterday?" Jeff asked.

"No, not yet."

"I spent most of the day at the flat on Juniper Avenue, talking to the tenants. Wallenberg owned the end three, would you believe. Jones had a room in the end one and all the other rooms are taken by ladies of the night. He was taking about £200 a week each off them, which works out at something between one and two thousand, over and above the rents. Not bad if you can get it. He had similar operations in Bradford and Leeds and God-knows where else."

"Jesus. We're in the wrong line of work."

The phone rang and it was the call I'd been waiting for. "Hello Prof," I said. "What have you got for me?"

"The body from Juniper Avenue..." he began.

"Oh, that body," I interrupted.

"You know very well which body I mean, Charlie. The time of death has proved most awkward to define. The heating was on in the room, but quite low, and as the room was fairly well sealed and as it's this time of the year there was little entomological corruption. I've had Sulaiman over from York but there's not much for him. We both agree that he's been dead for about two weeks. Say a minimum of ten or twelve days, but it's very imprecise."

"As long as that? What about cause of death?"

"Ah, now we are on firmer ground. Cardiopulmonary arrest. A massive heart attack to you. No doubt about it."

"Brought on by what, would you say?"

"A bad dose of arteriosclerotic hypertensive disease."

"Yes, Prof, but what caused him to have that heart attack at that time?"

"No idea. I'm not a bloody soothsayer."

"You're the nearest to one I've ever met. Dave said he looked as if he'd been scared to death."

"He did, didn't he? But a heart attack is a pretty scary experience, especially if you're alone."

"No other marks on his body?"

"No, none."

"Natural causes?" I suggested.

"That's what I've put."

I thanked the professor and replaced the phone. I'd wondered if a cattle prod left marks, but evidently it didn't. And I wondered if the prof had been right about Wallenberg being alone.

"Natural causes," I said to Jeff. "He died of a heart attack."

"So he cheated us."

I shrugged. "Maybe, maybe not."

I rang Lorraine and passed the information on to her that Pony's Tail was dead and Doo-gie had been charged with murder. There might be a crumb of comfort in it for Ludmilla. "How is she?" I asked.

"She's doing well," Lorraine told me. "She's lodging with a family from her own country and they can give her a job as a waitress."

"Good. I hope it works out for her. Remember me to her, please."

I was passing the front desk when the sergeant covered the mouthpiece of his phone and told me there was a call for me. "One of your women, Charlie," he said with a conspiratorial wink.

"I have no women," I growled. "That's why I'm such an aggressive so-and-so. I'll take it in my office."

I ran up the stairs and reached across my desk to grab the phone, expecting it to be Lorraine again. "Priest," I snapped into it.

"Is that... Inspector Priest?" a voice enquired, hesitantly.

"Yes," I replied, sidling round to my chair. "How can I help you?"

"It's Sonia Thornton, Charlie. How are you?"

Sonia! My kidneys leapt into an impromptu congo and my spleen accompanied them on duodenum. "Hi! I'm fine. How about you?"

"I'm fine, too, thanks. I see you've got someone for Tony's murder."

"Yes. Two of them, but one's already dead. Listen, Sonia. I still have your photograph albums. I've had one picture copied but you can have the rest of them back. I was going to ring you and return them one day."

"There's no hurry, but, well, I wanted to ask you a favour."

"Ask away, Sonia. I'll help if I can." Providing it didn't involve swimming with great whites or sky-diving without a parachute, I was at her disposal.

"There's this function," she began. "Yorkshire Sports Personality of the Year. It's at the weekend and will be on television. They send me tickets every year but I never go. It's not on live TV. They record it and show it in the New Year. All the local sports people will be there, with some famous TV celebrity I've never heard of fronting it. It's mainly footballers, of course, and cricketers. But there's athletes there, too."

"Sonia..."

"Leeds rugby union team did well this year, so they stand a good chance of the team award. Or Bradford Bulls. Jane Tomlinson should win the individual award. I hope so. She deserves it."

"Sonia…"

"There's a meal, to start with, I believe, before the TV bit starts. And after the speeches…"

"Sonia!"

"Oh, sorry, what?"

"Are you asking me if I'll vote for you?"

"Vote for me? Of course not."

"Don't tell me you want to nominate me?"

"No. Didn't I say? I was wondering… I was wondering… well, if you'd like to come. I know it's short notice, and I don't know if you are… you know… going with anyone. Or even married, but I don't think you are."

"Sonia! Are you inviting me, as your guest?"

"Well, yes, I think so. Was I gabbling?"

"Just a bit."

"Sorry."

"Will I have to wear a dinner jacket?"

"No. There'll be lots of footballers there in wide suits and kipper ties. And chewing gum. You could bring your three football medals along to show them." She gave a little giggle at that thought. "Sorry, am I gabbling again?"

"Yes." She remembered the football medals! She remembered my medals!

"I always do when I'm nervous."

"And are you nervous?"

"Mmm. I've never done this before."

"Really?"

"No."

"In that case, Sonia, I'd better say that I'm thrilled to bits that you thought of me and I gladly accept the invitation. Saturday, did you say?"

We've been seeing each other ever since. We had Christmas lunch with Dave and Shirley and spent Boxing Day with Sonia's parents in Ilkley. From there we drove to the Lake District and had four days in a log cabin owned by one of the sergeants and did some walking. Sonia was worried about her knee but it stood the strain without any problems.

First time we entered the cabin I said: "Allocation of tasks: you do the cooking and washing up; I'll chop logs, empty the ashes and keep the fire going."

"It's a gas fire," she replied as she switched the light on.

"Blow me down, so it is!"

"Huh! So what's your favourite meal?"

"Peanut butter, bacon and banana sandwiches."

"Is that three sandwiches or one?"

"One."

"I'll try to remember. Is there anything else I need to know about you, Charlie Priest?"

"Just one thing," I said, dropping our rucksacks in a corner and turning to her.

"What's that?"

"I'm too embarrassed to mention it."

"Force yourself."

"OK. I'm, well, the truth is, I'm scared of the dark."

263

"Really?"

"Yep. Terrified."

She reached out and placed her arms around my neck. "Oh dear," she said. "We'll just have to see what we can do about that, won't we?"

It was a Saturday morning near the end of January when I found the letter and photographs from the Home Office Immigration Department. Sonia was working at High Adventure and I was sitting in Gilbert's chair, going through his *In* tray. He was playing in a four ball, or a ten ball, or left-handed with your laces tied together. Something like that. It was addressed to the East Pennine Chief Constable, with copies to Distribution list D, and the CC had passed it on to Special Branch. SB had appended a brief note and bounced it to CID, which was me.

I swung my feet up on to the desk and started to read. It said:

Reference: Ludmilla Mitrovic
We can confirm that Ludmilla Mitrovic entered this country on 10th November 2003 via Leeds and Bradford airport and has not left the country. Suggest CID be requested to check on her whereabouts.

The letter from the Home Office read:

Reference: Ludmilla Mitrovic Case CLMB 439.26.04
Approaches have been made to the Home Office by the Albanian ambassador regarding the whereabouts of Ludmilla Mitrovic. She entered the UK on November 10th 2003 and has not been heard of since. Her parents, who are Kosovan Albanians, now living in Albania, are growing increasingly concerned about her. She apparently came to this country intending to take up a short-term position of a nanny to a doctor working at Heckley General Hospital, but attempts to contact the doctor have proved fruitless. Ludmilla is aged nineteen, of slightly above average height and has long blonde hair. Could you please investigate her movements. Photograph a)

attached, is of Ludmilla, and b) attached, is believed to be of her fingerprints. This case is being handled by Cynthia Bouvier, extension 2217, to whom all information should be addressed. Negative replies are not required.

It was signed by an under-secretary, but whether that was his title or a boast, I didn't know. I unpinned the over-exposed snapshot of the girl I'd last seen six weeks earlier and propped it against the phone. In this photo she looked much younger and happier. She was holding one hand above her eyes, shielding them from the sun, and was wearing a flowered dress. There were mountains in the background and the sky was cloudless.

It was an ordinary photo, like I'd seen hundreds of times before in old scrapbooks. Apart from the mountains it could have been taken anytime in the 40's or 50's in rural England. The girlfriend of a young man about to be called into the army, enjoying a last day with him. That's what Ludmilla was: an ordinary girl. But forces were at work in her country to create extraordinary events. Racial hatred and religious intolerance were channelled and exploited by groups who didn't care who or what they destroyed in their lust for power. Her parents had fled their homeland, like countless ancestors before them, in a ceaseless ebb and flow of humanity looking for somewhere safe to raise their children. Could it happen here? Some would like it to, no doubt about it.

The fingerprints were on an actual size contact print, presumably made after they had been lifted from something that had belonged to Ludmilla. I placed them in my pocket, put everything else back in the envelope and addressed it to myself.

Our fingerprints department loves it when you call on them unexpectedly and ask for a favour. "C'mon," I insisted. "I get you all the decent jobs. Without me it would be all stolen cars and TICs. Where's the fun in them?"

The officer who'd worked with me on the Wallenberg case came over. "What's the problem, Charlie?" he asked.

265

I pulled the photo of the prints from my pocket. "49, Juniper Avenue," I said. "How do these compare with the marks you found on the walls?"

"I thought it was natural causes," he said.

"You know me," I replied. "No stone unturned Charlie."

"Can you leave it with me?"

"If you insist."

"How urgent is it?"

"It's not. Just sewing up the loose ends."

"Cheers. I'll ring you this aft."

Sonia rang, between climbers, to see where we were eating. I volunteered to cook and she said she'd be at my house about seven. "I should be home," I said, "but let yourself in if I'm not." The SOCO rang shortly after I replaced the phone.

"We have a match," he declared. "The prints all over the walls of that room are from the same person as the ones you brought in. Is that any help?"

The photo of Ludmilla was now pinned above my desk, next to the calendar. I looked at her, decided she needed a break. "Not really," I said. "Elimination purposes only. They're from the daughter of a previous tenant."

"Fair enough. Shall I destroy them, then?"

"That's what the law says. Thanks for helping."

"No trouble. I'll stick them all in the shredder. Don't come again for a while, please."

I found my diary and copied a number on to my telephone pad. After six rings I was transferred to the BT Answer 1571 service. I tried again, several times, without luck, so I decided to leave a message.

"Hello Lorraine," I said. "This is Charlie Priest. Tell Ludmilla to send a postcard home. Her parents are worried about her."

On the way home I called in the supermarket and bought crusty bread, shallots, tomatoes, peppers, root ginger, coriander, mussels and tiger prawns, with a bottle of Chilean Sauvignon Blanc. I put the wine in the freezer and propped the recipe book against the microwave. After a few minutes of

266

cleaning the mussels I decided something was missing. I walked through into the lounge and put a CD on, with the volume wound up loud so I could hear it while I prepared the ingredients.

It was Bruce Springsteen. As I reached the kitchen he started singing and I joined in at the chorus. *Born... in the USA...* we sang, top of our voices, with Springsteen accompanying us both on guitar and me doing my best on the wooden spoon.

THE END